Bone tugged at his [illegible] t was futile. The twosome watched him in amusement and waited till he'd calmed down. Then the queer, Judy, stepped forward and tugged at Bone's belt. When it was loose he undid the top button and the fly, then wrestled Bone's trousers down until they were resting on Bone's ankles. Then he delicately hooked his hand into Bone's Y-fronts and did the same with them. Bone stared at the scalpel in horror. Terry said, 'At first, Jaime wanted you dead, but then he came up with a better idea. He thought as he'd lost what he considered the most important thing in his life, then it was only right and fitting that you suffer the same. Guess what we all decided you'd miss most . . . ?'

Also by Iain Blair in Sphere:

TRUE
DUFF

BONE

IAIN BLAIR

SPHERE BOOKS LIMITED
30/32 Gray's Inn Road, London WC1X 8JL

First published in Great Britain by Sphere Books Ltd., 1977

Published by arrangement with the author's agents

TRADE
MARK

Set in Intertype Pilgrim

Printed in Great Britain by
Hunt Barnard Printing Ltd.,
Aylesbury, Bucks.

Chapter 1

It was a typical Scottish morning for that time of year. The sky was murky grey and lowering; soft rain danced against the windscreen. Off in the distance the clouds had parted, in such a manner as to allow the harsh morning light to shine through in the form of a cross.

Jack Bone yawned and stuck another cigarette between his lips. His mouth was already stale from too many full strength Capstans and all night vigil. He blinked sleep from his eyes and, after drawing untasted smoke deep into his lungs, started to hum a tune

The Edinburgh road was unusually quiet and for once there weren't speed merchants hell bent on suicide every mile or so. The road from the capital to Glasgow was a notorious death trap.

Jack Bone was feeling good despite his tiredness, the job he'd been asked to do was complete, and not only that, but done well in his estimation. He'd also tied it up a whole day sooner than he'd expected. His belly rumbled, reminding him that it was over twelve hours since he'd eaten. He chuckled to himself at the thought of the cliché Babs would have uttered in similar circumstances. The full, red lips would have parted lusciously and ingenuously;

'My stomach's beginning to think my throat's been cut,' she would have said. Her voice guttural Glasgow, the vowels occasionally stretched when she remembered to try and speak 'posh'.

Bone blew smoke at his reflection in the windscreen and promised himself a bath, a plate of bacon and eggs and a good grind. Preferably in that order.

The outskirts of the city flashed past, horrendous architecture that would have won a gold star for bad taste anywhere. Slogans had been daubed in green paint (by Catholics; if it had been Protestants the paint would have been blue) on unprotesting walls: 'WEARRAPEOPLEANNAT.' Glaswegians have never been noted for their modesty.

Jack Bone grunted and relaxed; he was home again. Back amongst the people he liked and felt most at ease with. He was at one with the city and its inhabitants.

The battered Mini protested as he stuck his foot down and forced the speedo up to sixty. The car was old, tired and almost at the end of its days. He was going to miss it when it was gone; he identified a lot with it.

He wondered whether to pick Babs up before he went home, and decided against it. He could have his bath and grub and still have time to get to her place before she set out for work. He scratched a pockmarked cheek and wondered whether he could talk her into taking the day off. They could have a bit of a kip, take in an afternoon flick and then go out for a nosh. He grinned at the picture conjured up in his mind. It appealed.

Half an hour later he was approaching the new housing scheme where he lived. Castlemilk was rank upon rank of dreary houses that marched onwards till they disappeared over the horizon. Bone had long since decided that the scheme had been designed either by a fervent Presbyterian, or a sadist. Come to think of it, perhaps they were one and the same thing. Who else would have expected several hundred thousand people to live in a scheme where there were no amenities provided? There were no cinemas, pubs, social or sporting facilities, shops, theatres or even bingo halls. Just houses full of desperate people.

There was a clang as a stone bounced off the Mini's wing, and Bone slewed himself round quickly enough to see a group of filthy youngsters give him the V sign before they turned and ran to vanish up a close. He knew it was nothing personal, merely a sign of the times. And the place.

He parked the car and fixed the Krooklok. The battered hulk was hardly worth nicking, but in this neighbourhood there was always someone who'd do it just for practice. He noted that the drizzle had stopped.

Inside the flat he made himself a cup of strong coffee while the bath ran. When it was full he stripped, and eased his aching body into the luxuriating warmth. He grunted and lay back, occasionally taking the cigarette from his mouth so that he could blow smoke rings at the ceiling. It was an art he was trying to master.

When the water started to cool he climbed out and into a thick towelling dressing gown. He was stirring soft brown sugar into his second coffee when the doorbell rang.

'Mr Bone?'

The woman was old, and shrivelled like a prune. Fine hairs decorated the expanse of her top lip. Despite all this, it was still apparent to the discerning eye that she'd been a 'looker' in her younger days. Her male companion was equally old, and stared out at the world through rheumy eyes. He wheezed dramatically from the exertion of climbing three flights of stairs.

'Yes, I'm Jack Bone.'

The old woman ventured a smile.' I wonder if we might come in and talk? We have some business for you.'

'Aye, we have that,' said the man. He coughed into the back of his hand, a dry, racking sound.

Bone ushered them inside and gestured towards the living room. When they were both seated he said, 'I was just having a cup of coffee. Perhaps you might like to join me?'

'That would be most appreciated,' said the old woman.

Bone said to the man, 'There's something stronger if you'd like?'

Shrivelled lips twisted into a smile and that was answer enough. Bone flipped open the door of the sideboard and pulled out the whisky bottle. He poured a large one. 'Water?' he asked politely. The white head shook from side to side. The man accepted the drink and sipped appreciatively. Bone noticed that long, thin, blue streaks snaked up from below the man's collar to vanish into the thick bush of his hair. There were also similar ones protruding from the cuffs that encircled his wrists.

'That's grand,' said the old man with relish. He squirmed his thin body further back into the plush of the armchair.

Bone made a cup of coffee for the woman and after he'd handed it to her and been politely thanked he sat down and waited. There was a slight nervous pause before she said,

'Our name's Foster. Mr and Mrs Foster.'

'I'm pleased to meet you,' Bone smiled. He was pleased to see the soft words had the desired effect of setting the old woman more at ease. She licked her lips and went on,

'We have a problem and we've been told that you might be able to help us. Would you be interested?'

'That depends,' Bone replied.

She said very seriously, 'Oh we'll pay of course. We don't expect anything for nothing.

Bone was beginning to take a shine to the old couple. They were his sort of people. 'How long were you down the pits?' he asked Mr Foster.

The old man's eyes opened wide with surprise. 'How did you . . . !'

Bone pointed to the blue streaks deeply etched into the flesh. He said, 'Coal dust, isn't it?'

The shrivelled lips twisted bitterly upward while a gnarled thumb wiped away moisture that had seeped from leaky eyes. 'Aye,' said Mr Foster, 'that's what it is.'

His wife carefully laid down her cup before lifting her old fashioned handbag on to her lap. She undid the gilt clasp and rummaged inside. When she finally pulled her hand out again she was clutching a roll of tenners which were held together by an elastic band.

'Three hundred pounds,' she said, 'all the money we own in the world.' She slid the elastic band from the notes and laid them on the coffee table.

'Please count it,' she said.

Bone was fascinated. He pointed a finger towards the bundle. '*All* the money you have?' he queried.

'Aye,' spluttered the old man into his handkerchief.

Bone rose and poured Foster a large one. As he did so he contemplated the fact that he'd been offered many things in his life, but never another person's all. As an act it cried desperation. He screwed the top back on the bottle and, after putting it away, lit himself another fag. He stared at the old woman through the mirror that hung above the sideboard. 'What's the problem, then?' he asked.

Mrs Foster glanced at her husband before replying. Then she said in a voice tight with emotion,

'We have a daughter called Heather. Two years ago she left home, and since then we've lost touch. We want you to find her for us.'

'What if I find her and she doesn't want to know? It often happens that way.'

Mrs Foster shook her head, 'You don't quite understand. I think you'll find she wants to come once she knows about her Dad. They've always been close, ever since she was a little lassie.'

Bone digested that before turning to the old man. 'And what is it she should know about you?' he asked.

He was rewarded with a grimace which turned into another bout of coughing and spluttering. When he'd caught his breath, Foster said,

'I've been given my final cards.'

Bone frowned. 'I don't understand.'

The smile was forced to the point of caricature. 'The doc's told me I'm dying. I'd like to see the lassie before I go, you understand.'

The only sound that broke the silence in the room was the rhythmic ticking of the cheap alarm clock which lived on top of the fireplace. Eventually the old man continued,

'I contracted "the dust" a few years ago and had to leave the pits. Shortly after that we moved here from Wishaw.' Wishaw was a small mining village situated a few miles outside Glasgow.

He took a deep breath which made his chest rattle.

'They said that as long as I took it easy and got lots of fresh air then I should have a good few years left in me.' A flicker of panic flashed across his face and then swiftly disappeared. 'Aye, well, it seems the doctors who told me that were a wee bit optimistic. According to this latest man I was recommended to, I'm at the end of the line.'

Bone rose and paced to the window. In the street below some kids were playing a game of football, twenty a side with coats and jerseys as goal posts. The din that wafted up was considerable. Suddenly Bone didn't feel hungry any more. Come to think of it, he didn't feel tired either.

'How long does this new doctor reckon?' he asked over his shoulder. It was the woman who replied, 'A month. Maybe a little more.'

Bone tried to imagine what it must be like being stuck down a pit for all of your working life. Two miles under the ground, huddled in a three foot seam. He thought of the dust granules that were everywhere, getting into your hair, your skin, your mouth, your ears and your very soul itself. But worst of all was the dust getting into your lungs, because when that happened it was only a matter of time before they lost their elasticity. That was what the quacks called pneumoconiosis, but which the men themselves referred to simply as 'the dust'.

If you were lucky you lived out your days as a gasping, spluttering semi-invalid. If you weren't, you were dead. Some miners had been known to say it was the other way round.

Bone wondered whether he should say he was sorry. It seemed inadequate and vaguely patronising, so he didn't. Instead, he asked,

'Any idea where Heather might be?'

Mrs Foster went back to rummaging in her handbag. This time she pulled out several sheets of cheap writing paper. 'This was the last letter we had from her,' she said.

The address scrawled on the upper right hand side of the first sheet was:

YORK MANSIONS
PRINCE OF WALES DRIVE
S.W.11.

'This is in London!' Bone exclaimed.

'Aye, that's where she went,' mumbled the old man. 'Said things in Glasgow were too tame for her, said she wanted to be in the hub of things. "Where it's all happening", was the way she put it.'

'How old is she?' Bone asked.

'Twenty-three,' Mrs Foster fired back immediately. She sat stiff and prim, her bright eyes never leaving Bone's face.

'And what does she do for a living?'

'She's a trained shorthand-typist, and a good one at that we're told. But she never did tell us what she was working at down in London.'

'She had a good job in town here,' broke in the husband. 'Worked for a firm of solicitors in West Nile Street. Very grand they are by all accounts.' He winked slowly as though this was something secret he was sharing with Bone. He squirmed further back into the chair after carefully setting his empty whisky glass on the floor.

Bone gazed at the money and had to admit to himself it was tempting.

He asked the obvious question, 'Been to the police?'

Mrs Foster nodded. 'They took the particulars and said they'd be in touch. That was five weeks ago.'

'So now she's officially listed as a missing person?'

'Aye,' confirmed the old woman.

Her husband went back to coughing into his now sodden handkerchief. His hands were trembling. 'You'll appreciate that time isn't exactly a thing I've got a lot of,' he said.

Bone glanced sideways at the loot and tried not to think of what he could do with three hundred portraits of the Queen. It was a lot more poppy than he was normally offered, and besides, apart from the Edinburgh job, things had been a bit quiet lately. He shrugged his shoulders.

'I'd like to help, but I'm afraid I can't. You see, it's my policy to work only in Scotland.'

The old man stared blankly, the coughing momentarily stilled. 'Surely you don't mean that?' he rasped.

The wife was rigid, her face set. She looked the picture of well controlled hopelessness. Her mouth opened, shut, and then opened again.

'Please, Mr Bone!' she pleaded. It was probably the only time she'd ever done so in her life.

'If the money's not enough,' said her husband, 'Then maybe we can . . .'

Bone cut in sounding more sharp than he'd intended, 'It's nothing to do with the money. It's just that like I told you, I never work outside Scotland.'

There was a pause during which the old woman's fingers fidgeted in her lap. The skin that covered them was stretched tight and dotted with brown spots; it was also heavily veined.

'Will you no' make an exception just this once?' she asked.

When there was no reply, her husband let out a great sigh and his head drooped forward. 'Aye, well there we are then. I suppose that's that,' he said. He dabbed at his streaming eyes with the hanky. Mrs Foster sat staring into space, her mouth pulled downwards in a fierce slash. Her drooping dugs heaved.

'I'm sorry,' said Bone.

'You were our last hope,' mumbled the old man.

Bone rose and walked to the window. He glanced at his watch and saw that if he hurried he would still have time to spend at least half an hour with Babs. He hoped again that he could talk her out of going to work. He thought of her lying in bed, the sheets thrown back and her top parts exposed. She always slept that way. He smelled her scent and heard the throatiness of her laughter.

The sound of slow, laborious scratching of pencil on paper interrupted his day dream and he turned to find Mrs Foster writing on his telephone pad. She licked the tip of the pencil and carefully underlined each word and number.

'In case you change your mind,' she said simply.

Bone made a mental note to pick up a bunch of flowers for Babs. She loved that sort of thing. To the old woman he said, 'You do realise it's nothing personal?'

'Aye,' answered her husband. The rest of his reply was lost in a fresh bout of coughing. His thin chest heaved and strained with exertion while his pale face became mottled as he spat gout after gout of thick mucus into the handkerchief. He gasped with relief when he was finally finished.

'Is there anything I can get you?' asked Bone. He glanced suggestively at the sideboard where the whisky was kept.

'No, no,' replied the old man: 'You've been more than kind as it is.' Clutching each other's arms the old couple made their way to the front door.

'I hope you find her,' said Bone.

The old man looked up from the landing below and smiled. 'Thank you,' he said graciously. His steel-shod boots clattered on the concrete steps as they made their way down into the street.

Bone sighed and ran a hand over his face. He felt rotten, as though he'd done the dirty on the old couple. He told himself not to be so stupid, London wasn't his territory and that was that.

In the living room he picked up the sheet of paper with the Foster's address on it. The writing was large and copper plate. Out of habit he memorised what had been written before screwing the paper into a tight ball and slinging it into the waste basket. Outside it had started to rain again.

He dressed swiftly and warmly, he suspected it was going to get a lot colder later on in the day. He buttoned his black crombie and then stuck a floppy, wide-brimmed felt hat on his head.

'OK?' queried the neighbour's kid at the close mouth.

'OK!' Bone repeated.

The kid stuck his hands in his pockets and sauntered off down the street. He walked in perfect imitation of the way Cagney had on the goggle box the night before. The kid was dreaming he was Public Enemy Number 1.

As he drove, Bone thought of his London days and the things that had happened to him in the Smoke. He'd been younger then, not long out the Army. He thought of the booze, the endless bottles that had come and gone as he'd relentlessly drunk himself into oblivion day after day, night after night.

And of course that made him think of Nick and Malaya.

As the memories invaded his mind Bone's throat tightened and his mouth went dry, the way it always did when he thought of the Corp. Sweat globules broke on his forehead as he groped for the fags. He coughed when some of the much-needed smoke went down the wrong way. Outside the windscreen it was Glasgow that was flashing past, but that wasn't what Jack Bone was seeing.

He was back squatting round a small camp fire in the Malay village of Mersing. He stared out at the South China Sea while all around him mysterious jungle noises jangled in the night. The air was sweet and heavy, salt mingled with the aroma of jungle flowers. He gazed into the flickering flames and listened to the 'put put' of the banyan boats as they chugged towards the reef and the islands that lay beyond.

Faces came and went, nearly all of them now dead. Dickie Smith, who had had most of his back blown away; Harry Levi, who died screaming from snake bite. But clearest of all Bone remembered Nick Byers, the Corporal who became his great mate.

Bone was back at the camp fire again as Mick punched a hole in the tin with his panga and then poured the condensed milk into the tea. 'Big treat tonight,' Nick said.

The young Bone grinned and gratefully accepted his cup. The tea was thick, the sort you could stand a spoon in. Bone swallowed a mouthful with relish. 'I hear we're going up country again,' he said after a while.

Nick Byers lay on his back and stared up at the stars. He was a big lad, strong and well-formed. He was nineteen years old and reckoned he'd already killed three men in hand to hand combat.

'First I've heard of it,' Nick said non-committally.

They smoked in silence, watching the silhouette of a navy frigate disappear over the horizon. When it was finally gone, they went back to watching the stars.

'You know what I miss most of all?' said Nick.

'What?'

'A really good pint of beer.' He rolled on his side. 'You ever drink Batham's Delph Ale?'

Bone shook his head.

'Best drink in the Black Country, that is. Whole of Britain as well, more than likely.'

Bone felt a bit of patriotism was called for. 'It'll have to go some to beat a pint of heavy,' he said.

Nick laughed. 'That's right. You stick up for your own kind, Scotchman.'

'Sco*ts*man,' Bone said wearily. 'Scotch is what you drink. Scots are the people.' He was fed up with pointing out the difference. He was also beginning to suspect that Nick did it deliberately to annoy him.

'OK! OK! lad, don't get your kilt in a twist!'

'And another thing,' said Bone vehemently, 'I don't like being called Scotch Jack!'

Mick chuckled. 'Don't be so touchy. It's only to identify you from "Welsh Jack".'

'Well I don't like it!'

Byers said gently, 'Then my suggestion to you is that you hurry up and get used to it. It's been my experience that those sort of nicknames tend to stick.'

There was a short lull in the conversation after that and then because he was genuinely intrigued by the Corporal, Bone asked 'What did you work at before you came in?'

'Me Dad's got a small shop out Warley way. I helped him.'

'Oh!' That was a bit of a disappointment to the young Bone, he'd imagined Byers to have done something more exotic. His faith, however, was immediately restored when the Corporal continued,

'I've got plans, mind you. Big ones.'

'What sort of plans, Nick?'

Byers pursed his lips. 'The Chinese in Singapore gave me the idea. Some of them have this thing of buying in bulk, keeping the prices down to an absolute minimum and making their profit on turnover. If I can raise the cash when I get back home, I might have a stab at trying the same thing in Birmingham. If the Chinese can make it work, then I don't see why I can't.'

Bone grinned. 'You never dreamt that up down Bugis Street.'

'You're right there. And you stay away from those Ki-Ti's, Scotch Jack. Stick your hand up one of their skirts and you'll be in for a shock.'

'I'm no nancy boy,' Bone growled, 'The only women I'm interested in are the real kind. The ones that have a fanny between their legs.'

Byers's tone was taunting. 'You make it sound as though you're experienced.'

'I am enough.'

The Corporal passed over a Lucky and they both lit up. 'Got a regular bird, eh?'

Bone shook his head. 'No. Nothing like that.'

'So you've just been at it with whatever you can get your hands on. With those . . . what do you Jocks call those birds in Glasgow? Hermies?'

'Hairies,' Bone corrected, 'And they're not the sort of birds I go out with. I like them with a bit of class. A bit of experience you ken.'

'Oh, I think I ken all right,' Byers said mockingly. Then as an afterthought, 'Why are they called hairies?'

'Working class girls. Too poor to buy a hat. The expression comes from the old days.'

'I see,' mused Byers. 'And what did you do before you came in?'

Bone's reply was evasive. 'Oh, a bit of this and that. Nothing specific if you know what I mean.'

'And what about your father?'

Bone stared out to sea. The tide was now in far enough for the waiting banyan boats to be able to slip over the reef. Their bobbing yellow lights moved as their engines crackled into life.

'He's dead,' Bone mumbled.

The Corporal turned to stare at him. He didn't say anything, he merely nodded his head. Bone felt the compulsion to go on.

'He worked on the railways, my Ma told me. He died of T.B. a couple of months before I was born.'

'That's rough,' said Byers, 'So your Mum brought you up, eh?' Bone closed his eyes. He didn't want to have to look at anybody or anything. It never ceased to amaze him how sensitive he still was about it. He felt foolish and juvenile.

'She died two years ago. Same as him, T.B.' he said.

'So who did you live with?'

'An aunt, until she threw me out. We didn't get on. She had a pig of a husband who got on my tits. One night he tried to throw me around, so I took a knife to him.' Bone's lips parted in a wolfish grin. 'I chased him all the way down the street in his underpants. I would never have believed he could run so fast.'

'So you didn't actually stick him, then?'

'No, I couldn't catch him.' Then, in a voice loaded with hate, 'But I would've if I'd caught up. I hated that man so much it actually hurt.'

'It sounds like you've had it a bit tough so far,' said the Corporal.

'I've got by,' Bone replied harshly. Then, more softly, 'I've got by.'

He kept his eyes closed until he fell asleep.

Jack Bone brought himself back to the present with a grunt as the dog-end burnt his fingers. He ground it out in the already overflowing ashtray, at the same time sweeping Nick Byers and Malaya clear from his thoughts.

He swung the Mini alongside the kerb by a flower-stall, rolled down the window and shouted to the spiv stallholder that he'd take a bunch of the red and another of the pink. There was a bit of fern mixed in with them and they had a good smell. He reckoned Babs would be delighted.

Five minutes later, he was striding up the slate-coloured stairs that led to the top of the tenement building where she lived. On the top floor right he came face to face with a nameplate which bore the legend in blue speckle, B. McGRATH.

With the flowers clutched in front of him he slid the key into the lock and pushed the door open.

A radio blared in the apartment, and from the direction of the bathroom came the sound of water gushing in the shower. Bone snicked the door shut and padded towards the bathroom. To get to it he had to go through the bedroom, and as he entered a D.J. announced the time in a bubbling southern drawl. He was half-way across the room when he heard the laughter.

He paused while his insides fell with a sickening thump. For the first time he became aware of the odour that permeated the bedroom; it was one he was familiar with. Both pillows on the bed were bruised, as was the mattress on both sides. The sheets had been pulled to one side, and he knew only too well what that meant.

He was turning back for the door when Babs's voice cried out, 'Will you stop it!' She laughed throatily, 'I have to get to work!' The reply was male and indistinct.

A second later the bathroom door burst open and Babs ran into the room. She froze with shock when she saw Bone.

The young man at her back was the Adonis type. Tall, husky, with a swarthy skin that had a permanent tanned look about it. His hair was jet and long, he had it tied back in a pony tail. All he was wearing was a jade Buddha dangling on the end of a golden chain. His look was supercilious.

Bone held out the flowers. 'Surprise!' he said. When she made no move to take them from him he threw them on the bed.

'Who's this?' asked the Adonis, 'Don't tell me there's a husband you forgot to tell me about?'

Babs blushed and dropped her gaze to the floor. 'It's a friend of mine,' she muttered. Then to Bone, 'You're back earlier than you said.'

Bone studied the young man and knew that, even if he hadn't met him under these circumstances, he would still have taken an instant dislike to him. He positively oozed arrogance along with an unnatural amount of self-confidence and poise.

'Don't I know you?' Bone asked.

The Adonis smirked. 'The name's Jaime Swan. Maybe you've heard of me.' He said it as a statement.

The name clicked and Bone knew why the face had been puzzlingly familiar. Swan was a pop star who played lead guitar with a group whose origins were in Scotland. Now they were big time with an international reputation. Swan, who reputedly had some Spanish blood in him, was billed as El Gato Grande: The Big Cat.

Bone was singularly unimpressed. His gaze slid to Babs and he wondered why she had done it. Was it because she was thirty-five years old and beginning to feel her age? Had she found it necessary to prove to herself she was as good looking as she'd always been, and could still trap the youngsters? Or was there more to it than that, could it be that she'd been stringing him along all this while and Swan was only one of many? Somehow he couldn't bring himself to believe that last possibility and he couldn't make up his mind whether it was because of his judgement of her character or merely his romantic streak coming out.

Babs waggled a toe in the deep pile of the carpet. 'I'm sorry, Jack,' she said.

Swan grinned. 'So it's that way!' He sat on the edge of the bed, mangling the flowers in the process. His eyes flicked from Bone to Babs and then back again. He indicated the phone.

'May I?' He didn't wait for a reply. He dialled a number and when he was connected, said jocularly, 'Les, get your ass round to that chick's apartment. Some geezer's come bustin' in and there might be a bit of aggro.'

He hung up, reached across to the bedside table and poured himself a hefty slug from a Tequila bottle. 'I hope you're not going to make trouble,' he leered at Bone. 'Because if you even begin to look like you're going to, then my bodyguard Les will kick the living shit out of you.'

Bone was still unimpressed. 'We say *shite* in this part of the country,' he said. Then turning to Babs, 'Put something on before the cavalry arrive.'

While she was wriggling herself into a wrap he said,

'How'd you come to meet lover boy here?'

Her reply was an indistinct mumble.

'I can't hear you!' Bone said loudly.

'RECEPTION!' She bit her lip and and went back to looking at the carpet. Every few seconds she reached up and nervously played with a lock of hair.

'Tell me about it,' said Bone.

Her voice was a whisper. 'The agency's doing a promotion on an after shave and Jaime's agreed to be the personality who pushes it. There was a photo session yesterday and the reception came after.'

Bone couldn't help the bitterness that spilled over in his voice. 'And I suppose there was the usual flowing champers which led to one thing and then another?'

Babs winced. 'Don't, Jack. I feel bad enough as it is.'

Swan said to Bone, 'You shouldn't take any notice of me, I'm just one of those ships that pass in the night. No doubt she'll be happy to come back to you once I've split.'

'You're a real charmer,' said Bone, 'And modest with it.'

'I'm beginning to like you, so I'll tell you what I'll do,' Swan's face lit up with a combination of laughter and malice. 'I'll give her back to you right now. She was a lousy fuck, anyway.' Babs sobbed and stuck a fist in her mouth. Her shoulders sagged.

A voice from the doorway said, 'So who's the aggro merchant, then?'

Bone gave the newcomer full marks for making a silent entrance.

'Right on cue,' said Swan, swinging his legs over the side of the bed. 'Say hello to Les, folks,' he added.

Les was tall and broad with it. He had a meaty face and even meatier fists. His accent was pure Bow Bells.

'Did you really mean that, what you just said?' Babs asked in a cracked voice.

Swan's already enormous grin grew even larger. 'Every word of it, baby. If I was giving marks out of ten, I reckon you'd score about two for effort. And even that's being nice to you.' To Bone he said, 'You want to get organised, chum. I'm sure you could do better than that slag.'

Babs made a sobbing noise and collapsed into a chair. Her shoulders heaved as she hid her face in cupped hands.

'Tell you what I'll do,' said Swan. He extricated his wallet from his velvet jacket, pulled out a twenty-pound note and laid it on the table beside the Tequila bottle. 'Go out and buy yourself a little pressy. I'm sure that'll make you feel better.'

Bone asked, 'Do you always carry on this way, or only when your gorilla's around?'

'Watch your lip,' said Les.

The anger that bubbled inside Bone was white hot by now. He glanced at the woman he'd been planning to marry and then across to where Swan was zipping himself into a pair of skin-tight trousers. The pants were so crutch-hugging they left nothing whatsoever to the imagination. Bone decided what he was going to do.

'I think you owe the lady an apology,' he said.

Swan looked incredulous. 'Eh?'

'You heard me.'

Swan laughed, and slapped his thigh. 'Oh, that's good, that really slays me!' he guffawed. 'Did you hear that, Les? I'm supposed to say sorry because his bit of skirt's rubbish in the kip!' His face contorted as he turned on Bone. 'Get knotted, mister!'

'Leave it, Jack,' Babs sobbed. She wiped her nose and studiously avoided catching anyone's eye. Her skin crawled and she felt unclean. She wondered whatever had possessed her to be so stupid as to allow Swan to come back to the flat with her. Shame welled through her, and all she wanted to do was hide in some corner. She knew she'd lost Jack Bone forever.

'I'm deadly serious,' said Bone softly.

Les tapped him politely on the arm. 'Take my advice. Drop it.'

'Better listen to him,' Swan brayed. He scratched the hairy chest beneath the see-through shirt. The jade Buddha was twirled back to front as though hiding its head in embarrassment.

'Please take that money back,' Babs whispered.

'I told you, it's for a pressy. Buy yourself something nice.'

'Please!' she wailed.

Swan regarded her with satisfaction. 'That's the way I like to see them,' he said. 'Begging!'

'That how you get your kicks?' Bone asked.

'Sure. Adds a little spice.'

'Tell me,' Bone asked quietly, 'If you weren't a guitar player, how would you earn your living?'

Jaime Swan frowned. 'Why?'

'Curious, that's all.'

'I don't know. It's the only thing I'm good at. Well . . . that, and screwing.'

Babs rose and, still without looking at anyone, crossed to the bedside table. She picked up the twenty-pound note and methodically tore it into tiny shreds. 'Now get out!' she hissed.

Swan coolly ran his gaze over the short red hair, the high-thrusting breasts and the boyish backside. Babs cringed under his glance, and he said maliciously, 'I'll say this for you, you're not bad looking for a bird so long in the tooth. It's just too bad you don't know how to use it.' He lit a pastel-coloured cigarette and effetely puffed smoke into the air.

'Perhaps you don't inspire her,' said Bone. Peripherally he was sizing up the gorilla, looking for any natural weaknesses. He still wasn't sure whether Les was a pro or just an enthusiastic amateur.

'Eh? What?' Incredulity was written all over Swan's swarthy face.

'You heard.'

'Listen, mister, I haven't yet met the chick who hasn't been turned on by me! All the gash I've known say I'm too much. I ain't ever had no complaints!'

Bone waved a thumb at Les. 'Maybe they've been scared to voice an opinion.' Then, with relish, he added, 'Have you ever stopped to consider why they sleep with you?'

'Because it's me. They fancy it!'

Bone started walking slowly towards the pop star. 'Are you sure it's you, or could it be what you are? You're interchangeable, Swan, you and a hundred other clowns. You're nothing but filth with an overinflated ego. If your life was to be summed up, you know what it would amount to? Well, I'll tell you. The answer's nothing. You're pathetic!'

He brought his hand up in a backhander that sent Swan

spinning across the room. The pop star cried out with fright and shouted for his bodyguard.

Les lowered his head and came in like a bulldozer. Bone grunted with satisfaction; the man was more brawn than brain. It was what he'd been hoping for.

Bone's stiffened fingers lashed out in a V, and Les screamed as they punched into his eyeballs. As he blundered past Bone kicked him full in the cobblers and followed that with an elbow under the chin which caused pink blood and bits of teeth to spatter everywhere. Bone then grabbed the stricken man by the scruff of the neck and propelled him headfirst towards the bedroom wall. There was a sickening thud as his bullet head battered into plaster and bricks. Les slid to the floor, where he lay in an unconscious heap.

Swan stood mesmerised, mouth agape and eyes bulging in their sockets. The swarthy complexion had faded to a muddy grey. His legs were trembling, and it could be seen that under his skin tight pants he was rigidly excited. He gulped and back-pedalled. 'You leave me alone,' he whined.

Bone advanced slowly. 'The lady still hasn't had her apology. How about it?'

Frenzied eyes swung from Bone to Babs. 'I'm . . . I'm sorry,' he mumbled.

'You'll have to do better than that,' said Bone.

Swan was getting hysterical now. He screamed, 'I'M SORRY!' and cowered against the window where Bone had purposefully trapped him.

Bone nodded. 'That's better.' Then to Babs out the corner of his mouth, 'What do you think of lover boy now?'

Her tone was vitriolic. 'He's a pig!'

'I agree.' To Swan he said, 'What was it you were saying about your women? Didn't you say you liked to make them beg? To plead? Wasn't that what you said?'

Swan gibbered and pushed himself even closer to the glass. His see-through shirt was a sweat-sodden rag.

Bone said, 'Well I think I'd like to play that game.' His hand lashed out to crack against first one cheek and then the other. Red weals sprang into life where he'd made contact.

'I'll give you money. How much d'you want, a hundred, two?' Swan croaked.

'You're not listening,' Bone admonished. His hand flashed again and crack followed crack. 'It's your turn to plead. Down on your knees, pig. Down!'

Swan's legs buckled and he sank to the floor. His entire body was shaking now. His eyes flickered towards the stricken bodyguard, but there would be no help coming from that direction. Les lay exactly as he'd fallen. Occasionally he made a grunting sound.

'Beg,' said Bone softly.

Lips quivered. 'Please . . . Please!'

Bone smiled thinly. 'Not to me. To her.' He indicated Babs. 'Beg her forgiveness for what you said. And make it sound like you mean it!'

'I'm terribly sorry for what I said about you. It was only a joke, I . . . ' He winced as Bone's foot connected with his ribs.

'I said mean it,' Bone whispered.

Tears welled and blurred Swan's eyes. 'Please forgive me,' he wailed.

Bone's hand descended to grab a handful of jet black hair. As he pulled the screaming pop star to his feet, he was using his other hand to heave up the sash window. When it was fully raised he grabbed Swan's wrists and smacked the man's hands directly underneath. Bone heaved and the window screeched down like some horrible, dull guillotine.

Jaime Swan screamed, a high, thin, piercing sound that might not have been human at all. He stared down at the mangled, bloody mess which only seconds before had been his fingers. Then a pain more intense than any he'd ever have believed possible hammered into him, and he fainted.

Bone freed the pop star before turning and walking to the door. He paused momentarily. 'You'd better call an ambulance right away,' he said.

Babs struggled to her feet. 'Jack!' she called. But she was too late, she was talking to an empty room.

Chapter 2

London had changed even more than he'd imagined. The King's Road had been transformed into a trendy strip of boutiques that seemed inhabited by an endless stream of pseuds. One thing that struck Bone was that none of the women in London, under forty that was, seemed to wear bras anymore. It was a fashion he approved of, although he was sure it would never catch on north of the border. The Church of Scotland and the Women's Guild would see to that. Just for a giggle and old time's sake, he crossed over into Clapham and went searching for the old wedge-shaped flat where he'd once lived. The house had gone, knocked down and replaced by a warren of yellow brick maisonettes. He wondered what had happened to the Polish landlady with bad teeth.

He found Prince of Wales Drive, drove on past the Fun Fair and drew up outside York Buildings. He was more than pleased with the Mini's performance during the journey south. 'Good lass,' he muttered as he patted the steering wheel, 'You did well.'

He walked through some swing doors and started checking flat numbers until he found the one he was looking for on the top storey. He pressed the bell and waited. When there was no reply he pressed again.

After five minutes he gave up and started the long haul down to the street again. Whoever was living in the flat now was probably out at work, so Bone decided to come back after six and try again. The address was the only lead he had to go on.

As he reached the swing doors, he saw through the glass which panelled them that a girl was climbing the stone steps towards him. He held the door open politely.

'Thankyouverramuch,' she said, and swung on past.

He was nearly to the car before the penny dropped. The voice had been Glasgow born and bred. Swinging on his heels he dashed after her, and pounded up three flights of stairs before he caught her again. She was inserting her key into a lock.

'If you're from the telephone, the bill's been paid,' she said aggressively.

He smiled and gave what he hoped was a sympathetic look. 'I'm not from the telephone. I wonder if I could have a word with you, please?'

The girl frowned, 'Here, you're no' one of these queeries, are you?'

Using his index finger he made a sign over the left part of his chest, 'Cross my heart and hope to die. I'm perfectly normal.'

The frown became a smile but she was still cautious. 'What's it all about?' she asked.

Bone groped in his pocket and pulled out the picture the Fosters had given him. 'Know her?' he asked.

'What makes you think I might?'

'Because she lived upstairs and came from Glasgow like you do. Us Scots are like the Mafia, we have a habit of sticking together, especially when we're away from home.'

'Are you a rozzer?'

Bone shook his head. 'Nope. Not even the private kind.'

The girl made up her mind. 'You'd better come in then,' she said. And then, as she led him through a dingy hall, 'My name's Susan Sweet. Mind Noddy!'

Noddy was a barrel with a funny horse's face painted on one end and a brown saddle slung over its middle. It was anchored to a heavy wooden base.

'I like to ride,' she said, 'And no cracks!'

In the kitchen she seated Bone at a long refectory table while she went about the business of making a pot of tea. Bone lit up a cigarette and studied her. She was small, thin, with the sort of wan complexion that comes from staying indoors too much. The hair was well acquainted with peroxide.

'What do you want Nova for?' she asked.

'I was told her name was Heather.'

Susan poured the tea into two tin mugs and passed his across to him. She indicated there was sugar in a pottery bowl. 'She changed her name not long after she came here.

Said she never liked Heather. Said it had about as much charm as a pound of mince.'

'You were quite friendly, then?'

'Oh, aye. Regular gasbags we were. We even worked together for a time, but the bar wasn't good enough for Nova. No, she had other ideas.'

'What bar was this?'

'It's in Clarges Street just off Piccadilly.' She peered intently at Bone across the table. 'Why are you looking for her?'

'She's gone missing and her folks would like to find her again. Her father's dying.'

Susan pulled a face. 'That's a shame. I know she was fond of the old bloke. Spoke of him quite often.'

'Did you know the police were looking for her?'

'Sure. I heard it on the grapevine. They've been up at Nova's old flat several times.'

'And what did you tell them?'

Susan grinned, which made her look very pixieish. 'Nothing. They never thought to ask me.'

Bone sipped his tea and gazed around the kitchen. There was a lot of pine and a number of copper pans in evidence. On one wall hung a poster of a huge elephant having a pee. 'Any idea where I can find her?' he asked.

'No. One day she was here, and the next she was gone without even a good-bye.' She helped herself to one of Bone's cigarettes. 'If it's any help to you, she was working at a place called "The Grumble Club" doing her hostess bit.'

Bone made a mental note of the name. 'What sort of place is it?' he asked.

'A casino, the expensive kind. Very exclusive clientele. At least that's what Nova told me, I've never been there myself.'

'And do you hostess in this bar of yours?'

Eyes flickered to meet his and then danced away again. They seemed to be smiling. 'I'm a waitress; the topless kind. All teeth and tits. The money's good and the tips are even better. And before you ask, the customers are allowed to look but not touch.'

'Was Nova so particular?'

Susan shrugged. 'She got around. She was good looking and knew it. As she herself said many times, she reckoned she was sitting on a fortune and somewhere along the line she was going to cash in.'

'What was she after? Money?'

'That and all the things it can buy. She wanted the good life while she was young, and respectability when she wasn't quite so young anymore.'

'Sounds like quite a calculating lady.'

Susan laughed. 'Wasn't she just! But then aren't we all, in our own little ways?'

'The cynics amongst us say that all women flog it. It's only their asking price which varies.'

'You sound bitter.'

Bone finished his tea and pushed the mug away. He was tired after the long drive down, and he needed a shave. He rose to his feet. 'Well thanks very much for the info. If there's nothing else you can tell me then I'll –'

She cut in, 'How long are you going to be in town?'

'I don't know. A few days. A week. Maybe a little longer.'

Susan Sweet gave him a long, hard look. 'If you haven't found a place to kip yet, I can offer you the spare room here.' She mentioned a price that was reasonable.

'Cheaper than a hotel,' said Bone.

'Well?'

He smiled. 'You're sweet, Miss Sweet. It's a deal.' He went back down to the Mini and hauled out his scuffed plastic case. She showed him into the room and he dumped it on the bed.

'Pleasant dreams!' she shouted after he'd showered and shaved. With the daylight dancing on his face he fell fast asleep.

Later that evening he cut a piece of broccoli and stuck it into his mouth. It had been covered with melted butter and had lemon juice squeezed over it. 'Very good,' he confessed, 'There's more to you than meets the eye.'

'I'm not just a pretty face, you know,' Susan teased. 'And before you say anything about me cooking for you, it's as cheap to feed one as it is two.'

'So who's complaining,' said Bone, getting stuck into the casserole, 'I'm not proud.'

She pointed to his badly pitted face. 'Hope you don't think I'm being rude, but what caused that? Acne?'

He shook his head. 'Smallpox. Contracted it in the Far East during the fifties.' He tapped his cheek with the butt of his fork. 'This was the result. Not very nice, eh?'

'Oh, I don't know. I think it makes you look very butch.'

'Are you sending me up?'

Her eyes twinkled. 'What do you think?' Then seriously, 'What were you doing out in that part of the world?'

His lips set as he tried to hold back the memories. He ran a hand through thinning sandy hair; he'd allowed it to grow long at the nape of his neck so that it curled over his shirt collar. 'I was one of those green kids who went out and fought in Malaya when they had the trouble there.'

'You look sad when you say that.'

'Yeah. And if you don't mind, I prefer not to talk about it.'

Susan lowered her head and stared at the plate set in front of her. She thought of the one and only time she'd ever fallen in love, and how he'd conned her out of more than a thousand pounds and run off with another bird, leaving her in the club. Since that day she'd carried an ache inside her that had never gone away. She'd had the kid and then had him fostered. It was a decision she knew she'd regret the rest of her life.

'I know what you mean,' she rose swiftly and crossed to the fridge, where she pulled out a bottle of cheap white plonk. Saying, 'You can't really stomach this stuff if it's at room temperature,' she filled a glass to the brim.

Bone made patterns in his gravy. 'Not for me, thanks.'

'I've got a little drop of brandy, if you fancy that?'

He shook his head. 'Thanks anyway, but I don't drink alcohol of any kind.'

Susan laughed and then took a long pull at her drink. She shuddered and immediately filled the glass to the top again. 'What a ridiculous thing!' she said, 'Whoever heard of a teetotal Scotsman? I didn't think they bred such an animal!'

'I'm a member of A.A.' he said quietly. And then as a joke, 'And I don't mean the Automobile Association.'

'Oh!' she said, 'How long have you been on the wagon?'

'Ten years.'

'And do you still feel like . . . ?' She trailed off, not quite sure what she was trying to say.

Bone said it for her. 'If you mean do I still want a drink, then the answer is yes. Once an alcoholic, always one. The Association doesn't cure you, nobody can do that. What it does do is to help you stop and try to keep that way. One drink, just one, and within a couple of days I'd be back to the way I was ten years ago. A drunken slob who would sell his grandmother for even a smell at that bottle over there.' He jammed a fag into his mouth and lit up, streaming smoke at the table.

Quietly and without saying anything Susan gathered the dirty dishes together and piled them in the sink. She washed, dried and put them away. 'I'll have to go to work now,' she said, looking at her watch.

'I'll give you a lift,' Bone offered and went looking for his Crombie.

When he dropped her off at Clarges Street she pressed a Yale key into his palm. 'I won't be in till about four,' she said. She looked as though she might say something else, but in the end she thought better of it. Bone sat and watched her, listening to her platform shoes as they clattered away along the pavement. She turned and waved before disappearing into an open doorway. He was left with the impression of a white pixie face. It seemed to him he couldn't remember one which looked more vulnerable

He'd already searched through the phone book to discover that thc 'Grumble Club' had an address in Bloomsbury just behind the British Museum. After getting well and truly lost in the one way system that surrounded the area, he eventually found it. He'd deliberately worn his one and only suit in honour of the occasion.

The outside of the club was not impressive. A rather dirty candy-striped canopy, guarded by a greasy gentleman who could only be Maltese. Bone paid his fiver entrance fee and stepped inside.

There was the clickety-clack of the roulette table overlaid by the hum of conversation. The punters were a mixed bunch, but seemed mainly to fall into the middle-aged male variety. There were lots of birds with low cut dresses and fixed smiles. Without exception their eyes were cold.

'Would you like someing?' She was petite and Chinese.

She wore a flame-coloured *cheomsang* that was slit to her thigh. Bone glimpsed a black frilly garter. 'Perhaps you like to entertain yourself at the gaming tables?' she added.

'What's your name?'

She made a small, bowing motion with her head. 'Li Soong, but you may call me Petal. I am here to look after you and arrange anything you might require.'

'Anything?'

'Most things can be arranged.'

Bone nearly laughed out loud. He'd been away from London too long, and had forgotten his Cockney rhyming slang. Grumble was the shortened version of Grumble And Grunt . . .

So this was the exclusive club that catered for the best clientele! He wondered whether it was pride or sheer fantasy that had made Nova lie to Susan Sweet. The place was an out-and-out clip joint operating a string of call girls on the side.

'Let's have a drink,' he said. He ordered whisky for Petal and a Coke for himself. 'Is there someplace we can sit and talk?' he asked.

Petal smiled and started hustling. 'You no wanna play roulette or cards? I think you make lots of money tonight. I think you look a lucky man.'

'I'd rather talk.'

She pouted. 'Aw!' and took his hand in hers. 'I much rarrer watch you at the tables. We can talk there if you wanna.'

Bone thought her act was about as subtle as a sledgehammer. He nodded his agreement, knowing he'd have to make a few bets if he was going to get any change out the girl at all. En route to the tables he asked, 'How long have you worked here?'

'About a year,' she replied, fluttering her eyelids. Several of the other girls watched her enviously, obviously thinking she had a ripe one on her hook.

Bone watched the game for a few minutes before buying some low denomination chips. He ventured a quid on black and watched it come up. He let it ride and won again. Petal squeezed his arm. 'See, I knew you were going to be lucky!'

'Yeah,' said Bone. He placed a quarter and an eighth which

went down, so he went back to playing colours. During the next fifteen minutes he won a tenner.

A hot thigh rubbed against him. 'Bet the numbers,' she whispered.

'Last bets, ladies and gentlemen, please!' the croupier intoned. His shifty eyes swept the table.

On an impulse Bone threw two pound chips on to number twelve, the day during the month of August on which he'd been born. 'Last of the big time spenders, that's me,' he grinned.

The white ball whirred round and round, then clacked as it rolled over the numbers. Petal squealed when it plopped into the number twelve slot. Bone collected his seventy quid and steered the protesting girl away from the table with the excuse that you should always get out while you were ahead. Out of the corner of his eye he saw the croupier shoot her a glance that said, *get him back again*.

Bone collected more drinks from the small bar and squeezed the pair of them into a tiny, plush booth. He noted that the embossed wallpaper behind the girl's head had begun to peel and that the fancy lampshade on the wall was festooned with cobwebs. From another booth close by came the garrulous tones of an American as he chatted up his hostess. Bone wondered idly how much the Yank would be taken for that night.

'You wanna play again in a few minutes, eh?' she grinned. She squirmed closer and laid her hand on his leg. Childlike fingers made walking movements till they were resting on the inner part of his thigh. Pink lips parted provocatively. 'Or maybe you like girl for the night? Can be arranged. You like Petal?'

'I think you're gorgeous,' he lied.

'You wan I arrange?'

He peeled ten quid off his wad and slipped it down the valley of her breasts. 'Did you know a girl called Nova Foster?' he asked.

The calculating eyes became even more so. 'Sure, she used to work here.'

'Know where I can find her?'

The hand was removed from the inside of his thigh and the ten quid disappeared into the slit of her *cheomsang*. She tapped her teeth with a long fingernail while she studied him. 'You the police?'

It was a question he'd long since got used to. 'Nope,' he replied, 'A friend.'

Her eyes flickered from side to side. 'I might be able to help you but, ah . . . '

Bone got the message. He peeled off another ten and stuck it in her decolletage. He looked inquiringly at her and was rewarded with a cynical smile and an upraised eyebrow. He added the same again.

'You have to take me out and then I take you to someone who know. Wait for me at the door while I go get my coat.' She slid out of the booth and waggled her way towards the rear of the club. When she disappeared behind a silk screen Bone rose and sauntered towards the entranceway.

In less than five minutes the Chinese girl had rejoined him. She gave him a soft smile and led him into the night.

'That'll be twenty-five, mac,' said the Maltese doorman.

Bone stopped. 'What for?'

The Malt nodded towards the girl and then stuck out his hand. The other he kept conspicuously in his right hand jacket pocket, where it made a bulge. 'House percentage,' he said as the notes were counted out.

'Where to?' asked Bone.

Petal clung to his arm and flashed him a trusting smile. 'No too far, but it best we take a taxi,' she said.

During the cab ride Bone tried to question the girl further, but she steadfastly refused to answer. She told him to be patient and she would see he found Nova. She snuggled up beside him, and the drive was completed in silence.

The address she'd given the driver was in Marylebone, and there they were dutifully dropped. Petal led him round a corner and along a street till she eventually stopped before a shop that sold porno mags.

UNDERSTANDING BONDAGE said a caption in the window. There was a picture of a girl tied to a table. She was looking over her shoulder with great pleasure at her very red looking bum. 'Whatever turns you on,' said Bone as he was led up a flight of rickety stairs.

When he entered the room at the top of the flight, two things happened simultaneously. The lights went on and the door slammed shut behind him. He found himself confronted by two muscular gentlemen, both of whom he reckoned to be in their late twenties or very early thirties. They were both well dressed and intelligent looking. Behind him Bone heard the rapid *ratatattat* of heels on wood as Petal rushed down the stairs. He relaxed his body as much as he could, bent his knees a fraction and waited for the play.

'We hear you're looking for Nova Foster,' said one of the heavies and nodded in a friendly fashion. 'That true?'

Bone admitted that he was. He'd already taken in the fact that the only furniture the room contained was a large double bed, a washbasin and a tatty wardrobe. He reckoned he knew what the room was used for.

The second man said, 'I wonder if you'd care to come and meet our boss? He'd like a word with you. Tonight, if possible.'

'Does this boss of yours have a name?'

The man cleared his throat. 'I'm sure if he wants you to know he'll tell you that himself.'

Bone instinctively knew these two were in a far different class from the muscle who'd been guarding Jaime Swan. These were pros and, he was willing to bet, good at their job. He asked,

'If that's the case, then why didn't Petal take me to him direct?' He waved a hand round the room. 'Why this?'

'A little precaution on our part,' said the second man. 'We wanted to have a look at you first. Also, the boss would like to see you at his home, so we wanted to make sure you weren't the type who was going to make any fuss.'

'And if I don't come?'

The first man said smoothly, 'Then we'll arrange something else at your convenience. But I'm sure you will.'

'Does your boss know where I can find the girl?'

Second man shrugged. 'We're only carrying the invite, mister.'

It seemed to Bone he was stirring up a lot more than he'd bargained for. He wondered what connection Nova Foster had had with this lot. He had already decided, however, to go with them; after all it was a lead, and that was what he'd been looking for. 'OK, let's go then,' he said.

En route downstairs again they passed several closed

doors, and from behind one of them came muffled, passionate noises. His guess about the rooms had been correct.

One thing he didn't have to guess about, though, was the fact that at least one of his companions was carrying a shooter. He'd heard the faint chink of metal on wood when the first man had knocked against the door coming out.

Outside in the street they climbed into a gleaming black Bentley, Bone and the second man in the back while the first drove. Second man offered round small cigars which Bone declined, he preferred to stay with his full strength gaspers. He puffed smoke while the machine whispered through the night.

The car threaded its way through north London, past King's Cross and a sign that said they were now at the Angel. Five minutes later they pulled into an impressive Georgian square. First man parked the car and then, flanked by the pair of them, Bone was led up a short flight of steps. The door knocker was an evil-looking brass satyr. Its eyes were crossed and its tongue protruded in a leer.

A maid answered the knock. Her eyes flickered over the threesome and she gave the briefest of smiles. 'This way please,' she said. They were ushered into a basement room that had been laid out as a combination den and bar. Bone sat on a button-down leather Chesterfield and gazed around. First and second man sat at the bar. There was a wait of about three minutes before the door opened and a man wearing jeans and a sweater entered. Below the thatch of iron grey hair the eyes were piercing blue ice. The man crossed to stand in front of Bone, who immediately rose, and the man extended his hand.

'Thank you very much for coming, Mr Bone. My name is Duff.'

Glasgow wasn't that far away from the big action for Bone not to have heard whispers. He'd heard a great deal of this Duff, and knew him to be the head of the very powerful north London gang.

'I'm pleased to meet you,' he said.

Duff crossed to the bar. 'Drink?'

'Anything soft that you might have.'

Duff smiled and poured a Coke. 'Jonno? Jimbo?'

First and second man shook their heads respectively. Duff

nodded and said, 'Well, I think that'll be all for tonight. I'll see you in the morning.'

The heavies muttered their farewells and silently exited. Duff sipped a whisky, and then glanced at his watch. 'Anything lined up for tonight?' he asked.

Bone said he hadn't, and accepted a cigarette from the silver box proffered to him. It was a pleasant surprise to discover the fag to be Turkish and of an obviously superior blend.

Duff said, 'In that case, I wonder if you'd like to join us for dinner? My wife and I've invited a few guests, nothing formal, and we were just about to sit down and eat when you arrived. There's a few things I'd like to talk over with you later.'

For the first time Bone noticed that Duff had a slight accent. He put it down to being either Canadian or American. 'If one of those things is Nova Foster, I'll be happy to stay,' he replied.

'Then that's settled. Come and meet the rest of our guests.'

As Bone was ushered into a combination dining and reception room, a dark-haired, doe-eyed woman swept forward to meet him. 'How kind of you to come Mr Bone,' she said. She was dressed in suede trousers with matching top.

'I'm pleased to meet you, Mrs Duff.'

She smiled. 'My friends call me Anya.'

Bone did just that. There were eight other people in the room, apart from himself and his hosts, and he was introduced to each in turn. One was a film starlet with a German background, who clung to her escort, a scruffy painter type. There was a Labour M.P. whom Bone seemed to remember as having held government office at some time. He had a fishy handshake and a wet smile, and his eyes looked as though the corpse had already been buried for a week. Bone recalled that the M.P. had a name for being very left wing. He took an instant dislike to him. Of the other five guests, one was a young girl, he reckoned about eighteen, two were matrons, whose husbands were the hard-faced variety who wore Savile Row suits and huge diamond rings.

Duff was beside him when the starlet gushed, 'And what do you do, Mr Bone? You look terribly important.'

Bone found the girl irritating. She exuded false sincerity, the sort of bird who, if she thought you could do anything for her, would be all over you like a rash. The paint on her face looked as though it had been laid on with a trowel. But what annoyed him most of all was the fact that she was covered in perfume, the same sort that had been Babs's favourite.

'I'm a sorter,' he growled.

The starlet giggled. 'Goodness me, don't tell me you work for the Post Office?'

Bone glanced sideways to find Duff watching him, the craggy face lit up with amusement. Bone said,

'Where I live, there are a lot of people need things doing for them. When that happens, they come to me and I sort it out. Understand?'

The starlet giggled some more. 'How frightfully interesting! Isn't it, Morrie?'

Her artist friend nodded that it was and puffed on his king sized home made rollup. Bone caught the sweet smell of griff.

'And what sort of accent is that I detect?' Morrie asked. His eyes were vacuous and faraway looking. He was having another little party inside his skull.

'Glasgow,' Bone said.

'And some marvellous people have come from there,' smarmed the M.P., joining them. He flicked a dank lock out of his eyes. 'John McLean, for instance, eh?'

Bone took in threads that had cost at least a couple of hundred, a gold Omega that was worth a few bob and shoes which he recognised as hand made. If he'd inquired, he'd have discovered them to be by Kurt Geiger. 'Roll on the revolution. I'm a Nationalist myself,' he said.

The M.P. would have started a political discussion if Anya hadn't rescued them by announcing that dinner was ready. Bone sat where he was told, and found himself with his hostess on one hand and the starlet on the other. It had been a long time since he'd found himself in company like this, so he hoped he'd remember which knife was which. Not that he was impressed by the company anyway; with the exception of Duff and his wife he considered them a bunch of slobs. Especially the M.P.; that sort made him want to puke.

Bone made what small talk he could and waded through the nosh. He steadfastly refused the wine, and eventually the waiter got the message. He talked mainly to Anya, and found her entertaining; to his surprise she knew a great deal about events north of the border. She listened with sympathy to his argument for devolution and the desperate need for a workable Scottish assembly. He said he drew the line at complete separation, although at one time he had been strongly in favour of it.

'You love your country very much,' Anya said when he finally came to a halt.

Bone grinned, showing a lot of teeth. 'Ever heard the chestnut about the two Englishmen marooned on a desert island?' She shook her head and he continued, 'Well they never got around to talking to each other because they hadn't been formally introduced. Now if that had been two Irishmen they would have immediately had a fight, but if it had been two Scotsmen, you know what? The first thing they would have done would be to form a Caledonian Society.'

Anya laughed and made him repeat it to Duff. He'd no sooner done so than the starlet launched into some dreary joke that Bone was sure everyone was bound to have heard before. He eyed the starlet with distaste. She was the type who hated anyone even edging into the spotlight when she was around. He would have bet his Y-fronts she was lousy in bed.

After the sweet they repaired to the reception side of the room where brandy, port and coffee was served. Bone noted that neither of the two hard-faced characters had said much up until now. They spoke only when spoken to. During the entire meal their eyes had barely strayed from watching Duff.

Half an hour went by before Duff strolled over to Bone. 'If you'd like to come downstairs, we could have that chat.'

Bone nodded and let him lead the way. He noted that the hard-faced men watched them intently as they left the room.

Once downstairs, Bone settled himself into the chesterfield and waited while Duff poured himself a drink. All the time he was wondering what Nova Foster had done to get herself in the big league with cats like Duff.

'How did you know my name?' he asked for starters.

Duff hooked a leg over a bar stool. 'Do you know who and what I am?'

'Yes.'

'Good, that saves time.' He had ignored Bone's question. 'Do you mind telling me a little about yourself?'

Bone told him about his life in Glasgow, the way he helped people out in return for whatever fee they could afford. He spoke about Glasgow as though it were a woman, one he was intimate with and cared for. Warmth crept into his voice.

Duff listened in silence, the ice-cold eyes never once leaving Bone's face. When Bone was finally finished he asked him several leading questions about the criminal set-up in the city. The questions were all probing, and showed a great deal of insight into the Glasgow syndicates. After that Duff said,

'And now you're looking for Nova Foster. Why's that?'

Bone explained about how the father was dying from pneumoconiosis and how he'd been asked to find the daughter and get her to contact home before her old man finally snuffed it.

'How are you doing so far?' Duff asked.

'I'm doing all right. It's early days yet.'

Duff stared at the ceiling and appeared to turn something over in his mind. 'How much are they paying you?' he asked.

'Three hundred. That's all the money they have in the world.'

'Well, I suppose no one can pay more than that.'

'That's what I thought.' Bone allowed a few seconds to tick by before going on. 'Do you mind if I ask what your interest is in all this?'

Duff slipped from his stool and went behind the bar. He poured a large Malt over some ice cubes and then topped the glass up with milk. Bone winced.

Duff said slowly, 'You will appreciate that the "Grumble Club" is only one of many, all varying types, that my organisation and I run in north London.' He came round the front of the bar again and started to pace up and down. 'During the past few months I've begun to suspect that something's going on in certain parts of the organisation, that somebody's being naughty. I think money isn't reaching me which should be. In other words, somebody's on the fiddle. Trouble is, I suspect, but so far I cannot prove.'

'And you think Nova Foster might have been tied up in it in some way?'

Duff shook his head. 'Not at all. What I *do* think is that inadvertently she stumbled on to something and got scared, shit scared. Enough to make her light out one day, to do a disappearing act.'

Bone digested this. 'Have you anything concrete to back up this theory of yours?'

'No, just a feeling. The Foster girl was ambitious, and I'd recently promised her a new job in one of the better clubs. The other thing is that she left without collecting her wages and commission for the past month. That added up to nearly seven hundred pounds.'

'From what I've heard of her so far, it's not like her to leave that sort of loot behind,' said Bone.

'Precisely.'

'And you think that whatever it was she might have stumbled on might be connected with this stray money of yours?'

'It's possible, which is why I very badly want a word with the girl.'

Bone asked the obvious question. 'But surely, with your contacts, you should be able to trace her?'

'Not a sniff,' Duff replied, 'I've had two men on it since the day she took a powder, and they've drawn a complete blank.' He crossed to a bookcase and swung a section of it away from the wall to reveal a safe. He twiddled with the knob, spoke into a concealed mike, finally gave a chromium plated bar a twist to the right, then groped inside and pulled out a massive wad of notes, most of which he stuffed back inside again. The residue he laid on the chesterfield beside Bone.

'I'd like to hire you,' he said.

Bone blinked, for the moment caught off balance. 'To do what?' he asked.

'The same thing her folks hired you to do. Find Nova Foster; only if and when you do, I want you to call me and let me know.' He pointed at the stack of notes.

'There's three grand there. Find the girl and I'll replace

what you had to spend in expenses and also add another three. What do you say?'

'Why me, Mr Duff?'

'I've told you, my boys are getting nowhere fast, and besides, I like your style. I think you're the right man for the job. Call it a feeling again.' He sipped at his drink, eyeing Bone through the glass.

Bone played for time, not entirely sure if he wanted to get mixed up with Duff and his organisation. 'It's a lot of money to lay out on someone you hardly know.'

Duff grinned, his lips a thin line. 'I know more about you than you think,' he said softly.

'One thing must be clearly understood. I work my way, and I work alone. I don't function properly otherwise.'

'Suit yourself. All I ask is the occasional phone call to let me know how you're getting on, and of course the big one when you find her.'

'*If* I do, and let's face it, if she's stumbled on to what you suspect then she might be the late Nova Foster by now.'

'I'll pay the full amount for that information as well.'

Bone picked up the notes, it was more than he'd held in his hand for a long time. 'You know if you'd asked me I'd have given you the phone call anyway?'

'Yeah. But I like to pay my way. Besides, I reckon six grand is more incentive than three hundred.'

Bone made up his mind. He rose. 'It's a deal,' he said, and held out his hand.

They shook on it.

Chapter 3

Fleet Street was alive and growling just like it always was at that time in the morning. Bone paid off the cabbie and walked up a rain-slick alleyway; his feet clumped on the cobbles as he penetrated the gloom.

Once inside the pub he made his way through the Saloon bar into the Public.

Matthew Pamm was engaged in pursuing his favourite sport, and one he'd worked relentlessly at for over thirty years. Drinking Irish whiskey. The bony shoulders were hunched, the monkey face wrinkled. He wore the same old tweed jacket that he'd done time out of mind, its only acknowledgement to the passing years being the recent addition of leather patches on the elbows. He stared into his glass of Bushmills as though it was a crystal ball.

'If you'll talk to an old friend, I'll buy you another,' said Bone. 'You're looking well. Not a day over a hundred.'

Pamm looked up, and his face creased with delight. He sat back on the wooden bench and stared up at Bone. 'It's the gargle that does it. You know it'll be the death of me yet.'

Bone had been right, Pamm looked at least double his fifty-odd years. 'I know,' he said. He pushed his way through to the bar and ordered a large one for Pamm and a lime and soda for himself, added a mountain of ice and made his way back to the table.

Pamm took a large swallow and sighed with pleasure. He reached across and touched the back of Bone's hand in a gesture meant to convey his delight at seeing his old friend again. He nodded towards the soft drink.

'I'm proud of you.'

Although he knew it would be futile, Bone said, 'There's always room for new members.'

'I'm incorrigible. Besides, I own shares in the stuff!'

For a little while they sat and reminisced about the old days in Glasgow, when Pamm had been based there working for the Scottish version of the parent paper.

'Great days, me handsome. Great days,' said Pamm. He made a sign at the barman and a few seconds later fresh drinks appeared in front of them. A passer-by called out and pleasantries were exchanged. Then Pamm turned again to Bone.

'So, what brings you down here?' he asked, 'I thought Glasgow was your beat?'

'I'm doing a job and it's favour-asking time.'

A bushy eyebrow was raised. 'Me?'

'You still on the news desk?'

'Not for the past six months. They thought upstairs that I was getting a bit old for all that running around, so they've shifted me over to features.' He grinned and tugged at his yellow-stained white beard. 'A move I like. Gives me more time in the rub a dub dub.' He cleared his throat. 'Why?'

'I need some info from the old Bill. I thought you could help.'

'I presume it's not the sort they're going to give you if you were to walk in off the street and ask for it?'

'Right. They've been inquiring about a missing bird, Scots lassie by the name of Nova Foster. I'd like to read what's on the report.'

Pamm whistled. 'Possible, but difficult.' He rose, 'Let's see what happens. Come on over to the office and I'll make a couple of calls.'

Pamm hobbled through the press with Bone in tow. Outside, Bone asked him what was wrong with his legs, and was curtly informed that old age was creeping on apace. That and arthritis. For the first time Bone noted that his friend's back was now slightly twisted and one shoulder drooped lower than the other.

They made it safely across the street and into the glass and steel building that housed the paper Pamm worked for. They went down a flight of stairs, through swing doors and emerged into the case room. Rows of men sat playing the keys of their machines which punched out lead type. In a glass-panelled office a reader sat and listened to his assistant calling out the copy. The air smelled of ink and bustle, a smell Bone liked and never got tired of. The first time he'd come across it was when he was a lad in the Boy's Brigade and had been taken on a conducted tour of the old Glasgow Citizen.

They passed through the machinery room, where the giant presses hummed with excitement as they hammered out the early morning editions. Matt Pamm had a swift word with a gaffer before leading Bone through another door into the relative calm of the teletype room. Here, machines whirred as they spewed out reams of cream coloured printout. This was the news coming in from Reuters, AP, and the other wire services.

As they walked, Bone explained about the Foster girl. 'She's been calling herself Nova since she came south, but she was christened Heather.' He went on to give Pamm the background about how her old man was dying, but said nothing about Duff.

Pamm's office (he confided gleefully to Bone that he was one of the very few in the building who had one all to himself) was tiny and covered in heavy-duty cork. Hundreds of sheets of paper were pinned to the wall, most of them covered in scrawls and hieroglyphic comments.

'Take a seat,' said Matt. He opened a drawer and pulled out a half empty bottle of Bushmills. He poured a large one before plonking himself in front of the ancient, scarred roll-top desk which dominated the room. The typewriter that had pride of place might have come out of the Ark.

While his friend talked on the blower, Bone thought back to the story Matt'd told him years ago when they'd been well and truly guttered together one night. Once Matt had had a wife and kid whom he'd taken on a driving holiday in Italy. Half-way up a mountain road Matt had become desperate for a pee, so he'd parked the car and run across the road to get behind some bushes. When he came out a few minutes later, the car was gone, and he was just in time to see it fail to make a bend. At the end of the thousand foot drop the car exploded like a bomb when it hit the rocks. The inquest had laid the blame on mechanical failure, but Matt had never been fully convinced. He had the nightmarish idea that he might not have engaged the handbrake fully. Before that day Matt Pamm had been a purely social drinker.

Pamm hung up. 'I think we're on, but I won't be able to get you the guff until tomorrow. That OK?'

Bone nodded that it was, and made arrangements to come around next morning. He wanted to go through that report with a fine toothcomb to see what he could pick up. He was wondering about boy friends, as it seemed to him that a good looking doll like Nova was bound to have a regular stashed away somewhere, and made a mental note to ask Susan Sweet about that as well. He glanced at his watch and decided it was too late to ring the Fosters in Glasgow. He wanted another word with them to see if they'd been able to remember the names of any friends Nova might have mentioned. He'd asked them before he'd come away, and drawn a blank. It seemed Nova was the tight-lipped kind when it came to her private life, but he'd told the Fosters to keep thinking about it. He also promised himself a trip to the bank first thing; he didn't like the idea of walking around with three thousand in his pocket.

Off in the distance Big Ben chimed out the hour.

'There's a spare bed in my gaff if you're short,' said Pamm. 'That is if you don't mind putting up with an old piss artist like myself.'

Bone grinned and told him that he was already fixed. He described Susan Sweet and the set up in Battersea.

Pamm tugged at his beard. 'Some people have all the luck,' he said.

Bone knew his friend to be kidding; Pamm had never been involved with another woman since the death of his wife. He was strictly a one-woman man. He rose and said his good-byes, the arrangement being that they'd meet next morning in the boozer while Matthew drank his breakfast. Pamm swung round in his chair, fixed spectacles on his face and then rolled a fresh sheet of paper into the typewriter. As Bone let himself out the office, the noise that followed him was like machine-gun fire.

Bone knew there was nothing more he could do that night, so he decided to go back to Battersea. When he got there he made himself a cup of coffee before climbing into bed and switching out the light. He stared at the ceiling and thought of Babs. Night was always the worst for him, that was when he wanted a drink more than at any other time.

He wondered again why Babs had allowed herself to be screwed by a turd like Jaime Swan. He wouldn't have minded quite so much if it had been someone he could've respected, but a creep like that! He remembered how it had been good between them and the amount of laughs they'd had together. He smelled again the perfume she'd been so fond of dousing herself in. On the journey down from Scotland he'd kept the car windows open for the first hundred miles after he'd caught a whiff of it.

He knew he was probably a fool and should have tried to be more understanding about the Swan episode, but that was the way he was, and he was too old now to change. He'd known from the shocked look on her face that she'd realised that, no matter what she said, no matter how she tried to explain it, he would never have anything to do with her again.

He was drifting off to sleep when he thought of the Chinese girl called Petal. He heard her laugh and knew it wasn't really her he was hearing, but another Chinese girl, a long way off in time. The laugh swelled until it filled his head, and suddenly he was young again with a face that wasn't pitted and scarred. He'd been considered handsome in those days.

Nick Byers was high on Tiger beer. 'God damn the cow!' he roared and threw an empty bottle at the wall of their rented flat. It burst with a bang. Nick stared sullenly out of the window at the carpet of lights which was Singapore.

'She's gone out with someone else. I know it. I know it!' His bunched fist smacked into his palm.

Bone had never seen his mate this way before, and was surprised to find that it rather frightened him. 'You don't know that for certain,' he said.

The top from another bottle of Tiger rattled on the floor. 'I know, and so do you! Why else would she stand me up if it wasn't because she'd found someone else? She knows I'm only here for the three days!'

'Her father says he'll have her ring once she gets in. All you can do is wait.'

Nick snorted, and half the beer gurgled down his throat. Some frothed over his lips and ran in trickles down the side of his chin. He wiped them away impatiently. 'Never fall in love, Scotch Jack! Never do that thing. There's not a piece of gash that's worth it.'

'That wasn't what you said last week.'

'Fuck last week. We were up the jungle then, and you need some illusions to keep you going.' He rattled the window. 'Damn you, Beverley Robertson! Damn your rotten black soul!' He made a gesture that took in the flat. 'And to think we blew money on this lot just so I could be alone with her during my leave! Nice and cosy with all mod cons.' Then, vehemently, 'Piss on it!'

Bone wiped sweat from his brow. 'Well, I suppose that's Americans for you.'

'She isn't American. She's English, the family come from Hove. She only speaks with a Yankee accent because she's spent most of her life in the Bahamas.'

'Tell me, Nick, is she well off?'

'I don't know, although I suppose so. Her old man's a director in that firm he works for, and you couldn't exactly call them a small affair. Why? What in the Hell's that got to do with it?'

'Nothing. Just wondering.'

Nick crossed to the phone and glared at it. 'I wonder if I should try again?'

'Her father said . . . '

'OK! OK! I get the point.'

'Listen, why don't we go for a swim and cool off?'

Nick Byers snorted again and finished off his beer. The bottle went the way of its predecessors and ended up as fragments on the floor. He said, 'Listen, kid, I came hot-foot to Singapore to get me hole, and me hole I am going to have. Is that clear?'

The young Bone sighed. 'All right. But how?'

Nick shook his head despairingly. He said, 'For a bright kid you can sometimes be a trifle slow on the uptake. I'll paint a picture for you; now that the fair Beverley has toddled off with some other geezer, where is it natural for two enterprising squaddies like ourselves to go sniffing for a bit of nookie?'

'You mean pros?'

'You got it in one.'

Bone shook his head. 'It's not that I'm a prude or anything, but Christ, you know how much syph there is flying around just now. I don't fancy ending up flat on me back with only a galloping dose to keep me company.'

'No problem, not if you use your loaf and like the Boy Scouts always go prepared.' He patted his chest pocket. 'As a naval acquaintance of mine used to say . . . ' He broke into song, during which he capered grotesquely on the spot, 'It's only me with a packet of three, Barnacle Bill the sailor!'

Bone laughed. 'Well I'll only come if you promise to give me one.'

Nick handed over the American-made condom. It had the name SHEIK emblazoned on the front of the foil. 'Be my jest,' he grinned.

As they elbowed their way through the crowded streets Bone said, 'What do you think, should we try one of the massage parlours?'

Nick rubbed his jaw. 'I rather fancy getting a bint back to the flat. We could do a Dutch sandwich if you like.'

Bone frowned. 'What's that?' He gulped when it was explained. Much as he liked Nick, he couldn't see himself sharing the same woman with him. He despised himself for his shyness.

'I think I'd prefer one to myself,' he muttered.

A little further on, Nick said, 'You know, I've got a theory about women. Pick a right slag, a really horrible one, and I bet she's a fantastic grind. They have to compensate for being ugly, you see.'

'Sounds reasonable enough. If you can stomach it.'

'You can always buy a paper bag,' Nick laughed, 'And you know what they say? There's no need to look at the mantelpiece when you're poking the fire!'

Despite his mate's sudden jocularity, Bone knew him to be still deeply upset at having missed out with Beverley. For months now, ever since their last leave, he'd done nothing but rabbit on about her. He'd written to her the week before, telling her to expect him and how he was going to rent a flat so they could spend as much time as possible together. There hadn't been time for a reply.

'What type do you fancy?' asked Bone, 'Chinese, Singaporian or Malay?'

'I don't care, just as long as she's not a western bint. I don't want one of those tonight. Something exotic with a bit of spice about it; none of this "close your eyes and think of Britain" caper.'

At Nick's insistence they stopped in at a bar so he could refuel the already considerable load he was carrying. His sudden elated mood vanished as suddenly as it had come, and Nick became sullen and morose. He downed three large gins and tried to pick a fight with the owner. He was asked to leave and, after much shouting and protest, did so.

Nick leaned against a stone building and stared in fascination at a caged mongoose. His eyes were glazed, and every so often his knees buckled slightly. 'Something really ugly, really horrible, that's what I want. They make the best fucks you know, did I tell you that?'

'Yes,' said Bone wearily, then, 'Don't you think we should jack it in for tonight and go back to the flat?' They'd just been thrown out of the third bar in succession, and he was scared the redcaps would pick them up.

Nick said thickly, 'Good idea, but first we pick up the whore. Follow me!' He stumbled off down the street.

The madam had a figure like a blown up balloon, which was a pity, because sometime in the past she'd been beautiful. The vestiges of that beauty could still be seen, despite the puffed-up features and gross tissue. She listened sympathetically while Nick Byers mumbled his wants. A bargain was struck and the price agreed before she turned to Bone.

'And what about you?' she smiled.

Bone felt butterflies racing up and down his spine. For the fat woman scared him more than a whole jungle full of guerrillas had done. He gulped.

'Not for me. I don't want a woman, thanks. It's just my friend here.' He wondered why he was being so polite.

Nick rounded on him. 'What do you mean? I thought we were in this together,' he said garrulously, and swayed as he spoke.

'Well I've changed my mind. I'm not interested, and that's that. You can do what you like but I go back solo!' His lower lip jutted out determinedly.

Nick laughed. 'OK! OK! Don't get your knickers in a twist!' He turned to the fat madam. 'So let's have a shufti at this gargoyle you've promised me, then!'

The bird who slunk through the bead curtain was Chinese and subservient. Although she could only have been in her early thirties, she looked positively ancient to the young squaddies. She had warts on her neck, and one eye had a tendency to wander. At some time in the past her nose had been broken, and whoever had set it had done a lousy job. It careered towards the right side of her face and the wandering eye. She had two upper front teeth missing.

Nick Byers whistled. 'My God what a roach! It's enough to give you the screaming ab-dabs just to stand and look at it!'

'I hope you've got a paper bag at home,' said Bone.

'My name is Mai Ri Rer,' said the girl in a surprisingly pleasant voice. She bowed her head and looked humble.

Nick guffawed. 'Hear that, Jack? She's called Rider!' He put his arm round the woman's shoulders. 'I'll tell you what, pet, we'll call you Nookie for short. How does that grab you?'

Her face split into a hideous grin. 'Nookie Ri Rer? I rike, but what it mean?'

'I'll do better than tell you. I'll show you!' Money changed hands and the threesome plunged into the scented night.

By the time they'd got back to the flat Nick had almost sobered up. 'Still want to go through with it?' Bone asked.

'I paid me money and I'm getting me hole. I said I would tonight and I bloody well intend to. Besides, I told you about these ugly ones . . .'

'Sure, I know. They're so good they'll suck you in and blow you out again in spangled coloured bubbles. Good luck!'

Nick, already tugging at his flies, vanished inside the flat's one bedroom. They'd tried to get one with a double bed, but the best they'd been able to come up with was two singles.

Five minutes later there was a rap on the front door.

Bone gawped as Beverley Robertson breezed past him. 'I was over seeing a girl friend, and when I got home Daddy told me that Nick was in town. I've come right over.' She looked around expectantly.

Bone's mind raced. 'Come on into the kitchen and get some coffee. He's gone out, but he should be back at any moment. Didn't you get his letter?'

Beverley frowned. 'No. I haven't heard a word from him for a couple of weeks now.'

Bone plugged in the kettle and mumbled something about mail going astray. 'Milk! It's in the other room. Excuse me, Bev!' With an idiotic smile plastered all over his face he fled the kitchen.

Nick was in mid-performance. 'Here, it's true. They really are fantastic,' he grinned. 'You changed your mind and decided to join in?' The woman pinned under his body writhed like a speared eel.

'You've got a visitor,' said Bone.

'Who?'

'Beverley.'

The smile vanished. 'You're joking!'

'I've never been so serious in my life.'

Nick gazed down in horror at the Chinese whore. There was a soft plop as he pulled himself free. Nookie Rider made gurgling noises and clamped her legs round his waist.

'You like suckee now?' she asked.

'Jesus H. Bastarding Christ! You've got to help me!' howled Nick.

'How? What can I do?'

Nick had disentangled himself and was dressing as fast as he could. Nookie Rider watched in puzzlement. She said sadly, 'You no like me? Me no good fuck?'

'You're great, doll, it's just that something's come up.' Nick whirled on Bone. 'Get stripped off and get in there beside her. Leave all the explaining to me.'

'What!'

'Listen, you wouldn't let an old mate down, would you? Not in his hour of need? Now you get in there with Nookie and I'll square it with Bev.'

'But Nick, I . . .'

Nick whipped a knot into his tie, spat on his palms and rubbed what cropped hair he had left into position. 'Please, Jack! Just this one thing for me.'

'Look, why don't I wait here with Nookie and you take Bev out someplace?'

'Because I want to take her to bed, stupid, and these are the only two in the flat. And I can't see any way of getting Nookie out without Bev seeing her, so will you just shut up and do as you're told! Get in that kip and look as though you're enjoying it, will you!'

The young Jack Bone groaned and started to strip. 'What I do for mates!' he moaned. He moaned again when he crawled in beside the Chink bird and got a close up view of her face. He felt queasy, and gagged at the thought of kissing it.

'I'm the second shift,' he mumbled. And then, 'Look, no matter what happens, don't mention it was the other chap who brought you here. You came with me. Understand?'

'I unnerstand. I give you good time. You see.'

Bone fell backwards as the Chinese girl launched an

offensive. Her clothes were pulled to one side and he glimpsed a stomach raddled with stretch marks. Hands flew everywhere, and he was astonished to find he was getting excited. He would have bet that was impossible under the circumstances.

'Well, hello, Jack,' said Beverley, standing framed in the doorway. She gave a superior smile as she took in the scene. 'Who's your friend?'

'My name Mai Ri Rer,' said the Chinese woman toothily. 'I verry good bang bang girl.'

The smile became malicious. 'I bet you are.' Her hand flicked the light switch and the room was plunged into darkness. There was the rustle of falling clothes and then the slippery sound of skin on skin. 'Don't mind us. You carry on, Private,' giggled Beverley from the other side of the room. Then, viciously, 'I'll say this for you Jack Bone. You have a marvellous sense of style and taste.' Nick joined in the laughter.

'You come to me,' whispered Nookie Rider, 'I make you good fuckee.'

And she did.

Three days later their leave came to an end and they went back up country. It wasn't long after that that Nick felt he was pissing over broken glass and began to get worried. So did Bone, who in the flurry of the moment had forgotten to take his SHEIK condom to bed with him. Nick hadn't bothered with Bev; after all, she was the woman he loved!

Nick's dose was confirmed and he started a course of penicillin injections. Just to be one the safe side, Bone had a test done and was verified clean. Nick never spoke to or contacted Beverley Robertson again.

Bone blinked his eyes open and found himself staring up at Susan Sweet. She handed him a cup of tea. 'Sleep well?' she asked.

He nodded, and inquired the time. When she told him, he said, 'You didn't spend much time in bed.'

'I'm one of those people who don't need much sleep, and it comes in handy sometimes. Your breakfast will be ready in five minutes. I made you porridge, seeing you're a Scotsman.'

Bone pulled himself into his clothes and had time for the three S's before she called him through. The porridge she dished up wasn't porridge at all but some horrible, pulpy, hot cereal. He ate a few spoonfuls and swore that it was just like mummy used to make.

Then Susan produced a small, elaborately beaded handbag and said, 'I came across this at work last night and remembered Nova had lent it to me. I found this inside; probably nothing, but I thought I'd better show it to you, anyway, just on the off chance.'

The business card was pearly pink with a swirling pattern. The inscription read,

SHAWKI COSTANDI
JEWELLERY GOLD AND SILVERSMITH
RAAD & HANI STREET. NO 6.
TEL–236–306–BEIRUT.

The back of the card was covered in a mass of calculations which had been worked and then re-worked numerous times. The final figure was 230,000, and this had been heavily underlined in black ink. There were several exclamation marks after it.

'What do you make of it?' asked Susan.

Bone laid the card down face up. 'Doesn't mean anything to me. You sure it was hers?'

'Positive. She only bought the bag the week before I borrowed it, and in the end I never used it. I was late and in such a rush that night I left it at work.'

Bone mused, 'Maybe she's been knocking off some rich Arab and this was his calling card. Maybe he was trying to talk her into joining his harem.' They both laughed.

'It's not so funny,' giggled Susan. 'It happens.'

Bone pursed his lips and studied the card again. 'Did she have any connections in Beirut?'

'Not that I know of.'

He told her then about the Grumble Club and the sort of clientele who infested it. He said that Nova had certainly been supplementing her income by doing a bit of brass nailing on the side, a fact he'd confirmed with Duff.

Susan nodded. 'I'm not surprised. I told you she was ambitious for bread.'

'What about fellas? Was there anyone in particular?'

'There were quite a few, but the faces changed regularly. They always seemed to be the same type, you know the ones, a big car parked outside and an air about them that says they're not exactly short of a few bob. Playboy types with a big tip for themselves, the sort you get a lot around the clubs.'

'But no-one in particular?'

Susan accepted one of Bone's full strength gaspers and coughed as she lit up. 'That's a bit rough first thing in the morning,' she wheezed, and went on, 'There was one bloke I used to see from time to time, seemed to pop up at odd intervals. If they were having it away together then I suppose he'd be the closest thing she'd have had to a regular. Mind you, there might well have been somebody I knew nothing about. All I can tell you is what I saw here in the flats. Nova wasn't exactly one to shoot her yap off about her men friends.'

'What was this bloke like?'

Susan considered the question. 'Tall, dishy and talked with a plum in his mouth. You know, the la de dah Kensington type, only there was more to his accent than just that.'

'How do you mean?'

'I'm not quite sure. Some of the words he used were a bit odd, things like tiffin and . . . oh yes, once when he was going home he said he was off to his "basha", I think it sounded like.'

Bone nodded. 'It's a word they use in India. Think he might have been one of your pukka sahibs?'

'It's possible. He certainly struck me as the colonial type.'

'Did he have a name?'

'Well, he was introduced to me as Rupert, but no surname I'm afraid. He was one of these guys who're always very smartly dressed, in fact most of the times I saw him he was dressed in a tux. The full bit.'

When Bone ascertained that there was nothing else the girl could tell him about Rupert, he excused himself and made for the telephone, where he rang the Fosters. He asked them if they'd been able to think of anything else that might help him, but they hadn't, and so he told them he'd be in touch, rang off and went looking for a taxi.

The only acknowledgement Matthew Pamm made to the fact that it was morning was to add some water to his Bushmills. Bone ordered two large ones and lined them up in front of his friend.

Pamm beamed. 'You owe me fifty quid. Bent law comes expensive nowadays,' he said, and slid a red folder across the table to Bone. 'They're all photostats. Read, memorise and destroy.' He giggled. 'Touch of the James Bonds, eh?'

Bone paid the money and huddled closer to the wall light. Slowly and methodically he read each report.

'Any joy?' asked Matt, sipping his drink.

Bone shook his head and slipped the reports back into the folder.

'Nothing here I don't know already.' He rolled the folder with both hands and then crammed it into his inside pocket, adding, 'I'll probably see you later.' As he was going through the door he heard Pamm calling for his elevenses.

The Grumble Club looked even tattier than before in the daylight. Bone banged on the flaking paint door and then rang a bell for good measure. The door squeaked open, and the greasy Maltese peered out.

'What's your problem, Mac?' the Malt demanded.

Bone said he wanted to see the manager on private business. The Malt grinned. 'Get lost,' he said and started to swing the door shut again.

Bone whipped the cigarette from his mouth and flicked it into the Malt's face where it struck in a shower of sparks. The Malt yelped and automatically clutched at his eyes. The breath whoofed out of his body when the elbow ploughed into his gut, and, groaning, he sank to the floor.

'What's happening here?' demanded a new voice.

Bone turned to face it. 'You the manager?'

'I am.' His eyes flicked nervously from Bone to the stricken doorkeeper. He said with a hiss, 'I hope you have a good explanation for coming bursting in here!'

The Maltese rolled on to his front, pushed himself to his knees, and the silver fang of a switch blade zipped into life. Bone took a step forward and let go with a kick that would have won acclaim at Murrayfield. There was the sound of crumpling bone and the Maltese gurgled as his head snapped backwards. Blood spewed from his mouth.

Bone said, 'You'd get on a lot better if you'd stop and ask a few civil questions first.' He stooped and picked up the fallen knife, which disappeared into his Crombie. To the manager, he said, 'I'm working for Mr Duff and I want some information. Check me out if you like.'

The manager's eyes narrowed. 'I'll do just that. What's your name?'

'Jack Bone.'

The manager turned on his heel and vanished into the gloom. Bone strolled forward and wrinkled his nose in disgust. The smell of fear hung like a pall in the empty club, mingling with the sour scent of sweat and sex. The perfume they'd tried to dampen it down with was disinfectant.

The Maltese struggled to his feet, clutching a mouth that hung in tatters. 'I'll get you for this,' he said thickly and staggered off into the deeper recesses of the club. Bone shook his head. 'He's been watching too many late night movies,' he said to himself.

A door opened and the manager smarmed in. There was a fixed, ingratiating grin on his face and he was washing his hands in the best Fagin tradition. 'I'm sorry about that little misunderstanding, Mr Bone,' he crooned, 'But these things do unfortunately happen sometimes. Now, what can I do to help you?'

'A bird called Nova Foster worked here before she disappeared. Did she happen to leave any personal effects behind?'

The manager frowned. 'I'm not quite sure. I'll have to ask the cleaners, they should know.'

He ushered Bone along a dingy corridor and into a changing room where a row of metal lockers lined one wall.

'Maisie!' the manager called, and a few seconds later an old hag appeared from behind another door leading off.

'Yeah, she left a few odds and ends,' the hag grumbled after Bone had put his question. 'I shoved them in a cardboard box in case she should ever come back.' She sniffed. 'Not that many of them do.'

Bone conjured up a fiver and pushed it in her overall pocket. 'Mind if I have a peek at them?' he asked.

The raddled face broke into a sunshine grin. 'For you, ducks, anything. I'll get it.' She leant her bucket and mop against the lockers and vanished back from where she'd come. Seconds later she emerged, triumphantly carrying a small box. Bone emptied the contents on to the floor and went through them item by item. There was a Gossard bra, size 36 C, a packet of different coloured paper panties, a half completed book of crosswords, an unopened box of Tampax, a packet of Durex and a bottle of tomato ketchup.

'Great girl for hamburgers,' said Maisie, when Bone looked surprised.

There was also a piece of cardboard folded in two. When Bone opened it he saw that it was a receipt for a Hittite clay pot, circa 1800 B.C., which was stamped with the government seal guaranteeing authenticity. The address was,

TOMOZA'S SHOP
BYBLOS–LEBANON
PHONE 940–489.

This was the second time Bone had come across something which connected the girl with that part of the world. 'I'll keep this,' he said, and stuck it in his pocket.

'One more thing. There's a Chinese girl works here called Petal. I want her home address.'

The house, when he eventually found it, was a crumbling horror in Notting Hill Gate. He pulled the appropriate bell and waited.

'Yes?' demanded the voice through the squawk box.

'Gas, lady. There's been a leak reported. Can I come on up?'

The buzzer went on the lock and he pushed his way inside. He climbed four flights and found the flat situated round the back.

The door opened almost immediately after he'd rapped.

For a split second he wasn't sure, and then he took in the telltale slender shoulders and slight bulges at the chest. The tall, statuesque bird was wearing a double breasted suit, shirt and tie while her hair had been cut in the traditional short back and sides.

'Let me see your id card,' she demanded in a rich baritone voice.

Bone decided to try a little charm. 'I've a confession to make. I'm not really the gas man. What I want is a few words with Petal.'

For the second time that morning a door started to slam in his face. His foot shot out and wedged itself in the crack.

'Listen, lady, I'm being polite so far. All I want is a few words with her.'

The dyke grunted and threw her entire weight against the door. Bone lost his patience. 'Oh, to hell with it,' he said, and countered with his thirteen stone. The dyke bounced backwards against the inside wall.

'I'll call the police!' she snarled.

Bone walked on past and searched till he found Petal in the bedroom. She was struggling into her slippers and dressing gown, having obviously just woken up.

'Hello, Judas,' he said and sat down beside her. He was amused that it was the only bed in the flat, and that both sides had been slept on.

Sleep vanished from Petal's eyes as she snapped wide awake. She cowered away from him. 'What you want?'

The dyke stood in the doorway clutching a pair of scissors in her hand. 'Lay a finger on either of us and I'll stick these into you,' she said.

Bone stared at her. He saw a woman who was the model type and beautiful with it. She had blonde hair, fair skin and a rangy boy's figure. If it hadn't been for her sexual inclinations she would have been a cracking piece of crumpet.

'What a waste,' said Bone. 'Look, why don't you go through into the other room and play with a dildo or some other such jolly? I promise you, all I want from your playmate are words.'

The point of the scissors wavered and then sank a few inches. The dyke plonked herself on to a stool. 'I stay here,' she said defiantly.

Bone had the mild satisfaction of seeing that she was blushing. To Petal he said, 'There was a bloke called Rupert used to hang about with Nova sometimes. Ever come across him?'

Petal modestly drew the front of her dressing gown more

tightly about her. Slant eyes wandered from Bone to the dyke and then back again. 'How you fine me?' she asked.

'The manager of the Grumble coughed your address.'

'I no believe you! He no do such a thing, it one of their strictest rules.'

Bone grinned. 'Then let's just say it was all done by mirrors. Now, what about chum Rupert? Good-looking smoothie, white, might well have had an Indian background. You know, the Raj and all that baloney.'

Petal nodded. 'I know the one you mean. He used to pick Nova up some nights when she no score. Officer man, I think. We get a lot that type round the club.'

'Did Nova ever mention his surname?'

'No, but I did hear it once. One of the croupiers know him from another club.' Her face screwed up in concentration. 'What he call him? Edmunds? Edwards? Yes, that's it. Edwards!'

'Was he a heavy punter?'

'Not at our place, but I t'ink he was at the Carlton Sporting. That's where a lot of the big action takes place.'

'And this croupier who knew Edwards; he still around?'

Petal bent her head as Bone lit her cigarette for her. At the other end of the room the dyke snorted and looked furious. Petal said, 'He was Spanish, working over here without a permit. He go home some months ago. Maybe he still there, maybe he somewhere else now. He the travelling type.' Then, leaning closer, she said in a very serious tone of voice, 'I sorry about last night. You no hurt in any way?'

'They only wanted a chat.'

She smiled and touched his chest. 'Good, I pleased.'

The dyke ground her teeth together to make disapproving noises. She glared jealously at Bone. 'Got what you came for now?' she asked, and crossed one velvet covered leg impatiently across the other. She wanted this man out of her home, away from her woman. She thought Bone looked typical of his species, cruelty and arrogance his middle names, and her skin broke out in gooseflesh at the thought he might touch her. There had only ever been one man in her life, and that had been when she was fifteen. He'd forced her, first one side and then the other. He'd made her do unspeakable things. Loathing and hatred flooded through her. They had no softness these men, no understanding. They'd never heard the word sensitivity.

'I'll see you to the door,' she said, and rose.

Bone jotted down the phone number. 'If I think of anything else, I'll ring,' he said. 'And I'm sorry to have bothered you.'

'Try not to come back. You're not welcome,' said the dyke. She held the scissors purposefully in front of her in a hand that trembled slightly.

'What a bloody waste,' repeated Bone as he made his way back down the stairs. The door slammed shut behind him.

Chapter 4

The Carlton Sporting Club was an ornate gilt and maroon plush palace. Bone edged through the mixed bag of punters and made his way to the bar, where he ordered a tomato juice and Worcestershire sauce. Then he lit up and took in the scene.

There were a lot of women about with glazed expressions and wearing too much tom. Most of them seemed to have high-pitched, nervous giggles and fluttering fingers. The lady of the night was Luck and it was to her that the vast majority of the men present were plying their suit. Underneath the opulence and expensive perfumes, the prevalent smell was the same old sour one that had permeated the Grumble. Fear.

A couple of chinless wonders strolled across to the bar and ordered large gins and tonics. Their sharp-edged voices dripped what, in their world, passed for breeding. From the conversation it emerged that one of them had dropped a 'packet' at Sandown, and after a minute Bone broke in in his best Kelvinside.

'Excuse me, but I wonder if I could buy you chaps a drink? I think you might just be able to help me.' He smiled, and tried not to look too much like a peasant.

'Oh I say, that's jolly decent of you. What do you say, Messy?'

The one called Messy looked suspicious. He said truculently, 'Depends what sort of help the gentleman needs.' He succeeded in making the word 'gentleman' sound like an insult.

Bone swallowed hard and kept on smiling. He paid for the booze and shovelled the change back into his pocket, then said, 'I was in here a few months ago and lost rather heavily at the tables. In fact, I was flat. Came over here for a drink and bumped into a marvellous chap who loaned me a tenner and told me to get back in the game. Would you believe it, my luck changed right there and then! When I finally got out of the game the chap had gone, and I never did repay him the money. This is the first time I've been back since.' Inwardly Bone congratulated himself on his performance. He reckoned it was in the Oscar class at least.

'And you think we might know him?' asked Messy.

'I thought you might. I gathered from your conversation you are regular visitors here.'

'Yes . . . By the way let us introduce ourselves. I'm Robin Fitzhugh, and this is Messina Broughton. His friends call him Messy.'

Bone presented himself, at the same time ordering up another round. He noted cynically that no well-manicured hands flashed towards tuxedo pockets. It seemed the upper classes didn't mind mingling with the plebs as long as the plebs did the paying.

Messy was staring imperiously down at Bone through slightly watering, puffed-up eyes. He looked the picture of debauchery. 'And what makes you think we might know this chap?'

Bone's forced smile widened. 'I'm no expert on these things, but I think you might have gone to the same school.' Like nearly every Glaswegian ever born he hated the English aristocracy, especially the decadent kind. He fought down the impulse to kick the slob in the shins.

'What was his name?' asked Robin Fitzhugh. He picked the lemon out of his drink and chomped on it.

Bone said slowly, 'Rupert Edwards. Mean anything to you?'

Fitzhugh frowned and stared off vacantly into space. He

slowly shook his head from side to side. 'Not to me, old thing. How about you, Messy?'

Messy pursed his mouth, which suddenly transformed his face into that of a queer. 'Never heard of him; couldn't have been at my school after all,' he said.

'Thanks anyway,' said Bone He nodded and turned back towards the bar, lit a new fag and drew the harsh grey smoke deep into his lungs. He blew the smoke out in a thin stream which travelled for at least three feet before it broke up and started to disperse, then took a deep breath and followed it with another. Only then did he lose the almost overpowering desire to make a mess out of Messy. After that he did a bit of mingling, during which he picked out the types he thought might be able to help him. During his travels he noted that there were several hard-faced types dotted around the premises at strategic points.

A slick piece of crumpet gave him the eye and smiled provocatively. She wore a wedding ring and a dress that could only have been an original by someone expensive. Bone ignored her, he had no intention of being someone's piece of rough for the night. The woman's smile changed to one of disappointment, and she allowed herself to be swallowed up in the ever swirling circus. Bone picked out another small group which he reckoned were in the league he was after, and sauntered over. It took him five minutes to get an intro to the youngsters, whose average age he judged to be about nineteen. This lot were polite and eager to help, but once again no-one had any knowledge of Rupert Edwards. Bone said his thanks and moved off.

He was homing in on another likely gathering when he was stopped by someone tapping him on the shoulder. He turned round to find himself face to face with a grinning Robin Fitzhugh.

'I say,' said Robin, looking the worse for gin, 'I think we know the chap you're looking for. Meet Tiggers!'

Tiggers was so wet he could almost have been poured. Bone gagged at the virulent B.O. which suddenly wafted in his direction. Tiggers had a problem, and even if his best friends were telling him he certainly wasn't doing anything about it. Bone puffed furiously on his cigarette and sent up a smokescreen while Tiggers said through splayed teeth, 'I've already had a look around but I'm afraid old Rups isn't around tonight. In fact, now that I come to think of it I haven't seen him for a few weeks.' Red, blubbery lips worked their way up and down as he added lecherously, 'Maybe he's found himself a new popsy and that's taking up all his time, what?' He and Fitzhugh brayed, which made the crystal chandelier dangling above their heads tinkle from the repercussion.

'You're sure he hasn't been around for a while?'

'Well, I almost live here, and I haven't seen him.'

'He comes here quite a lot then?'

Tiggers nodded. 'Marvellous fella. Great one for the tables you know. Nerves of steel, that one.'

'Does he lose a lot?'

Irritation flickered across Tiggers's face and Bone knew he'd started to intrude on forbidden ground. The 'chaps' had their own codes and sets of rules, and discussing someone else's gambling losses, in front of strangers anyway, was extremely non-U. Bone went on swiftly, 'You wouldn't happen to know where I might be able to find him, would you? I really would like to thank him and repay the cash he lent me.'

Tiggers honked his nose in a grey-looking handkerchief and then cleaned each nostril thoroughly. When he was finished he tucked the handkerchief into the top pocket of his dinner jacket and arranged the edges in a fan-shaped display. Bone stared in fascination at the dried up bogey which quite clearly showed.

Tiggers said, 'I don't really know him all that well you know, not exactly one of our set. I couldn't tell you which other clubs he might go to, although . . . ' he clapped his hands together, suddenly, 'I can tell you where he lives, if that's any good. Perhaps you could drop him a line?'

'What a marvellous idea!' said Bone. He pulled out a biro and a scrap of paper before staring expectantly at Tiggers.

The address given him was at the tail end of Chelsea where it merges with Fulham and is known as The World's End. While Bone scribbled, Tiggers explained, 'It was during one of those infernal cabbie strikes, and I was absolutely stranded. Anyway along comes Rupert in his car and jolly well offers to give me a lift home, absolutely super of him I thought. He was going on somewhere to the other end of town, and en route we stopped at his place while he picked up a few things he needed. After that he whisked me home and dropped me off right at my front door.'

Robin Fitzhugh said brightly, 'Hope we've been able to be of some help, old thing.'

Bone said they had, old things, and after making thank you noises threaded his way towards the door. He'd decided there was no time like the present to go inquiring at The World's End.

As he retrieved his Crombie from the cloakroom he saw the bird who'd tried to pick him up, reflected in the huge mirror which lined one wall. The bird caught his glance and winked; it seemed she was getting bolder as the night went on. A second later she was joined by a beetle-browed man who thrust his arm through hers and gently propelled her towards the door. There was time for a last, wistful smile before she was escorted through revolving doors and out into the night.

As Bone drove towards Chelsea he fantasised about what she might have been like in bed. He gave that up when the face pictured in his mind started to waver and change into Babs's face.

At length he turned the Mini into Edith Grove, and found a parking space. The house, when he located it, was bland and uninteresting. There were five bells to choose from, and as none of them had names alongside he started at the top and pressed the button. He heard the echoes of a jangling sound, and lights flashed on.

'Yes?'

She was old, white-haired and wore a sweater with holes in the elbows. Bone nodded politely and said, 'I've come about Mr Edwards . . . '

She cut in briskly, 'I'm sorry, but the flat's already gone. I let it over a fortnight ago.' She glared at him as though he might try and dispute this fact. False teeth clicked together.

'I see,' said Bone. Then, 'I wonder if I might come in and have a word with you? I didn't actually come about the flat, but rather to see a Mr Edwards himself.'

The woman cackled mirthlessly. 'Why, did he owe you money too?'

'Quite a bit, and that's why I'm trying to get in touch with him. I don't suppose he left any sort of forwarding address, did he?'

The woman pulled the door open and said, 'You better come on in. I'm just making a cup of tea, if you'd like one.'

Bone said he would, and was ushered into an old-fashioned kitchen. There was an open coal fire which was part of a black lead grate. Above that was a wooden mantelpiece which had a brass rail running its entire length. A kettle bubbled and sang on the hob.

'This takes me back,' said Bone. He pointed to the grate. 'I think I must have been a kid the last time I saw one of those.'

The woman chuckled and poured boiling water into a fancy patterned teapot. She counted in two heaped spoonfuls of tea before saying, 'And another for the pot,' and stirred the brew, then put the lid on and set it to draw beside the fire. Then she said matter-of-factly,

'You look like the police, but you're not. So what are you, then?'

Bone studied the woman and decided there was no point in lying to her. She was the type who could see right through you. 'I'm afraid I told you a bit of a story at the door there. Edwards doesn't owe me any money. I'm just looking for him.'

She made *harumphing* noises and poured the tea. When she'd dosed hers with sugar and milk she sat back in an over-stuffed chair and stared frankly at Bone. Her eyes were bright and piercing.

'Why?' she asked.

Although the room had been wired for electricity it was lit by gas lamps that sputtered where they were mounted on the walls. They cast weird, flickering shadows around the room, shadows that danced and twisted in an ever-changing kaleidoscope. The light itself was yellow and soft. Bone said, 'It's actually a Scots girl called Heather Foster, or Nova Foster as she calls herself now, that I'm after. I think she might be with Edwards, or if not at least he might know her whereabouts.' He went on to give the woman the rest of the story, leaving out his involvement with Duff.

There was silence when he finished. A cat materialised out

of the shadows and sat preening itself in front of the blazing fire. Bone watched while it completed its toilet.

'I know the girl you mean,' said the woman at last. 'I met her and Rupert once on the stairs, and he introduced me. Pretty girl I thought, but with wanton eyes. That one was no stranger to men, not by a long chalk. Although I never mentioned it to Rupert, wasn't my business and even less my place to say.'

'Did you get the impression they were quite close?' Bone asked.

'She never stayed the night here, if that's what you're asking. I don't allow that sort of thing in my house. I'm no prude; any of my people can entertain whoever they like in their rooms until twelve. Then it's outski. Those are my rules.'

Bone hid a smile and nodded to show that he understood. 'But surely you can make an educated guess?' he asked.

The woman sipped her tea and then bent down to scratch the cat's neck. The animal miaowed and proceeded to rub itself sensuously against her heavily varicose-veined leg. She said, 'Rupert was an attractive man, and he certainly had his fair share of women. I can vouch for that. But just lately he's been keen on this Nova you're looking for, although why her I'll never know. She was a common piece of goods, for all her accent and upbringing. And Rupert usually showing such good taste too!' She shook her head. 'I never could understand what he saw in her. Unless it was bed. Some men are funny that way.'

'They were having . . . an affair, then?'

'Of course they were! Rupert wasn't the sort to go in for one of those platonic relationships. And believe me, neither was she!'

That gave Bone one answer that he'd been after. He closed his eyes, laid his head against the antimaccasar and luxuriated in the heat that played against his face. A clock chimed the hour and a piece of coal sparked. He opened his eyes again, gazed into flames and watched them writhe in their own miniature hell. It all belonged to a different age, another world almost.

'Progress isn't always for the better,' he said softly.

The woman smiled and lifted the cat on to her lap. She

smoothed black fur flat with stroke after long stroke. 'There was a lot of bad things about the old days,' she said, 'But there was a lot of good ones too.' She sighed.

Bone knew he'd have to shake himself out of his peaceful mood. He had a job to do. Reluctantly he sat upright and asked, 'How much rent did Edwards owe?'

'I went to my sister's for the night, and he must have moved his stuff out then. It was a week before I found out, even. *And* he was supposed to give me a month's notice that he was leaving!'

'What sort of visitors did he have generally?' asked Bone.

The woman sniffed. 'Lady friends mainly, and most of them I never saw more than once. The occasional man, and as best I can remember they were all as well spoken as Rupert. He was terribly well-bred, you know, he never said but I expect he went to a public school. You can always tell, can't you?'

Bone offered the woman a gasper and was surprised when she accepted. He'd thought she looked the non-smoker type. 'How about his living? How did he earn that?' he asked.

The cat leapt to the floor and stalked in front of the fire. It paused for a moment to stare at Bone and then, with a contemptuous flick of its bushy tail, it disappeared once again into the shadows that abounded in the room. The woman said, 'Never had a regular job as far as I knew. Always slept in late, midday before he usually got up. And never any trouble with him paying the rent and suchlike.' She pursed her mouth cynically. 'Until the last week, that is.'

'How about mail, did he get much?'

'Not a lot. In fact, now that I come to think about it he got very little.'

Bone felt it all slipping away. The lead had been a tenuous one to start with, and now even that was running slap bang into a brick wall. He was beginning to understand why Duff's men hadn't been able to come up with anything.

He thought of the three grand that had already been given to him and the other three should he manage to locate the girl, and smiled inwardly, Duff was right. It was one helluva big incentive when money came stacked like that.

'I don't suppose he ever mentioned any parents or where they might live, did he?'

The woman frowned. After a few seconds she shook her head. 'I can't remember him ever saying. If he had, I'm sure I would have remembered. Although he was always friendly and quite chatty, he never did let much drop about himself. Except the army of course, he occasionally used to talk about that.'

Bone leaned forward. 'I don't suppose he ever mentioned which regiment he was in?'

The woman repeated her head-shaking performance. 'He did mention something about India once, but I can't remember whether it was to do with the army or not. I'm afraid I'm not really being much help to you, am I?'

Bone smiled. 'You're doing just fine. It's me who should be apologising for putting you to the bother of answering questions like this.'

The woman stared into the fire and it seemed she was far away in her thoughts. 'Oh I don't mind. It's a bit of company after all. You get quite lonely living on your own you know, but then I'm hardly the only one who has to do it. Mustn't grumble, must we?'

Bone rose, smiling. 'One more thing. I don't suppose you have any addresses belonging to friends, relatives, anything I might be able to follow up?'

The woman poked the fire till it glowed a deep, satisfying, cherry red. She tapped the poker on the grate and then laid it carefully in the hearth. Her back creaked audibly as she did so.

'I can't help you there either. Sorry,' she said.

Bone paused in front of the dresser and stared down at the faded brown photo which stood there. Its frame was made of ornately carved heavy silver. The young man who gazed out on the room was fresh-faced and wearing a uniform of World War I.

From behind Bone the woman said, 'My husband. Killed at Passchendaele.'

'How long were you married?'

Her voice was sad and forlorn. 'Three weeks. Not a lot, is it?'

'No,' Bone agreed, 'Not a lot.' He pulled out a biro, and on a scrap of paper scribbled Susan Sweet's telephone number. 'Get in touch if anything comes up which you think I should know.' He counted out six fivers and laid them beside the paper. 'Buy pussy some Kit-E-Kat,' he added.

Outside in the Mini he ran over what few facts he had and decided his next course of action was to contact the army. They must have a file on Edwards, and perhaps he could glean from it the address of his parents, if they were still alive. He was hoping their son would have kept in touch with them, and the thought made him smile ruefully in the darkness. It was a lot of 'ifs'.

He was about to drive off, when one of his warning premonitions hit him. Fairy fingers raced up and down his spine while the flesh at the back of his neck went chill. His eyes slid towards the driving mirror.

There were two more parked cars in Edith Grove, and from that distance he couldn't tell whether or not they had occupants. The street itself was lined with hedgerows, and whoever it was out there could be lurking behind those. Bone didn't doubt for a moment that someone actually was there; the fairy feet were old companions and ones who'd never let him down yet. He decided to play bait.

He got out of the Mini, locked the door and strolled down towards the main road. He passed the garish World's End pub and turned into a dark sidestreet. Here the houses that stood in silent rows were crumbling and Victorian, and many of them appeared to be derelict. Most of the street lights were smashed, the bulb holders like pitted eye sockets that glared sightlessly out into the night. The foetid stench of dog shit mingled with cat piss was everywhere.

There was the faint ring of a footstep out of synch, and Bone knew the tail wasn't far behind. Ahead of him the skeletal structure of the gas works loomed out of the dark. He skirted a pile of smashed bricks, turned a corner and then ploughed his way over some waste ground. When he reached the girded metal he stopped and waited. A shadow moved, and there was the sound of rustling grass. The moon moved out from behind some cloud and for a fleeting instant the tail was in perfect silhouette.

Bone, his right fist balled in readiness, hunched and snaked forward to the next girder. The shadow moved again, and this time it was so close as to be almost upon him. Bone got ready to spring.

Then pain started at his hairline and swiftly worked its way upwards to explode inside his head. A constellation of stars that had nothing to do with the night sky appeared before his eyes and then he was falling. The tag from an old Scottish folk song whirled round and round in his mind,

'There's no' just one,
there's two!'

Although his body was completely paralysed and useless to him, he never quite lost consciousness. He knew he'd been sandbagged by a pro; if it had been an amateur he'd probably have been dead by now from a caved-in skull. At last he was roughly hauled to his feet and thrown against a metal girder. His arms were pulled round behind him and he dimly felt them being lashed together. While this was going on, the other man worked on his feet.

The mist and fog shimmered away and Bone found himself staring into a well-remembered face. The second one he'd never seen before.

'Gotcha!' said Les, Jaime Swan's bodyguard.

His companion, who bore a distinct resemblance to a rat, said, 'Here, I thought you reckoned this geezer to be a load of bother?' He came forward and patted Bone's cheeks. 'He was simple. Dead simple.'

'Don't mind Judy. He's got a peculiar sense of humour,' said Les.

Judy simpered and acted coy. He pulled out a surgeon's scalpel and started to trim a nail with it. 'I'm ever so nice really,' he lisped. Then, 'When you get to know me better, that is!'

Les said, 'You shouldn't have done what you did to Jaime, you know. He was most upset when the quacks told him he'd never play his guitar again. He doesn't like you, Mister Bone. He doesn't like you at all.'

Bone watched the scalpel wink with reflected moonlight. His throat was dry and he had trouble breathing. His head ached like a thousand hangovers rolled into one. 'Why bring pouf in boots here?' he asked. 'Couldn't you do the job on your own?'

Les smiled maliciously. 'Judy's a specialist who enjoys

his work. He's probably the best there is in his field.'

Bone knew they were waiting for him to ask, and hated himself for doing so. He managed to make some saliva. 'What field's that?' he croaked.

Judy's lips twitched as he pared another nail. 'Pity about your girl friend,' he said. 'According to Les here she was quite a looker.'

'You talking about Babs?' Bone demanded.

Les nodded. 'Jaime laid the blame at her door. Said if it hadn't been for her it wouldn't have happened. He was very upset, you understand. Not thinking clearly. But it wasn't my place to tell him that. I only carry out orders.'

'What did you do?' Bone said through clenched teeth.

Les cocked an eyebrow. 'Only what I was told to.' He made slicing motions with his index finger. 'Chop! Chop! If you know of any Mau Mau looking for a white bird, you can tell them you know one already got the tribal markings.' He laughed while Judy snickered.

Bone tugged at his bonds, knowing it was futile. He wasn't scared any more, only angry. The twosome watched him in amusement and waited till he'd calmed down again.

'Fag?' asked Les and stuck one between Bone's lips.

'Do you mind!' said Judy, pretending to be insulted. He stepped forward and tugged at Bone's belt. When it was loose he undid the top button and then carefully slid the fly all the way down. He then dropped on to one knee while he wrestled Bone's trousers down till they were resting on his ankles. Then he delicately hooked his hand into Bone's Y-fronts and did the same with them.

Bone's stomach muscles heaved in anticipation. He stared at the scalpel in horror. Les said, 'At first Jaime wanted you dead, but then after he'd thought about it for a little while he came up with a better idea. He thought, as he'd lost what he considered the most important thing in his life, then it was only right and fitting that you suffer the same. Guess what we all decided you'd miss most?'

Judy chuckled. 'My! My! But isn't he a big boy?' he crooned. He held Bone in his hand for a moment and then dropped him again. 'Like the man said, I enjoy my work.'

Bone spat out the cigarette and tugged again furiously at the ropes that bound him to the girder. He felt wetness on his wrists and knew that he'd only succeeded in ripping and tearing the skin. Judy pulled out a small leather strap and used this to strop the scalpel. When the cutting edge was finally to his satisfaction he grinned.

'And don't think you might die, you won't. I'll make sure of that. After all, that's what the clients pay me five grand a go for.' The scalpel glittered evilly in his hand. 'Say good-bye Dick,' he added and, bent forward.

The click that came out of the night at that moment might have hung in the middle of inverted commas. A voice said lazily, 'Drop that right away, or I'll blow your head off.'

It was obvious from his tone that the speaker meant every word he said. The scalpel twisted as it fell into the grass.

'Has he done it?' the voice demanded.

'Yes,' said Bone. He could hardly see for the sweat that clogged his eyes. Breath whistled out of him and he found himself shaking.

'Now take three steps backwards, the pair of you,' said another voice from the same direction.

Les's eyes flickered from left to right as he judged his chances of making a dash for it. His body had only moved a fraction when the first voice said, 'Do that and you're dead.'

Les froze on the spot.

It was Jonno, Duff's man, who was on the end of the .45. The gun disappeared while he undid Bone, and just so there would be no mistakes made there was another click and Jimbo stepped out of the darkness. Les and Judy stared in fascination at the black eye of death hovering at a point aimed directly between them.

Bone buckled his belt and gratefully accepted the cigarette offered him by Jonno. He dragged smoke into his lungs and wasn't surprised to note that his hands were still shaking. 'What brings you out here on a night like this?' he asked in a quavering voice.

Jonno jerked a thumb towards Judy. 'We saw him watching you at the Carlton. When you left he teamed up with his mate here and the pair of them tailed you. We mentioned it to Mister Duff, who said it would be a good idea if we followed.'

'It was,' said Bone. 'And I'll thank him for his concern when I get to a phone.'

Judy whined, 'We didn't know this geezer had any connections with Mister Duff. Honest we didn't.. '

Les broke in, 'We wouldn't have touched the contract if we'd known Mister Duff was involved. We're not that bloody daft!'

Bone confirmed that they were telling the truth. 'This is from another business, up north,' he explained.

Jonno said quietly, in his strangely high pitched voice, 'I'm glad about that, because if you'd been making a play against Mister Duff then there could have only been one possible outcome for you. Do you understand?'

'Yes,' they said together.

Jonno turned to Bone. 'What do you want done with them?'

Bone walked forward till he was standing facing Judy. His hand swept up to crack against the queer's cheek. 'You are a horrible little man, the sort who wants to make me spew.' To Jonno he said, 'Let them go. They won't catch me like they did a second time.'

Jonno said softly, 'There won't ever be a second time. Mister Bone is a friend of Mister Duff's. Anything happens to him and you end up as a new motorway. Clear?'

'Yes,' they chorused.

'Then get lost.'

Les and Judy scampered back towards the main road and the place where they'd parked their car. Jimbo pulled a flask out of his inside pocket and offered it to Bone. 'This'll steady you,' he said.

Bone shook his head and replied that he didn't drink. He flipped the end of the cigarette away and immediately lit another. 'Any time I can do a favour for you lads, all you have to do is ask.'

'We're only doing what we're paid for,' said Jonno.

'I know that, but it was my skin you saved tonight. You never know, you might come to Glasgow some time and need a bit of help. If that ever happens, you know who to get in touch with.'

'Thanks,' said Jonno gravely.

They were half-way back across the waste ground when Bone threw up.

Chapter 5

Bone was ushered down a flight of stairs into the same basement den he remembered from his previous visit.

Duff was waiting for him. 'I'm glad you decided to drop by.' He said, 'I was wondering how you were getting on.' He gestured Bone to a seat and then picked up an internal telephone built into the bar.

'I wonder if you could come down for a few minutes and bring your box of tricks with you. Our friend Jack Bone's been in the wars,' he said. A voice that Bone recognised as Duff's wife Anya crackled from the other side.

Bone protested that it wasn't worth the bother, but Duff waved his objections aside. While they waited for Anya to appear, Jonno made his report about the night's events.

'Nasty,' said Duff when it was concluded. 'You're lucky Jonno saw that creep tagging you at the Carlton.'

'I know,' said Bone softly, 'And I well appreciate it. I want to thank you for telling them to come after me.' Then he made the Glasgow offer to Duff that he'd already made to Jonno and Jimbo. Duff smiled mysteriously. 'I might just take you up on that. And perhaps sooner than you think.' He told Jonno and Jimbo that they could go for the night, and as the two heavies disappeared up the stairs Bone said,

'Good men, those.'

'The best,' Duff replied. 'I always have the best. It's the only way to do business.'

Anya bustled in at that moment, clutching a metal box. She was wearing a powder blue dressing gown, and from the way it clung to her Bone knew there was nothing underneath. Her hair had been swept back in a chignon and her face had already been cleaned of all make up. The brown, doelike eyes seemed even more huge against the creamy skin. It struck Bone that she was probably one of the most beautiful women he'd ever come into contact with.

A butler appeared, carrying a large silver tray which contained a pot, cups and saucers plus a plate covered in small brown bread sandwiches.

'I thought the you might fancy a bite to eat,' said Anya. 'Spey salmon appeal?'

'My favourite vice,' said Bone, and meant it.

Anya cocked an eyebrow but said nothing. She clucked when she saw his bloodied wrists, the skin raw and torn where he'd rubbed and pulled against the rope. She opened her box and set to work.

'She used to be a nurse,' said Duff, 'And a good one at that. I can personally vouch for her.'

Bone winced as Anya wiped away the congealed gobs of blood which crusted his wrists. She rinsed the cloth in a bowl of piping hot water, and the water turned pink and then red.

'I'm really a big baby,' said Bone. He winced again when she applied some liquid from a blue bottle.

'I think you'll live now,' she replied, and wound a bandage round each wrist. As she was tying the final knot Duff said,

'Coffee or Coke?'

Bone plumped for the coffee and was delighted to see that his favourite soft brown sugar had been laid on. He was surprised to find himself ravenous and swiftly made inroads into the salmon sandwiches. 'Delicious,' he mumbled between mouthfuls.

Anya made a few minutes' polite conversation and then excused herself, saying she was tired and that anyway she presumed they had business to discuss. When she'd gone Bone said,

'You're a very lucky man, Mister Duff. I envy you.'

Duff paused behind the bar and his eyes glittered as he stared at Bone. 'Thank you. I accept that as the compliment it was intended to be.' Then, 'Why don't you tell me your version of tonight? I always like to know the reason why something like this happens.' He pulled on the china pump that projected above the bar, and beer gushed into a narrow glass. When he'd poured his pint he took an appreciative swallow. 'Nothing to beat a good pint of Ruddles,' he said with satisfaction.

'You're a beer man, then?'

'When it's good. None of this keg muck. Straight from the wood, that's the only way for it to be.'

Bone said, 'Ever try Young's Special? That's another great one.'

Duff stared over the rim of his glass. 'You sound like a connoisseur.'

'I was at one time. A mate of mine got me started on it, a Black Country man who swore by a brew called Batham's Delph Ales.' Bone grinned. 'We had a few right piss-ups on that stuff. A right brew it is.'

Duff hunted round the bar for a pencil and then made Bone repeat the name. He jotted it carefully down. 'I'll try some of that,' he said, 'If it's still being made, that is.' He sat on a chair facing Bone.

'Now, tell me about tonight and how you're getting on with finding Nova Foster.'

Bone explained about Babs and Jaime Swan, amused at the fact that he was actually telling these details of his life to another man. It crossed his mind that he and Duff were very much alike and that perhaps this was the reason he found it easy to relax in the other man's company. Two words popped into his head; 'empathy' and 'sympatico'. He reckoned they existed between himself and Duff.

When Bone came to the end of his story Duff sat for a little while lost in thought, and then rose to pour himself another pint. 'Ever been to the States?' he asked. When Bone replied that he hadn't, Duff went on, 'Lousy beer made over there. Schlitz, Pabst, Blatz, Miller High Life, none of it worth a monkey's wank.'

Bone said, 'I had thought of going to America some time for a holiday, if I could ever raise the money.'

Duff laughed cynically. 'Take a tip from me; don't. That country isn't worth a damn any more, it's already on the way out.' He added reflectively, 'You know, you might find this hard to take coming from a guy who earns his money the way I do, but the States has no soul any more. No soul at all.'

'I sometimes think we're going the same way,' said Bone.

Cynicism played round Duff's mouth. 'Maybe. But I'll tell you this,' he raised his pint in front of him and manipulated it so that it sparkled in the light, 'Any country that can brew beer like this still has a lot going for it.' There was a pause and then he said, 'anyway, back to business. Things aren't looking too bright in this Nova Foster caper. The little lady's covered up her trail rather well.'

Bone said, 'There might be something you can do to help me here. Rupert Edwards was in the army at one point, my own personal guess would be the Brigade of Guards or one of the other top class regiments, and somewhere there's a file on him. I'd like to have a shufti at that file.'

'You think he and the girl are together, then?'

Bone blew a perfect smoke ring and felt proud at his accomplishment. 'It all adds up that way. She takes off, and at the same time so does the bloke she's been knocking off. It's too much of a coincidence. No, I say find Rupert, and my money is that Nova won't be far away.'

Duff nodded. 'I'll see what I can do about the file. I'll get in touch as soon as I have anything for you.'

The clock on the wall said the new day was getting well into its stride. Bone yawned and suddenly felt dog tired. 'Thanks for the grub and medical attention,' he said, and rose to his feet.

As they walked up the stairs Duff said, 'These two references to the Lebanon rather interest me. What do you make of them?'

Bone shrugged. 'Nothing so far. I'm not even sure if they're relevant.'

'Nevertheless, I think they're worth bearing in mind. If Nova has gone abroad, that might well be the sort of place she'd choose to go to. Especially if she's had connections there in the past. And don't forget there are a lot of clubs there, and that's the sort of life Nova's used to.'

Bone was thinking of the business card Susan Sweet had found in Nova's evening bag and all the scribbled computations that had been scrawled on the back. He got the feeling there was something in those figures that should make sense to him, something he was missing. He made a mental note to have another look at the card before he went to sleep that night.

The two men said good-night at the door and Bone made his way to the Mini. As he slid behind the wheel it struck him anew just how close his escape had been that night. Sweat broke out on his forehead at the thought of being emasculated for the rest of his life. His hands squeezed the wheel till the knuckles and finally the fingers grew white.

A picture of Babs conjured itself up in his mind. Her face floated in and out of view while from far off came the sound of her laughter. He saw her face glistening with sex sweat and felt the coolness of her cheek next to his. The cloying smell of her perfume invaded his nostrils, while in his mind's eye he saw their naked bodies matching rhythm for rhythm, heart beat for heart beat, ecstatic cry for cry.

'Oh Jack, Jack,' she whispered, her hands fluttering up and down his back, 'I love you. I love you.'

He wiped a damp strand of hair away from her forehead and kissed the spot that had been covered. Beneath the make-up her skin was smooth and silky. In all the time he'd known her she'd never once had a blemish.

She'd sit in front of the mirror for hours, brushing her hair first one way and then another. He'd found her vanity amusing and had told her so. Babs laughed and replied that he wanted her to look her best for him, didn't he? She said she wanted to look beautiful and not let him down. They'd both smiled at that knowing it to be a white lie.

Then the face in his mind crumpled with fear and started to dissolve and blister as acid ate its way through her flesh.

'*Bastards! Bastards!*' he mumbled.

Then it wasn't acid any more, but a flickering cut-throat razor like the one Terry had used.

'Chop! Chop!' the man said. Steel sliced through skin and the living flesh parted like soft, warm butter. How many times had the steel hissed redly through the air? Four? Five? Six? The flesh would heal, after months of excruciating agony, till the great day arrived when the bandages could be removed for the last time. Then the horror would be reflected in her eyes as she gazed at the disfigurement which scoured her face. Tramlines running from cheek to chin. Ugly, hateful! The face staring out of the mirror wasn't hers, couldn't be! She was beautiful, always had been. The monster pretending to be her was an imposter!

Then the scream would rend the air as the full realisation dawned. There would be Valium after that, mingled with soft words of hope. Talk of plastic surgery and the miracles that could be performed with the knife nowadays. Cosmetic surgery would become the god she lived with and prayed to.

Bile rose in Bone's throat and he forced the pictures from his mind. He lit up and blew smoke furiously at the dashboard. Inside his head, Les's voice reverberated round and round.

'Mau Mau! Full tribal markings . . .'

'Oh, Babs,' Bone muttered, 'Oh, Babs.'

When he got to the flat in Battersea he found that Susan Sweet was home and making tea. For a moment he stood astonished in the kitchen doorway, before dropping his eyes. He cleared his throat. 'I'm sorry. I didn't realise,' he said.

Susan shot him an amused glance before reaching for another cup. 'Come in and take the load off your pins,' she said, 'And stop looking as though you've never seen a woman's tits before.' As she poured the tea she went on, 'I often walk around this way at night. You sort of get used to it in the job I'm in. Becomes sort of second nature. I often say it's a bit like losing the habit of wearing shoes. It's sheer hell when you put on a pair again and try to walk around.'

She was wearing a Royal Stewart skirt and slippers. Her waist was slim, her breasts small and firm. The nipples were dark brown, the aureoles covered with a myriad of bumps and her skin was so white it might never have been directly exposed to sunlight in her entire life.

'How'd you get on sleuthing it?' she asked.

For the second time that night he recounted his story. When he got to the bit about Judy, Les and the gasworks her eyes grew so large he was sure they'd pop out of her head.

'Bloody hell!' she said when he'd finished. Her exposed skin blossomed with a crop of goose bumps and she shivered. 'It's horrible even to think about it.' She gazed into her cup. 'I'm sorry about what happened to your lady friend . . .'

'*Ex*-lady friend,' Bone cut in.

That made Susan smile. 'You want to use the telephone? Maybe the lady would like to hear from you in her time of need?'

Bone shook his head. 'Later perhaps, but not now.'

'OK, suit yourself. You know your own business best.' She clicked her fingers, suddenly remembering something. 'Nova's Ma rang. Said you were to buzz her no matter what time you came in.'

Bone's chair scraped on the floor as he hurriedly pushed it back. He strode swiftly to the phone and dialled the Glasgow number. It was answered almost immediately.

'Jack Bone here, Mrs Foster. You said I should ring.'

'Oh aye, aye. It's just that I came across something today and I wondered if it might be of any help to you. Thought I'd telephone just to be on the safe side.'

'What is it?' Bone asked.

The line crackled with static. Mrs Foster said, 'A postcard Heather sent us a few months back. It says on the back that she's having a wee holiday and thoroughly enjoying herself. She says she'd like to go back there someday and spend longer.' Mrs Foster's tone changed to one of apology. 'It's probably not important at a', but ye did say to let you know of any wee thing I might remember or come across.'

'You did right,' said Bone. 'Tell me; this postcard wasn't from the Lebanon, was it?'

Mrs Foster laughed. 'Och, nothing as grand as all that! No, it's from a place in Wales. I canna pronounce it, so I'll have to spell it out for you.' After she'd done that she went on, 'The name of the hotel is the Eryri.'

Bone thanked her and, after making sure there was nothing else she could tell him, inquired after her husband. His health was the same, but according to the doctor that was to be expected. When the final deterioration started it would be rapid and that would be the end. Bone said he would be in touch, and hung up.

'Worthwhile?' asked Susan Sweet.

'Could be,' replied Bone, 'I'll sleep on it.'

'I took the liberty of putting a hottie in your bed. Hope you don't mind?'

He smiled: 'All the comforts of home?'

Susan reddened and the resulting flush spread down her neck and across her breasts. This amused Bone, but at the same time puzzled him. He failed to see why an innocent jibe should produce such a reaction.

Susan picked up a silk shirt and twirled it round her shoulders. After she'd fastened it she stacked the cups in the sink. 'Not quite,' she retorted, and flounced from the room.

There were some bangings and clatterings from her bedroom before her light snapped off. Bone paused outside her door.

'Susan, I'm sorry. I honestly didn't mean to offend,' he said. Her reply was silence.

The noise of the telephone ringing jangled him awake. He groaned when he looked at the clock and saw that it was well past eleven. The incident at the gasworks had drained him physically, and this was the body's reaction to recharge its batteries. Bone stumbled from his bed, clawed his way into a dressing gown and made for the phone.

'Good morning,' said Duff. 'And how are you today?'

Bone made the usual mundane pleasantries while at the same time rubbing sleep from his eyes. He could tell from the stillness in the flat that apart from himself it was empty and he wondered where Susan had got to. Then he wondered if she was still mad at him from the night before.

Duff said, 'I've made those inquiries you asked me to, and my sources have come up with the files of three Rupert Edwards who've been in the British army.' He chuckled. 'Want to hear the bad news?'

Bone had already guessed. 'Go on,' he said.

'The first one was with General Gordon at Khartoum. The mad Mahdi and his fuzzy wuzzies did for him.

Bone groaned. 'And number two?'

'Fought in the desert war against Rommel. Died of enteritis at a place called Wadi-El-Har. He was seventeen at the time.'

'And the third?'

'Now you're in luck here, he's still alive.'

There was a pregnant pause, and Bone knew there was a catch coming up. He played straight man. 'Do you know where I can find him?'

'Sure. Chelsea Royal Hospital. He's an old age pensioner there. Let me see . . . ' There was the sound of rustling paper. 'According to this, he was born in 1886. What do you think?'

'If he's been giving Nova Foster a run for her money, I think I'd like to ask him his secret.'

They both laughed and then Duff said, 'Sorry to be the bearer of bad tidings, but there you are.'

'You're sure there couldn't be another Rupert Edwards who your contact missed?'

'I asked him that question myself, and according to him the answer's no way. The British army's gone all modern and that means the record department is fully computerised. You feed in the relevant data, and a few seconds later out pops what you want to know. He told me that the records go back to the time of Wellington.'

Again it was the brick wall where it seemed all roads ended. Bone rubbed his forehead and took stock.

'What now?' asked Duff.

Bone remarked, 'As Newton once said, for every action there is a reaction. Likewise, for every problem there's an answer. I'll be in touch.' He heard Duff laughing as he hung up.

He made himself a cup of coffee, using some soft brown sugar that he'd managed to get hold of, lit the first gasper of the day and took himself back to the phone. He rang Glasgow to ask Mrs Foster the one point he'd forgotten to get the night before, then called Directory Inquiries and asked for the number of the Eryri Hotel in Llanberis. When he finally got through he asked for the manager.

'Yes?' The voice was as Welsh as leeks.

'I wonder if you could help me? I'm trying to trace a –'

The manager cut him off in mid-sentence. 'Are you the police?'

Bone paused for a fraction of a second as he considered whether or not to take the risk. He decided against it. 'I'm afraid I'm not.'

'Then I can't give you any information over the telephone. If you come to see me personally, perhaps I might be able to help you. Good-bye.' There was a click followed by the dialling tone as the manager hung up.

'Thank you very much,' said Bone and followed suit. He turned to find Susan Sweet staring at him. Her face looked even paler than usual.

'How's tricks?' she asked.

He waggled his eyebrows up and down in what was supposed to be a Groucho Marx impersonation. 'Win a few. Lose a few.'

'And that was one of the losers, eh? As a matter of interest, has anyone ever told you you smoke too much?'

'Frequently.'

'Then why don't you cut down?'

'Because, young lady, I've cut out the whisky and wild, wild women. It's the only vice I've got left in this world and I fully intend to keep on revelling in it!'

Susan grinned. 'You can be quite funny sometimes. I like you when you're like that.'

Bone strode to the window and peered out. The sky was blue and the sun had put in an appearance. He said, 'You should get out and get some fresh air. You look terribly peely wally.'

Susan laughed. 'Peely wally! That's an expression my mother used to use a lot. I haven't heard it in ages.'

'You sound homesick.'

'Sometimes. But I've been away too long now. I've grown away from it all up there.'

'You like your life here?'

'It has its good points.'

'That doesn't answer my question.'

Susan's mouth twisted downwards as she fiddled with a knife lying on the table. 'Some of it's good and some of it's bad, but then isn't that the same wherever you go?'

'Yes,' said Bone, 'That's true.'

Susan joined him at the window. 'I've got a couple of days off work, so maybe I'll just use some of the time to go for a nice walk like you suggest. I'll do that if you promise me to try and cut down a little on the fags. Is it a bargain?' She stuck out her hand.

'It's a bargain,' Bone said solemnly. They shook on it.

He shaved and was in the middle of dressing when the idea struck him. He poked his head round the kitchen door. 'If you fancy a breath of real fresh air, I can arrange it,' he said.

Susan, her expression cautious, looked round from the sink. 'What do you have in mind?'

'I have to drive up to Welsh Wales. How about coming along to keep me company?'

She said slowly, 'What exactly does "company" entail?'

Bone kept a straight face and said very seriously, 'Well, actually I'm lusting something terrible after your body, Miss Sweet, and this is all a devious plan of mine to lure you into the countryside where I can ravage you to my heart's content. Fancy a bit of ravaging?'

Her face cracked into a smile. 'Do we stay overnight?' she asked.

'Yup! And as an added attraction, I promise you your own room with key, lock and all.'

She looked away and for a moment Bone thought she was going to colour again. 'I'd love to come, then,' she finally said in a small voice.

An hour later they were in the car and heading north-west on the road to Bangor. At first the girl was tense and nervous, occasionally glancing at Bone out the corner of her eye, but as the miles sped past and they got deeper and deeper into the country she finally began to relax.

'You should get out of London more often,' said Bone, 'It suits you.'

Susan rolled down her window and sucked in a lungful of air. She closed her eyes and sighed. 'You can actually forget how good the country smells,' she said.

He allowed some time to elapse before he asked the question that had been bothering him. 'Tell me something. How is it a bird like you becomes a topless waitress?'

She was immediately on the defensive. 'Well, why not? It's a perfectly good job and it pays decent money!'

Bone shook his head. 'You're just not the type somehow.'

'And what does that mean?'

He groped for the right words. 'Well, for a start, I think you're basically very shy.' She started to protest, but he ploughed on, 'I don't mean by that you're not experienced, sophisticated even. It's just that . . . you seem to me to be too sensitive to expose your body voluntarily.'

'It's not immoral, you know!'

'I'm not saying that,' he insisted softly.

Susan stared out of the window, and whatever she was seeing wasn't the countryside. When she spoke, her voice was so low Bone had to strain to hear. She said, 'I left school when I was fifteen and went to work in a shop. I was selling groceries for the Co-operative.' She smiled thinly. 'I had big plans in those days; I was going to go to Langside College to study shorthand and typing. I was going to become a big time secretary and make a lot of money. You know the sort of thing?'

'Yeah,' murmured Bone.

'That was one of the things about Nova I used to envy. She actually did it. She had it made in Glasgow, but it wasn't enough for her. She wanted the bright lights and the glitter that goes with them.' Her tone became cynical. 'There's a rotten, dirty world behind the glitter for most people. You soon find that out.' She was silent for a little while then, and the only sound that pervaded the car was that of wind whistling through the side windows. At length Susan continued,

'A couple of years went past, and then a couple more, and somehow things never got done. There I was, rapidly getting older and still dishing out packets of tea and biscuits. There weren't many fellas either, and certainly no prospects of marriage. For some reason I just didn't click with men. I put them off.'

Bone lit a cigarette and passed it to the girl. She took it without looking round. After a few puffs she went on, 'So I did what a lot of other girls before me have done. I packed my bags and came to the Smoke. And that was where I met Robert.' She swallowed hard and her eyes filled with moisture. The single tear was followed by another and then another.

'Did you love him?'

Susan forced a smile, 'I loved him so much I thought I'd die of it. You know something, he was the first man I ever had, and when I told him he gave me a funny look, as though I was lying to him. I should have known then what he was. I should have seen through him.'

'Love's a funny thing,' said Bone, 'It sometimes causes blindness in people who've got nothing wrong with their eyes.'

Susan smiled again and dabbed at her wet cheeks. 'Anyway, I'm sure you don't want to hear my sob story. I'm probably boring you to death.'

'No, tell me about this Robert,' said Bone. He knew the girl wanted to talk, wanted to get it out of her system.

'I suppose it all sounds so corny and naïve when I put it into words. He'd no sooner moved into the flat with me, when he lost his job. Of course, that meant I was supporting him. He did get some money from the National Assistance for a while, but that dried up and it was all down to me. At first he tried to get more work, but then he took ill and the doctor said he was to take it easy for a few months.'

'And that was when you started doing your topless waitressing?'

'Well, the money was good, better than any other job I'd been offered, and at that time we needed every penny we could lay our hands on.'

Bone said, 'You realise, of course, that if he was ill and had a doctor's line then his money shouldn't have been cut off from the National Assistance?'

Susan's grin turned sour. 'I told you it would sound naïve.'

Bone shook his head. 'So what happened then?' he asked.

'One night I came home to find Robert with one of his mates. I was tired and went off to bed. I was just falling asleep when the door opened and in came someone I thought was Robert. Only it wasn't, it was his mate. There was a struggle before the mate finally managed to pin me down. I can remember those wild eyes peering at me out of the darkness. "Lie still, you bitch!" the mate said, "You've cost me ten quid, and by Christ I want me money's worth in fucking!" I don't remember much more about the rest of that night. I know I stared at the ceiling a lot, when the mate wasn't crawling all over me that is.' She paused. 'You know, it's funny, but even after that I never stopped loving him.'

'How long did it go on for?' Bone asked.

Susan said woodenly, 'About six months, and then I discovered I was pregnant. He actually talked me into believing that we would get married, and on the strength of that I gave him the thousand pounds I'd saved up so that he could put it with his own money and make the down payment on a house.'

'And you never saw him again?'

She nodded. 'He used to take half the money and leave the other half for me. Then, in the end, he took it all.'

'And the baby?'

'I had it fostered.' Tears streamed down her face. 'I'm sorry,' she choked and fumbled in her bag.

Bone reached in his pocket and hauled out a packet of

multi-coloured tissues. 'Use these,' he said. There were times when he hated the entire human race, and this was one of them. He pushed his foot down on the throttle and the speedo crept up past seventy. The Mini rattled and shook as Bone worked off his anger.

'I'm all right now,' Susan said after a while.

'Was there another woman?' he asked.

'It took me a long time to admit it, but I think there was near the end.' She laughed hollowly. 'Some other sucker that he could leech off.'

'You got a really raw deal,' said Bone.

Susan stared out at a field full of cows. Overhead, a crow cawed as it wheeled through the air. 'It's a raw world,' she said harshly.

Llanberis was one of those sleepy Welsh villages made out of grey stone, superstition and other fey things which only a true-born Celt would understand. The hotel, when they found it, lay huddled beneath a lowering Snowdonia. The wind that whipped down from the mountainside was as cruel and cold as a hag's tit. Bone shivered as he slammed the car door shut and steered Susan towards the hotel entranceway. The atmosphere was cold and damp, the sort that seeps into the very marrow of your bones. Grey clouds eased themselves past Snowdonia and then fled across an ominous sky.

The hotel itself was typical of its kind; underneath the pretentions of grandeur it was third rate and seedy, and a suggestion of mustiness hung in the air. While they waited for attention at reception, Bone was aware of the girl's eyes flicking up at him from time to time. The pixie face had gone back to being tense and suspicious. Bone didn't take offence; he couldn't, after hearing her story.

He booked two double rooms, and shrugged when asked whether he wanted them together or not. 'It's immaterial,' he growled. The receptionist lifted a well plucked eyebrow and, after Bone and Susan had signed, handed over the keys. The rooms they were ushered to were side by side.

Susan said she wanted to take a bath and do a few things, so Bone arranged to meet her in an hour's time downstairs in the bar. He had a quick cup of coffee, sussed out who the manager and his wife were and then went for a walk. He wanted to go over all the details that had emerged from the tangle so far to see if he could come up with anything new.

He made his way over a stone bridge and squelched through short grass. A sheep with an orange circle stamped on its backside stared at him blankly. 'You don't know how lucky you are,' said Bone, and trudged past. He stopped by a clear stream and watched it ice its way downhill. There were frothy white bubbles floating on the water and he laughed to himself when he remembered that as a kid he'd thought similar bubbles to be fish.

'Look Jack, baggy minnows!' his mother had said as she pointed into the river Cart. Jack stared excitedly, but all he saw were the bubbles. Not like any fish he'd ever seen before, he thought. And then not wanting to disappoint his mother because he loved her he nodded his head. 'I see them! I see them!' he cried.

It was much later before he realised you were supposed to look *into* the water, not *at* it.

The top of the mountain was covered by cloud now, and Bone pulled the lapels of his Crombie up when soft rain started to feather against his face.

The more he delved into Nova Foster's life, the more he became convinced that Rupert Edwards was the key. But the key to what? It seemed to him that there was far more here than appeared on the surface – it was the story about the fish all over again. Up until now he'd been looking at the water, not into it. He knew he was right, the same way he'd known Terry was out there waiting for him in Edith Grove. It was instinct, the sense you developed in the jungle. Those who hadn't were all dead, alongside some of the ones who had. Bone sighed and lit a cigarette inside his cupped hand. The girl was right, he did smoke too much. The first two fingers on his right hand were brown and saffron from the nicotine. They smelled of lonely nights when he was scared to go to sleep in case the nightmares came. He knew he'd never stop smoking until the day they planted him.

Susan was five minutes late, and more elfin-looking than ever, when she finally came into the bar. She was dressed in brown suede trousers with a matching waistcoat. Her sweater was beige.

'Hi!' she said and slid on to the stool beside his. He asked her what she wanted to drink and when she replied brandy, he ordered up a large one.

'You're very extravagant, aren't you?' she said.

He smiled. 'Why not?. As my granny used to say, "the more you drink the bigger the divvy!" '

She laughed. 'Get away! I bet you can even remember your number.'

She was right. He could. '678434,' he reeled off.

Susan shook her head. 'It's amazing, but they never forget their Co-op numbers.'

For the first time Bone noticed the girl's ears. They were slightly pointed, and sloped away from her head at a more severe angle than was normal. This, combined with her narrow eyes and triangular shaped face, gave her the fairy look. He also noticed that sometime during the past few days she'd rinsed her hair, the dark roots now being gone and the colour a little softer than it had been previously. For some reason he found himself feeling paternal towards her. He wanted to put his arm around her and tell her she was safe now. Whilst he was about, none of the nasties would get her. There were no ideas of sex mixed up in his feelings. He regarded the girl as a companion, a daughter almost. He wondered if he was getting old.

For lunch he ordered up T-bones, and a half bottle of Chateauneuf Du Pape for the girl. She flushed, said he was spoiling her and then laughed when he agreed.

Bone carefully studied the manager and his wife when they sat down to eat at a table close by. The man had a belly and that peculiar florid face that only comes from a long-term over-indulgence in alcohol. The wife bulged and threatened to flow out of her lurex number. Her hair was piled high in a bouffant and looked as though it had been sprayed to petrification. It crackled like dead wood every time she moved her head.

Susan nodded towards the couple. 'Do you want to have a word with them now?' she asked.

Bone shook his head. 'Later tonight, after I've plied a bit

of gargle in their direction. That'll be the time to ask the funnies.'

Susan stared around her. 'I wonder what brought Nova to a place like this? I mean, it's so non-her,' she said in a puzzled tone.

'Maybe she fancied some rock climbing.'

She giggled. 'The only rocks Nova was ever interested in were the sort that go sparkle sparkle when you hold them up to the light.'

Bone grinned at that. 'Then it must have been a naughty week-end.'

'That sounds much more like the Nova I knew.'

After lunch, Bone made the girl wrap herself up warmly before taking her out on the mountainside for the fresh air he'd promised her. As they walked, he told her a little bit more about himself and the sort of life he led in Glasgow. She didn't press him for details on Babs, and he didn't volunteer them. He spoke about the sort of jobs he did for people, debts, bills, a quiet word in someone's ear. 'Usually nothing very glamorous. Quite humdrum really,' he said.

'But why do they come to you? Why not go to the police?' the girl asked.

Bone wiped his hands across his face, enjoying the refreshing wetness of the rain. His long, thinning, sandy hair lay plastered round the nape of his neck. He stood still and stared up into the leaden sky. That was what he'd missed most in the jungle, a grey sky bustling with wind. He closed his eyes and listened as it howled around him. He said, 'There are lots of reasons people don't go to the police, the main one being distrust. They'd rather have a bloke like me, one of them who they reckon understands. I've no personal axe to grind, I'm just a man for hire. They like the idea of that. Besides,' he grinned, 'not everything they ask me to do is strictly legal.'

Susan stared up at the mountain. 'I'm glad I came,' she said, 'Everything's so clean up here. I like that.'

Bone said, 'You mustn't shut off for ever. You've a long life ahead of you yet, you want to use it, not throw it away.'

She smiled tentatively. 'I know that, it's just . . . time that I need. Time to put the past into perspective.'

'See you remember that. We all make mistakes; the great trick is to learn from them and then go on.'

An arm curled round his and then fingers were crawling inside his Crombie pocket. They found and twisted round his thicker ones. 'I like you, mister man,' she said, 'I'm glad I asked you to stay.'

He smiled. 'When we get back to London, will you do something just for me?'

'Depends what.'

'Look for a new job.' He patted his wallet. 'And if you're short of the old mazoola, I'll fix it for you. I'm one of the filthy rich at the moment.'

Susan frowned. 'You'd do that for me?'

'I just said so, didn't I?'

'But why? You hardly even know me, and it's not like we're . . . ' she trailed off, and suspicion was back crowding her face.

Bone sighed. 'Does there always have to be an ulterior motive?'

'There usually is.'

His lips thinned into a line. 'Let's just say I like you and leave it at that,' he said.

They were half-way back to the hotel when she said, 'I wish I'd met somebody like you before.'

He didn't reply, nor did he look at her. He thought that the fingers curled round his clung with the tenacity of a frightened child. He felt a great deal of warmth towards the girl called Susan Sweet.

Darkness came early to that part of the country and as it did so did the trade that filled the long public bar. Most of them were young men with beards and anoraks, looking wild and smelling faintly unwashed. The few girls amongst them had rosy, well-scrubbed faces, and drank pints like their men. The unkind might have described them as homely. As the hours ticked by, the noise in the bar swelled both in volume and intensity. Then, as was inevitable in a Welsh pub, the singing started. Most of the songs were in Welsh, but occasionally the English faction would burst through with some rousing choruses of their own.

When the manager and his wife appeared Bone threaded

his way through the crowd till he was standing by their side. As the manager's drinks were placed in front of him Bone leant forward and at the same time appeared to stumble. The drinks were swept over and a glass shattered behind the bar. Bone immediately made profuse apologies, calling himself a clumsy fool, and a smile appeared on the manager's face when he ordered up replacements and made them doubles.

Bone paid with a flourish and then, before the moment was gone, swiftly introduced himself and Susan Sweet. In the background the choir thundered out *Men of Harlech.*

The manager's fat, lurexed wife gulped down her gin and tonic before treating Bone to a piggish grin. She gazed back down into her glass as though wondering where her drink had gone to. Bone knew the type; he fished again for his wallet and played at being a mug.

After the fourth round, all of which Bone had paid for, the manager hiccuped and said he and Mrs Hughes were going into the other, more select bar. Bone said that was a marvellous idea, and could he and Susan join them? The answer was, of course, yes, and the foursome trooped into the plastic and chromium setting which the Hughes obviously considered to be nearer their station in life. Bone did his benevolent act once again; he was sick of tomato juice so he switched to lime and soda, and started his patter.

'I must say we're really impressed with the hotel. Thoroughly enjoying ourselves, aren't we?' Susan nodded.

'You're only with us for one night, then,' said Mrs Hughes. The more she drank the more piglike she became.

Bone latched on to that. 'We weren't actually going to stop at all, but you'd been so strongly recommended to us that we felt we just had to.'

Mr Hughes swallowed the bait. 'Oh! Who recommended us?'

Bone gave him a dazzling smile. 'A friend of Miss Sweet's here. Nova Foster's her name, she came in . . . ' he frowned and pretended to be thinking of the date, 'Ah yes, October, the early part of October.' He rushed on, 'You must remember her, a beautiful girl.' He described Nova as best he was able.

The Hughes both frowned as they tried to prove how retentive their memories were and how conscientious they were at their job. First one head shook and then the other.

'I'm sorry,' said Mr Hughes, 'I'm afraid I can't place her.'

His piggy wife made a pyramid out of sausage fingers. She pursed her mouth and that made her double chins quiver. 'Although the name Nova does ring a bell. Not exactly a common one, is it?'

While they were all agreeing with her on that Bone reached into his inside pocket and produced the photo the Fosters had given him.

'Perhaps this might jog your memory?' he said. 'It's a very good likeness.'

'Of course! Of course!,' said Mr Hughes, clicking his fingers, 'We had several drinks with her and her husband. Charming couple. Absolutely charming.'

His wife took the photo and peered down at it. The frown came back to her face and she said slowly, 'But the name wasn't Foster. It was . . . ' She sucked on her lower lip while she tried to remember.

Bone said blithely, 'Foster's her maiden name. I thought Edwards was her married one?'

'No . . . I'm sure it was something double barrelled.' She shook her head from side to side.

Bone could see that more lubricant was in order, so he called the barman over. Mr Hughes made some vague mutterings about this being his round, but Bone stilled them with a nudge and a sly wink. 'It's all on the firm,' he whispered craftily.

The manager smirked and conspiratorially winked back. Beside him Susan said, 'You are thinking of the right couple, aren't you? He's tall, good-looking and talks very posh.'

'Of course I'm thinking about the right couple,' pig lady snapped, 'I never forget a face. And as for his accent, I remember distinctly remarking on it to Gomer. Didn't I, dear?'

'You did indeed,' her husband confirmed.

'I said to him that I thought the gentleman was well spoken enough to be one of the aristocracy. We do get them in here from time to time, you know.'

'I'm sure you do,' said Bone. 'I just wish we could remember their married name. It'll bother me now, you know. I'll be up all night thinking about it.'

Mr Hughes lumbered to his feet. 'Well, we'll soon sort this out. Early part of October, you say? I'll look them up in the book.'

Bone slapped a fiver on the table and told Susan to order another round while he went to the loo. He waited in front of the manager's office while Mr Hughes unlocked the door, then peered inside.

'So this is the nerve centre!' he exclaimed.

'That's right. Come on in. It's not really very exciting.'

While Hughes rummaged in a desk, Bone pretended to look about him. 'Here we are,' said Hughes as a heavy ledger-type book thudded on to the desk in front of him. He opened it up and swiftly flicked through well-thumbed pages.

'October, October,' he muttered over and over to himself, then grunted and a finger stabbed downwards. 'The wife was right, it was a double barrelled name. Room forty-nine, I remember distinctly.'

Bone peered over Mr Hughes's shoulder and ran his eye along the column marked forty-nine. The name was Edgerton-Forbes, and in the space where you wrote your permanent address, 'DATCHET, BUCKS' had been printed.

Chapter 6

Bone slumped against a tree and listened to the jungle night sounds. His hand shook when he reached for the water bottle and it was with the utmost difficulty that he managed to unscrew the cap and then lift the bottle to his lips. Tepid liquid splashed down the corners of his mouth to fall soundlessly to the matted jungle floor. Somewhere a monkey chuckled, and it seemed to Bone it was laughing at him.

He knew he was sick, worse than he'd ever been before. For two days he'd suffered from the hallucination that somehow ants had managed to burrow beneath his skin and now a whole colony of them were marching round and round his body. His face itched beyond endurance, and despite himself he occasionally fell into fitful slumber, waking to find his fingers hooked like talons and clawing at his cheeks. He hated himself for giving into sleep, despised himself for the weakness, but the tiredness had become so great he had little control over it any more.

The young Bone cocked his ear and listened. *They* were out there, waiting. They wanted to get him, kill him dead like they'd done to Robinson. He shuddered at the recollection of the body he'd stumbled across that morning. The eyes were gone, picked clean by a scavenger. The dead man's blood had turned to gas and this had blown the body up, stretching the waxy yellow skin tighter and tighter, till it resembled some gigantic, grotesque balloon. Robinson, whom he'd laughed and drunk with and to whom he still owed half a bar. Robinson, whose party piece was to stick his arse in the air and light his farts so that they shot out in a great *whoof* of blue flame. It had crossed Bone's mind that if the body kept on expanding the way it had it must finally explode.

Bone stared upwards at the matted foliage roof which obscured the heavens. If only he could get a glimpse of the stars, then he might be able to work out which way he was going. For all he knew he might be walking round and round in circles, or worse still, he might be walking straight into the area They were known to control. He knew that if he could find the sea he would have a chance. Ten miles south, and he was bound to fall in with some of their own patrols. His vision wavered and he teetered on the spot. The night whirled and he thought he was going to faint. He sucked in clammy air and the moment passed. He moved forward again.

Where the hell was Nick and the rest of the patrol? He stood in the middle of the Malayan jungle and felt more alone than he'd ever done in his entire life. Blind panic blossomed in his belly and it took all his self control and willpower not to go running maniacally through the trees.

Inside his mind, he pretended to be Fats Domino and sang,

'I found my thrill
on Blueberry Hill . . .'

He knew his body to be reaching the end of its tether. But if that was bad, then his mental state was worse. Insanity was lurking round every tree, a fat greasy smile on its face as it crooked a beckoning finger.

'On Blueberry Hill
where I found you . . .'

His face was on fire, a million red-hot needles trying to bore their way out. A muscle inside his right thigh was quivering non-stop, it had been that way for over a day now.

An unknown animal screamed, a high, raucous sound that reverberated round and round the treetops. Steam hung everywhere like a low-lying fog. His clothes were soaked and in many places lay plastered to his skin. Where they touched was agony, the incessant rub of drill on flesh almost unbearable.

'Where are you, Mick?' he screamed inside himself, 'Where the fuck are you?'

One moment the patrol had been together, and the next they were worming and squirming their way through the undergrowth as They blasted them from all points of the compass. Dickie Smith had gone down with half his back blown away and then Harry Levi had cried out, his face incredulous, 'It got me! The bastarding whore got me!' Harry tore his stocking down and gazed wide-eyed at the spot of blood oozing from his leg. 'Snake,' he whispered in a voice already growing cold, 'I stood on a bloody snake!'

It took him five minutes to die, and during that time his screaming could be heard for miles around. One of Them could have picked him off at any time, but They didn't, They preferred to let him suffer. Bone wondered why none of the rest of the patrol had done for Harry, but it was a question he already knew the answer to. Like him, they'd all been looking after number one and getting their arses out of the line of fire. Now they were split up, lost, and for all Bone knew he might be the only one left alive.

Inside he was singing Nancy Whisky now,

'Freight train, freight train, goin' so fast,
Freight train, freight train, goin' so fast,
I don't care which train I'm on
as long as it keeps rollin' on . . .'

He thought of Nookie Rider and the pleasure he'd found in screwing her. A hiccup of surprise rolled out of his mouth when he found he was getting excited. He wanted to laugh at the incongruity of it, but didn't. Instead he sang some more, and tried not to think of woman flesh.

Then Bone stood stock still and gazed in horror at the apparition which lay at his feet. His heart quickened and felt as though it would burst through his chest. He knelt on one knee and forced himself to take a closer look.

'Oh, you cunts, you fucking cunts!' he muttered to himself.

The head of the corpse had been cut across the crown from ear to ear, and the forward part of the scalp pulled down over the face. The skull dome had been sawn through and the brain removed. What was left of the skull gleamed a startling red and white in the pale light that filtered from above. But the head was far from being the worst of it. The chest had been opened from throat to abdomen and the sternum removed. The ribs had been cracked apart. What was left of the man's body skin was a bright, sickly shade of green.

Bone fumbled with his water bottle and forced more lukewarm liquid down his parched throat. At that moment he felt he would have traded his life if only he could have a fag and a glass of whisky first.

He knew They hadn't done this to the dead soldier. Even They didn't go that far. His eyes flicked from side to side and his scalp crawled as he tried to imagine what was out there. He knew the Sterling was in working order, but he automatically checked it anyway. Then he forced himself to roll the cadaver over so he could check the markings on the dead man's sleeve.

He experienced a feeling of profound relief when he saw that Corporal's chevrons weren't up. At least it wasn't Nick, his mate, that had been mutilated in such a fashion.

To one side of him he heard the faint click of a breaking twig and then a squeak of leather sliding across earth. Bone's lips drew back in a snarl and as the Sterling swung into position a red haze closed over him. He couldn't hear the defiant scream that tore from his throat.

'Wake up! Wake up!' the voice thundered in his ear.

Eyes starting, Bone sat bolt upright in bed. His finger was curled round the imaginary trigger of the Sterling and he knew he was squeezing it the way he'd done a thousand times before. The gun chattered and he saw the look of surprise on Nick's Byers's face as bullet after bullet stitched its way across his chest. Byers flew backwards in a flurry of blood, his body spinning as it crashed to the dank earth. A crimson trickle seeped from his mouth when he opened it to speak, but he was too late. Recognition faded into death.

For a second all was quiet, and then the treetops erupted into clamour. Birds screamed, monkeys protested, and a medley of other, unknown noises filled the night.

The young Bone, madness sapping his mind, stared down at the body of his one and only friend. 'Oh Nick, Nick, I'm sorry! I'm so sorry!' he cried. Then, stupidly, as though it needed saying, 'I didn't know it was you!'

Bone shook his head and dragged himself back to the present. His insides were griping, craving for a drink. The old, sick feeling was dancing in his gut demanding alcohol and oblivion. He screwed his hands into fists and gritted his teeth.

'No!' he said firmly.

He became aware that he wasn't alone in the room. Susan Sweet, a dressing gown hurriedly flung over her nightdress, stood staring down at him. He said, 'I was ill, you see, a lot more so than even I'd guessed. I was delirious, half out of my mind.' His fingers played an unknown symphony on his ravaged cheeks. 'I'd contracted smallpox from somewhere, although no one ever figured out how I managed it. I was the only one in the entire area who came down with it. I did have the vaccination, but for some reason it didn't work on me.'

Susan sat on the bed and took his hand in hers. 'Tell me about it,' she said. Outside the window dawn was breaking, and white, fluffy clouds were playing tag round the top of the mountain. There was the distant sound of voices and what might have been the snorting of a horse. A dog barked and was swiftly reprimanded by a scolding female.

Bone sweated and talked about Nick Byers. He spoke of the plans they'd had for when they were demobbed and how they were going to set up in business together. He talked and talked while the girl listened. Occasionally she passed the cigarettes to him and flicked the lighter into flame; but mostly she sat still and silent. When his story was finally finished she put her arm round his shoulders and drew him down to her breast. She rocked gently back and forth while at the same time humming the tune to an old Scottish lullaby.

Gradually the craving for a drink left him, and Bone knew he'd conquered it once again. If it hadn't been for the girl's sympathetic company he would have lifted the phone and dialled a Glasgow number. If his contact, a well known actor north of the border, hadn't been home then he would have rung the city's central A.A. office and they would have immediately connected him with one of their members on stand-by for just such an emergency as this.

Bone extricated himself from the girl's arms and strode to the window. 'Now you know why I started to drink,' he said harshly.

Incredulous, she asked, 'You mean that all this time you've blamed yourself for what happened?'

'Not any more. I did at first, but then I was made to realise just how sick I'd been. Besides, Nick should never have come up on my blind side like that. He should have made his presence known before stepping out of the bush.' Bone shrugged. 'But then who knows what state of mind *he* was in at the time, either.' There was a long silence before he added, 'It still doesn't alter the fact that I killed him. That's what I've got to live with.'

They ate breakfast and then loaded up the Mini with their overnight cases. Bone announced he was going to Datchet, but he would stop and drop Susan off at Battersea if she wanted. She didn't, and Bone was strangely pleased.

Four hours later they were there. Datchet was typical of many southern English towns and villages; fat and sleek, with an impression of laziness. In the distance were the walls of Windsor, while the meadows a scant mile away were the famous playing fields of Eton.

Bone found a telephone kiosk and thumbed his way through the local directory. He grunted when he came across the single entry which was the only Edgerton-Forbes in the book. The house was called THE WILLOWS.

They found it facing the river, a large, white house completely surrounded by a high wall. Bone swung open the wrought iron gate and, with Susan at his heels, strode through.

'Can I help you?'

She was in the winter of her days and boasted a parched, dry skin which still held its tan firmly ingrained like an old piece of well-chewed leather.

Bone smiled, 'I'm sorry to trouble you, but I'm looking for Mr Edgerton-Forbes. Is he at home?'

The woman's eyes flicked over him and then swung to Susan. It appeared they passed muster, because she said, 'He's round at the back doing some gardening. Follow me.'

Bone passed windows through which he glimpsed the Edgerton-Forbes lifestyle. As he expected it was genteel chintz, a leftover from the time of Victoria and the last heady days of the Empire. Bone grinned to himself at the recollection of the huge map which had dominated the school room when he was a boy. Most of the map was coloured red, and he could still hear Mr Barr, thc teacher, thunder, 'Every country you see coloured red is part of the Empire. From Canada in the west down here to Australia in the east. The sun never sets on the Empire, children. Remember that!'

Edgerton-Forbes was elderly, but still tall and slim, and sported a pencil-thin moustache. He held himself in the manner of a military man. He listened to his wife explain that Bone had come to see him before slipping off the worn gardening gloves and extending his hand. His grip was cool and firm, belonging to a man who knew who and what he was.

'Pleased to meet you, young fella. What can I do for you?'

Bone made the introductions on his side. 'It was actually Mr Rupert Edgerton-Forbes I wished to have a word with. You do have a son, don't you?

Edgerton-Forbes's face clouded and his eyes narrowed. His mouth pursed and tightened into a vice. He said thinly, 'My son's name is never mentioned in this house. I will not discuss him.' He was turning towards the house when Bone said,

'I'm sorry if I've intruded on something private, sir, but you see there's a young lady involved whose life might be in danger.'

Edgerton-Forbes paused 'From Rupert?'

'No. But it's imperative that I find her.'

A bushy eyebrow was raised. 'Then why come here?'

'I'm positive the girl's with your son, so I'm trying to trace her through him. She's vanished, you see.'

Mrs Edgerton-Forbes said 'Bo, I think we might invite these young people inside for some sherry. I'm sure they would welcome a little refreshment.'

Susan confirmed that they would, so, headed by the old man they were led inside. Sherry and biscuits appeared and after Bone had made his apologies and said that he was tee-total, Mrs Edgerton-Forbes rushed to the kitchen to make him coffee. While she was gone, Bone made his opening gambit.

'How long were you in India?' he asked politely.

Bushy eyebrows were raised in surprise. 'Now, how did you know that?'

Bone smiled. 'A whisper about it came out in my inquiries about your son. Mind you, it's easy to guess from looking at this room here.' He gestured towards the many Indian knick-knacks and souvenirs dotted around.

Edgerton-Forbes nodded. 'They represent thirty years before the colours. Deuced long time, what?' He sipped his sherry and grunted, 'You ever in the army young man?'

Bone said that he had been, mentioned his regiment and then spoke a little about his time in Malaya. He steered the conversation back to India, and soon the old man was avidly recounting his many exploits there. Bone listened politely and waited for an opportune moment. Finally, after many tales that ranged from tiger shoots to chasing the fierce Afghans through their mountain fortresses, he said, 'So Rupert was actually born out there, then?'

Edgerton-Forbes rose and poured himself another sherry. He said in a voice full of anger, 'Always gets me dander up just to think about him being a son of mine. He's a bad lot, don't ever doubt that Mr Bone.'

'Can I ask why?'

The old man coughed and straightened his back till it was proverbially ramrod straight. Half the sherry disappeared in a single gulp. 'He's a thief,' he said, 'A common thief.'

'Are you sure about that?' Bone asked.

'Of course we are! He was cashiered out of the army you know. Stole money fom his fellow officers. Can you imagine that? His fellow officers! I've never spoken to him from that day to this, and I never will!'

'Oh, Bo!' his wife said softly.

'Only child we had,' said the old man, 'And that's the way he turned out. Makes you think, don't it?' There was a pause before he went on, 'I often wondered afterwards whether we'd failed him in some way. Me not being home much, away a lot, you understand.'

'Yes,' said Bone.

The old man continued fiercely, 'But I came to the conclusion it wasn't any fault of ours. When he was a child you could see it in him; he was a lying, snivelling little sneak even then.'

'And he gambles a great deal,' his wife broke in, 'That's really what's the ruination of him.'

'Once it was his mother's diamond clip brooch. My present to her on our silver anniversary.'

She said quickly, 'But we don't know that for sure!'

Edgerton-Forbes snorted and finished off the remainder of his drink. 'Well it was most peculiar how the brooch came to be "lost" so shortly after one of his annual visits.'

'But we couldn't be *certain*!' his wife insisted stubbornly.

Edgerton-Forbes rounded on Bone. 'Now he's in trouble with some girl, eh? Well, it wouldn't be the first time.'

Bone told them about Nova Foster and how he'd been hired by her parents to try and locate her before her father died. He spoke about her job at 'The Grumble Club', leaving out the part that she did some brass nailing on the side, although it was obvious from the old man's expression that he guessed as much, and also made vague references to the fact that she'd seen something she oughtn't and now her life was possibly in danger.

'So how can we help you?' Edgerton-Forbes demanded.

Bone said, 'The only leads I've been able to get so far have all been through Rupert. Now that he's disappeared from London I thought I would contact you in the hope you might know his whereabouts.'

'Well, my dear, do you know? I certainly don't,' Edgerton-Forbes said.

His wife shook her head. 'He came here some weeks ago, on my birthday . . .'

'Only time he's allowed in the house,' Edgerton-Forbes broke in, 'And then only on condition he keeps away from me.'

His wife went on, 'He didn't mention anything about changing his address or anything like that.'

'Did he seem any different than usual?' asked Bone, 'Was he edgy? Irritable? Look as though he might have a lot on his mind?'

'No . . . ' Mrs Edgerton-Forbes replied slowly, 'I can't say that he was any of these things. Mind you it's a little difficult for me to tell these days, we've grown so apart you understand?'

'I see,' said Bone. It was all slipping away again. Another road leading up to the inevitable brick wall. He massaged his forehead and wondered where he could go from there. He was about to rise and say his thankyous when the old woman added,

'I do remember he had a sore arm. Complained about it all afternoon, not very brave our Rupert I'm afraid. Said it was to do with some jabs he'd had to have.'

Bone leant forward eagerly, 'You mean the sort of jabs you have when you're going abroad?'

She said, 'He didn't mention anything about that, but I suppose it's possible. Mind you, I would have thought Rupert would've already had most of those.'

'But they run out and have to be renewed,' Bone said. He rose and shook hands all round. When they got to the wrought iron front gate he added, 'I think you've told me what I wanted to know.'

Edgerton-Forbes coughed, 'Let's know if you find the girl will you? Sad business about her father.'

Bone said that he would and then after more farewells he and Susan disappeared in the direction of the Mini.

During the drive back to London Bone reached his decision. He didn't want to go abroad, but the thought of another three thousand quid was enough to tempt him. He would ring Glasgow and arrange to have his passport sent down and in the meantime he would make what necessary arrangements he could from this end. He also made a mental note to stop in at a local library and do a little homework. The Middle East, and the Lebanon in particular, were not areas he was familiar with.

He dropped Susan off in Battersea and before stopping by to see Duff made for the B.O.A.C. terminal in Victoria where he had himself inoculated against cholera. He then rang through to Canonbury Square and spoke to Anya, who informed him that Duff was out on business. She told him to park the Mini and then wait in front of the B.O.A.C. building where she would arrange to have him picked up. He agreed, hung up, picked up the phone again and dialled the woman in Castlemilk who did his cleaning for him. He told her where his passport was, made her write down Susan Sweet's address and told her to send it down registered mail.

When he stepped outside, Jonno was already waiting for him in a black limousine. Bone registered surprise and slid into the passenger seat. 'That was quick,' he said.

Jonno gestured to a small radio housed beneath the dashboard. 'I was already in the neighbourhood,' he explained.

As they drove through the crowded London streets Bone wondered whether it was psychosomatic, but it seemed to him that his neck was already stiffening up, the result of the jab he'd just had. He grinned ruefully and rubbed.

Jonno drove the car into Soho and turned right into Greek Street. He parked outside a building which, amongst others, boasted the legend, DE LISLE SOUND RECORDING COMPANY.

'Mr Duff's inside,' Jonno said. As he was locking the car door a warden hurried over, waving his book in the air. The accusations and reprimands turned to smiles, however, when he caught sight of Jonno's face. Fear sparkled behind pebble glasses.

'Oh, I didn't know it was you! I'm terribly sorry, sir,' the warden said, and hurried away.

'He's quite new,' said Jonno by way of explanation, and led the way inside. Bone noted that the car was parked on double yellow lines. 'It's great to have pull,' he muttered to himself.

The dolly bird receptionist leapt to her feet the moment they appeared. She wore thigh length boots and a skirt so short Bone reckoned she'd have to shave to avoid exposure. 'Mr Duff's in studio one,' the receptionist gushed. Eyelashes as large as bats fluttered.

Jonno nodded curtly. 'I know the way,' he said and headed towards the rear of the building down a corridor covered with heavy duty brown cork.

There was a red light on outside studio one and they had to wait a full five minutes before it winked into oblivion. Jonno pulled the door open and ushered Bone inside. In the control room, behind a panel busy with lights, knobs and slide controls, sat a trio of young men. They were all of the super-cool variety. One of them oozed into a mike, 'Great, darlin'. You were really coming across there. Have a breather and then we'll try another take. Just to be certain, okay? We all think you're terrif in here.'

A blonde-haired girl smiled back at them through the glass panel that separated them from the studio. She laid down her guitar and strolled over to where a peculiar-looking youth sat clutching a paper bag and a carton of milk. Even at that distance Bone could see that the youth's pupils were dilated in the extreme. On his face he wore a faraway look. Bone recognised him immediately as a famous pop star.

'Over here!' called Duff. He was sitting at the back of the control booth. An efficient looking woman in tweeds, holding pencil and notebook at the ready, sat to one side of him.

Duff waved Bone to a pew and said, 'I'm in the process of what the money men call "diversifying my interests". I'm about to make inroads into the pop scene.'

'There's a lot of mazoola there, I'm told,' said Bone. His eyes were flicking from side to side, taking it all in. The ambience was new and strange to him, and he found it disturbingly exciting.

Duff's finger stabbed towards the glass panel and the blonde haired girl who stood beyond. 'See that broad? Well, when I took her over a few weeks ago she was washed up, a has-been. And d'you know how old she is? Twenty-four. Now isn't that pathetic?'

Bone agreed that it was.

Duff continued, 'Six months from now she'll be a star, and in another six she'll be in the super bracket. And she's only the first of what's going to develop into a stable. You see, it's not only the loot from the records themselves, and believe you me that alone is quite substantial, but it's the gimmicks that go with it. The spin-offs, as they call them. You know the sort of thing, clothes, cosmetics, posters, personal appearances. And you know the great thing? It's all legit!' A thin smile lit up Duff's face. 'Well, almost,' he added.

'I wish you luck,' said Bone.

The smile thinned even further to give a chilling effect. 'Luck's got nothing to do with it,' Duff said evenly. He offered Bone a small cheroot and after they'd both lit up said,

'So, what's new?'

Bone explained how he'd finally located the Edgerton-Forbeses and how the wife had told him about Rupert's jabs. Duff listened intently and when Bone had finally finished said,

'It's not really all that much to draw a conclusion from, is it?'

'I agree. But it's all we've got.'

Duff smiled at that. 'You reckon Beirut, eh?'

This was the part Bone always found the most difficult. Trying to put feelings, emotions and instinct into words. Conclusions were easy, they were logical and could be explained step by step, but he'd never yet learned how to explain a hunch. He said, 'I certainly think it's worth a try. You see, apart from anything else I keep having this feeling that . . . ' He trailed off as he groped for words.

Duff's glittering gaze turned to him. He puffed on his cheroot till his face was hidden by a cloud of blue smoke. 'Go on,' he whispered softly through the swirl.

Bone said, 'I think there's more to all this than just a missing girl.'

'What do you mean?'

'That's just it; I don't *know* what I mean.'

Duff said, 'I told you what I suspect's going on in my organisation. Maybe that's the undercurrent you're sensing.'

'Possible.' There was a pause before Bone added, 'Is there something you're not telling me, Mr Duff?'

The smoke lengthened into streamers to reveal Duff's surprised expression. 'Who me?'

One of the super-cool trio said over his shoulder, 'We're ready when you are, Mr Duff.'

Duff said to Bone, 'I think you'd better go to Beirut and check it out. Call me the moment anything happens.' He stuck out his hand. 'Good luck.'

As they shook hands Bone said, 'Luck's got nothing to do with it.' He could still hear Duff laughing as he made his exit, and that puzzled him.

It hadn't been that funny.

Chapter 7

The Hotel Bristol had a lot in common with its little Welsh brother the Eryri. Outside they were both razzamatazz with pretensions of grandeur; inside it was a different story. Here, the mustiness of Wales had been replaced by the dust and general grot of the Lebanon.

Bone whistled tunelessly as he stood under the shower and listened to a jet bank in off the Mediterranean. The approaching roar changed to a scream as the plane played hop, skip and jump over the hotel roof. Windows rattled and furniture danced on the spot.

He wrapped himself in his dressing gown and padded through to the main room and the huge window which dominated the far end. In the distance the Med was blue and listless; it looked too tired to even raise a decent size wave.

Another plane winked out of the sky, circled round and then started its run in. A few minutes later the windows and furniture did a repeat performance. Bone groaned as he realised he was on the direct approach to the airport runway.

He opened the baby-sized fridge and took out a bottle of water. There was a card stuck to its plastic side which informed him in three languages, English, French and Arabic, that this was compliments of the manager. Bone took a long swallow and burped, then ripped the cellophane off a packet of fags and lit up his first duty free. He inhaled with relish; he was too much of a Scotsman not to appreciate saving money. Then he opened the window and stared out over the city.

That old, alien feeling of being in a foreign country came flooding back. He took in the heat, the architecture and the squalor of the side streets, in that order, and grunted in sympathy; like most Glaswegians, squalor was an acquaintance he was well familiar with. The streets below were bedlam, packed with continuous, moving streams of Wily Oriental Gentlemen.

Behind him there was a discreet knock on the door.

'Come in!' Bone yelled.

The girl who entered was young and wore a bright summer outfit. She carried a small holdall, which she immediately placed on the bed, and smiled, displaying dazzling white teeth.

'Mr Jack Bone?'

He nodded, for once lost for words.

'My name is Zena. I'm to help you in whatever way I can.'

Bone digested this statement while at the same time appraising the girl. She had long, thick, black hair which hung to shoulder length, a fresh, tanned complexion out of which shone two liquid brown eyes. Her figure was young and taut.

'I see,' said Bone, clearing his throat. He glanced at his watch; he'd landed in the city exactly one hour ago. 'And may I ask who sent you?' he enquired.

He was treated to another dazzling glimpse of the pearlies. 'Why, Mister Duff. Instructions came through from London late last night.'

There was another knock on the door, but this time it was the girl who called out. A waiter entered and placed a tray on a small table which lived between the room's two chairs. The girl perused the chit carefully before muttering something in Arabic and signing. To Bone she said, 'I thought we might have some coffee while we talk.'

Bone agreed that was a good idea, and excused himself to the bathroom where he hustled himself into fresh togs. He slicked back his long hair and, growling to himself about vanity, splashed on some after shave.

The coffee came in tiny cups, was thick and tasted like

watered-down mud. 'Delicious,' said Bone and beamed. Then, 'Now perhaps you might tell me what this is all about?'

Zena frowned. 'You didn't know I would be getting in touch?'

'No,' Bone was remembering Duff's laughter as he left the recording studio.

'Ah! That explains it,' she said.

'Explains what?'

'Why you're looking so puzzled.'

He eased his fourteen stone further back into the chair and listened to it squeak protestingly. It squeaked again, only this time more ominously, and he hoped it wasn't going to collapse under his weight. 'I'm all ears,' he said and gave what he hoped was coming over as a friendly grin.

Zena said, 'I'm to be your contact while you're here in the Lebanon. Anything you want, help, introductions, information, equipment, it's my job to supply.'

'And Mister Duff hired you?'

'Oh yes, we've worked for him several times in the past.'

'Who's we?' Bone asked.

'My brother and myself. Normally Hadje would have called on you today, but I'm afraid he's not available at the moment, so if you don't mind you'll have to put up with me.'

'I think I can manage to suffer that,' Bone said drolly.

The girl grinned, rose and crossed to the bed where she unzipped the holdall. She pulled out various parts of a rifle which she swiftly and expertly assembled. 'NATO FN general purpose machine-gun and rifle,' she said. 'I presumed you'd want to be armed during your stay with us, so I brought along a few things for you to choose from.'

Bone watched in fascination as she assembled another deadly piece of artillery. When she spoke, the tone she used was that a bird in Britain might employ while describing a new dress. 'Or you might prefer this, Israeli Galil rifle. Fires 650 56mm rounds a minute.' She hefted a tubular device. 'It can also be fitted with this Scotos 1 infra-red night light, very useful under certain circumstances.'

'Oh, I'm sure,' said Bone drily. He crossed to the bed and took the merchandise from the girl. It was light, compact and far more sophisticated than anything he'd ever come across during his army days.

'Did you say it was Israeli?' he asked.

Zena shrugged. 'So what, it's a good gun!' She delved back into her bag and this time it was two hand pieces she produced. One Bone recognised instantly as an old-fashioned .38 Smith and Wesson. It had a black butt and its barrel had been blued, a must for desert warfare.

The other gun was new to him. It was squat, somewhat rectangular and appeared to have a great many plastic components. Bone thought it ugly and vicious-looking.

'Ingram sub machine-gun,' said Zena. 'Very good at close quarters.'

Bone fought down the impulse to ask what a good-looking chick like her was doing with a bagful of goodies like this. Instead he said, 'And whose army am I supposed to be taking on?' He returned the hand guns to the bag.

Zena frowned. 'I don't understand.'

'What made you think I'd want a shooter?'

'All the men Mr Duff sends to us want guns. It's always the first thing they ask about.'

Bone laughed at the simplicity of it. 'Well I'm the exception to the rule,' he said. 'You can make this little lot disappear back to where they came from.'

After she'd repacked her holdall he added, 'You see, I don't really like guns. I had a nasty accident with one once.'

Zena replied, 'Well if I can't help you in that department, what can I do for you?'

He fished in his wallet and pulled out the pastel pink business card that Susan had found in Nova Foster's evening bag. He passed it across to the girl. 'I'm going to look up that character. Know anything about him?'

Lips the same colour as the business card puckered. She said slowly, 'I've heard of this Shawki Costandi. As far as I understand it, this address here is a front of his in the Gold Market.'

Bone sat on the edge of the bed and watched dust motes pirouette through the air. For some reason they reminded him of a scene from *Fantasia*. 'What does he deal in?' he asked.

'Anything that makes a profit,' replied Zena, 'Preferably

illegal, because there are bigger profits there. Drugs, arms, gems, that sort of thing.'

'Is he a wheel?'

She frowned: 'I don't understand you.'

'A colloquialism. What I mean is, is he a big man around town? You know, like Mr Duff is in London?' He flicked his lighter for the girl as she was about to light up. The smoke that wafted around him was rich to the point of being cloying. He recognised it as expensive Turkish, and stared in admiration as the girl blew a perfect smoke ring first go. He made a mental note to compare techniques.

Zena said, 'It's said he comes from a humble family who saved very hard to send him to study in the United States. His subject was economics. He returned from Harvard about eight years ago and since then his various enterprises have prospered greatly. Locally he's known as the man who owns the head of the God Bacchus.'

Bone smiled. 'Not literally, I hope.'

Zena laughed, a surprisingly liquid sound. 'No, it's the head of a statue which he brought up from the bottom of the sea. What makes it important is that it's been authenticated as an original statue to the God. That makes it very valuable.'

'I'll bet,' said Bone, 'Now just let me get my facts right. Bacchus was the God of wine and pleasure, wasn't he?'

'Yes, although his reputation had grown a little out of proportion over the years. I've never been there myself, but I'm told that this Costandi has a private club in Byblos. It was in the waters off there that he found the head, so he naturally enough calls his club the Club Bacchus. The head is reputedly on display in the centre of the main room.

'I'm surprised the government let him keep such a find,' Bone mused.

'I believe a deal has been made with them. Costandi is allowed to keep it until he dies, and after that it becomes the possession of the state.'

Bone dug again in his wallet, and this time the card he pulled out was the receipt for the Hittite pot. He grunted with satisfaction when he confirmed that the address of the seller was in Byblos. For the first time since he'd started tracing Nova Foster he actually felt he was beginning to get somewhere. He smiled at Zena. 'You still haven't told me how big an operator this character is.'

'That I'm afraid I don't know. All I do know is that he'll do anything for a profit, is considerably rich and has quite a few people working for him. If it's any interest to you, he's supposed to be extremely good-looking and charming with it.'

'It's not,' said Bone. He was wondering what business Nova Foster had with an operator like Costandi. Whatever it was, he was sure it had nothing to do with buying a Hittite pot. From what inquiries he'd made in London, pots like that were ten a penny out in this part of the world. Nova's was strictly souvenir stuff.

'So tell me about this Gold Market,' he suggested.

'As you probably know, gold is a lot cheaper in the Lebanon than in most parts of the world; consequently we do a great deal of trade in it. Most of the shops which do the dealing are concentrated in one area and that's what's called the Market.'

It sounded to Bone like another Hatton Garden. He rose and went searching for his jacket. Over his shoulder he said, 'Well that's where I'm off to now. Want to come along and make sure the taxi driver doesn't take advantage of a poor innocent foreigner?'

'That's my job,' Zena replied.

Bone wished she hadn't sounded so matter-of-fact about it.

Outside the hotel, Zena hailed a cab and they both climbed in. Bone told the girl he wanted a tour of the city itself before he went to the market and she passed this info along to the driver. He noted with surprise that the cab was a Mercedes, and Zena explained that this was common in the Lebanon; because of some trading agreements they were a cheap buy.

'Why the tour of the city?' Zena asked.

Bone sniffed. 'I want to get the feel of the place, allow the atmosphere to sink in. I want to hear the music.'

The girl looked baffled. 'What music?'

Bone laughed. 'The vibrations. The way it all hums.'

Later he blinked in surprise when they passed a spired building which bore the legend on its doors: CHURCH OF SCOTLAND. REVEREND ANGUS MCPHERSON, MINISTER.

'There are many Christians in Beirut,' Zena explained when he quizzed her about it. 'Don't forget your Crusaders spent many years here during the Holy Wars of that time. They succeeded in converting many of the locals.'

Bone twisted to face her. 'You sound cynical when you say that.'

Zena shrugged. 'Times were hard and your people were temporarily the masters. Besides, some Arabs will do anything if they think it will bring them a profit.'

'I know a few Scotsmen I could say the same of,' Bone remarked, 'Strikes me the two races might have something in common.'

'But I thought you were English?'

He chuckled. 'You're maybe good at speaking our language, but you're rotten at placing accents. I come from north of the Tartan Curtain and I'm proud of it!' He patted her on her bare arm. 'It may interest you to know you're the first Lebanese girl I've ever met.'

Zena smiled indulgently. 'Now it's you who's wrong. I may live in the Lebanon, but I'm a Palestinian by birth.' Fanaticism flared in her eyes. 'That's why my brother Hadje cannot be with you during this time. He has business to attend to across the border.'

Bone got the message. He dropped the subject and went back to watching the scenery. He had nothing against the Arabs, in fact he'd always got on well with the ones he'd had dealings with, but some of his best and closest friends belonged to the circumcised brigade. It was an argument he had no wish to get embroiled in.

Finally the cab drew to a halt, Bone reckoning he'd seen sufficient, and he paid the driver. He noted that the cabbie's eyes kept flicking from him to Zena and back again. The cabbie looked sick as Bone counted the correct fare into his hand.

They stepped through an archway and Bone gasped at the sight which greeted him. Shop upon shop, each with a window stuffed to overflowing with sparkling yellow, stretched out in all directions. Harsh, white light beamed from a thousand different sources to add the final frosting to an already gigantic gilt cake. Bone whistled.

'Who said "open sesame"?' he muttered.

Zena waved a well-tanned arm. 'The Gold Market,' she said, quite unnecessarily.

Bone stopped in front of the first shop and stared through its plate glass window. Rings, bracelets, pendants, watches, novelties, tie clips, chokers, 9ct, 18ct, 22ct. At the top of the pile was a solid chunk of the stuff, about the size of a baby's fist. A small card at its base announced it to be a 24ct paper-weight.

'I suppose that's for the man who has everything,' said Bone and moved on.

A dozen different languages hummed in the air around them. English was predominant, with French coming second. A fat shopkeeper bowed and tried to tempt them into his place of business. He gave a flashing smile which literally stunned Bone for a second. He'd seen many things in his life before, but never a set of solid gold teeth. He found himself wondering what carat they were.

'That's it,' said Zena and nodded ahead.

The sign above the door said SHAWKI COSTANDI: JEWELLERY, GOLD AND SILVERSMITH, exactly the same as on the pastel pink card.

'You wait here,' said Bone.

She crowded close to him. 'Don't you want me to come in with you?'

'No. The questions are my bag.' He patted her arm and then strode forward to the doorway.

A bell tinkled as he entered. Bead curtains parted and a roly-poly man greased his way in. He looked and smelled like he'd just stepped out of an olive oil bath. 'Can I help, M'sieur?' he crooned. Twin computers that passed for eyes dissected Bone on the spot.

Bone said politely, 'I'd like to speak to Mr Costandi. Is he available?'

'Aaah! Perhaps you would like to be seated?' Roly-poly gestured towards a yellow dacron chair.

'No thanks,' said Bone, 'I prefer to stand.'

Roly-poly moved behind a glass counter, where his fat stubby fingers found and played with an eye glass. He said silkily, 'I'm afraid M'sieur Costandi isn't here today, but perhaps I can help?' He made a vague gesture which took in the entire golden treasure trove. 'We have many fine things at reasonable prices if you are here to buy.'

Bone replied, 'My business is of a personal nature, and has to be conducted with Mr Costandi himself.'

'I see,' murmured the roly-poly man. The computers became laser beams which homed in for a second opinion. He coughed while fat fingers fiddled. 'Are you acquainted with Mr Costandi?' he asked.

'We've never met, but I'm looking forward to the pleasure.' Then, dangling a teaser, 'I think you'll find he'll be pleased to talk to me.'

Roly-poly nodded while he digested this. A sheet of yellow paper appeared from below the counter and this was spread before Bone. A gold pen was laid on top of it. 'M'sieur is staying in the city, I presume?

'I am.'

'Then if you would care to write down your address and telephone number, I shall see that M'sieur Costandi is informed that you wish to see him.'

Bone knew he'd have to settle for that at the moment. In block letters he wrote his name, his room number and the name of the hotel. He didn't bother with the phone number for the simple reason that he couldn't remember it.

'Can I expect to hear soon?' he asked.

Roly-poly shrugged and showed Bone the palms of his hands. The bell behind them *pinged* and a Yankee woman bowled in. The voice was mid-west, grating, the gear in bad taste. She was so loaded down with spangle she might have been a refugee from the top of a Christmas tree.

'I'll be waiting,' smiled Bone and made for the door. From the corner of his eye he saw roly-poly carefully fold the paper before putting it into his inside jacket pocket.

'Well?' Zena queried.

Bone gave her the story as they jostled their way through the press. Outside they hailed a cab, another Mercedes, and gave the driver the name of the Bristol. Bone sank into the leather upholstery and sucked in a lungful of perfumed night. 'So now we wait,' he said, 'As the saying goes, "the ball's now in his court".'

When they reached the hotel Bone suggested dinner together, and Zena agreed. She insisted he try Lebanese grub and, after joking that he didn't fancy sheep's eyes, he agreed.

When the food came it consisted of unleavened bread plus about a dozen bowls containing all sorts of goodies. Zena explained that the idea was to tear off some of the bread and, using this like a shovel, scoop up the food to convey it to the mouth. Bone wasn't surprised to find the new tastes novel and exciting. The only dish he declined was a plate on which sat an entire brain. Poker faced, he told the girl that he already had enough, thank you very much. This brought on a fit of the giggles and in the end he had to thump her on the back and help her to a glass of water.

After the meal they took coffee in the lounge, and talked. Bone was intrigued about what sort of business Duff might have in this part of the world, but when he attempted to question the girl on it she clammed up and refused to be drawn. What he did learn out of the conversation was that Zena was eighteen years old, a lot younger than he'd first imagined, and that her overriding ambition was to go back to Palestine. Her eyes shone as she talked incessantly on the subject, and during this part of the dialogue Bone smoked and kept his chat down to the minimum. The only direct question he asked was, 'Have you fought personally as a guerrilla?'

'Of course, it was my duty,' the girl replied avidly. Then, with enormous pride, 'I killed a man on my first mission.'

Bone stared into the dregs of his coffee and thought how sad it all was. He shuddered when he had the sudden vision of the girl lying dead on some forgotten battlefield. He thought of Nick Byers and wondered about the futility of it all. Then he wondered what the dead would have to say on the subject.

To Bone's amusement Zena insisted on escorting him to his room, where she checked that all was in order and as it should be. She dialled down to reception and in Arabic ordered some bottles of water and some ice. She also gave them instructions for an alarm call and, after hurried consultations with Bone, ordered his breakfast for the morning.

'You only really get service if you speak Arabic,' she explained after she'd hung up.

Bone said, 'You know, it's me that should be taking you home, and not the other way round. Do you live far away?'

Zena smiled. 'At the other end of the city, but while you

are here I shall be living in the hotel so I can be on hand should you want anything in a hurry.'

Bone raised an eyebrow. 'Won't that be inconvenient for someone?'

Zena frowned. 'I don't understand?'

'Well, isn't there a boy friend or folks you want to be with?'

She gave a soft, cynical smile, and suddenly she looked drawn and tired. She said in a tight voice, 'My parents were killed in the fighting some years ago and ever since then Hadje and I have been on our own.'

'And boy friends?' Bone asked gently.

'So far there hasn't been time for such a luxury. But perhaps some day the right boy will come along, and it will be good between us. This is what I pray for.'

On the pad of paper at Bone's bedside she jotted down her room and extension numbers. 'Call me if you need anything at all.' She shook hands. 'Good-night, and thank you for the meal. I thoroughly enjoyed your company.' A smile dimpled her cheeks. 'You're quite different from most of the men Mr Duff sends.' At the door she paused. 'I've had one or two misunderstandings with these men in the past. The services Mr Duff hires do not include my body. Is that quite clear?'

'Perfectly,' said Bone, 'Good-night, Zena. Pleasant dreams.'

He crossed to the window, opened it and stared out over the Mediterranean. The breeze that waltzed over his face was warm, carrying the night sounds. Traffic mingled with music, and underneath it all was the concentrated hum of humanity. Below him a neon light winked garishly on and off. It said GOLDEN BAR. Gold again, only the type they were dispensing came in a glass and promised oblivion.

He thought back to Heathrow and the blonde girl called Susan Sweet. 'Will you be coming back to London,' she had asked.

Bone shrugged, 'I've no idea.'

'If you do, there's always a bed for you.'

He suddenly felt awkward and didn't know why. What he did know was that he didn't feel paternal towards the girl any more. 'I'll remember that,' he said.

Behind him the tannoy squawked that it was departure

time. Susan looked lost and vulnerable. 'So,' she said. She smiled bravely.

'You have my address in Glasgow,' he said.

'Yes.'

'And whatever happens, remember your promise.'

A pale finger jerked across her left breast. 'Cross my heart and hope to die. No more tit shows.'

They both laughed and somehow, without him seeming to do anything she was in his arms. 'I like you mister man,' she whispered as she stood on tiptoe and kissed him. Then she turned and whirled into the crowd, leaving him with an impression of tears.

There was a knock on the door and Bone called out, 'Come in!' He thought it was either Zena back for something, or else the waiter with the fresh bottles of water. It was neither.

The man was about six foot six and built like a tank. When he removed his chauffeur's cap, a prematurely bald head flashed into view. Like every other Arab Bone had seen so far, he sported a Nasser moustache. He bowed slightly.

'Mr Bone?'

'Yes.'

'I believe you wish to speak with Mr Costandi.' His voice was warm and soft, oozing understanding and sympathy.

Bone glanced at his watch. It was midnight exactly. 'That's correct,' he said.

'My name is Paul, and I am Mr Costandi's chauffeur. If you'd care to accompany me, I'll take you to him.'

Bone briefly wondered whether he should buzz through to Zena and let her know where he was off to, but decided against it. The girl had looked tired and in need of her beauty sleep.

He grabbed his jacket from the bed. 'Lead on, McChuff!'

The big man paused. 'The name's Paul, sir,' he said. Then, amazingly for a man of his build, he strode down the hallway without making a single sound.

The car waiting for them was a Jaguar, a gleaming beast of a machine that had been polished with loving care. Bone climbed into the back and settled himself comfortably. He offered Paul a fag before lighting up.

'I don't smoke, sir,' said the chauffeur and eased the car

into gear. He gunned the beast into the traffic and turned down towards the sea.

Bone glanced up at Mt Lebanon and thought of the story Zena had told him over dinner. When the first tribes had marched out of the interior to come into contact with the mountain, being desert people they'd never seen or even heard of snow, and they'd pointed to its white capped tip in wonder. They thought the snow was milk, which afterwards partly gave rise to the expression 'Land of Milk and Honey'.

The Jag purred its way along the coast road, passing through villages which bore intriguing biblical names. Jall El Dib, Zouq El Kharab, Jounieh, Nahr Ibrahim.

'How much further?' asked Bone after they'd been driving for about an hour.

A road sign loomed out of the darkness and Paul gestured towards it. 'We're there, sir,' he said. The sign said BYBLOS, as Bone had guessed it would.

They turned in down past a ruined castle and the car bounced on a cobbled road. There was the sound of lapping waves as Paul parked beside the harbour wall, where about a dozen gaily-painted fishing boats rode smartly at anchor. 'This way sir,' said Paul and led on.

They passed through a patio dotted with tables and sun umbrellas closed for the night. The building itself was stone and incredibly old-looking. It was one storey high and its windows appeared Moorish in design. They skirted a fountain, an open air stone fire where several fish were being grilled by a chef, to make their way along the far side of the building. Paul stopped before the last of three studded doorways and knocked discreetly.

'Enter!' said a voice with a slight American accent.

Paul pushed the door open and, with Bone at his heels, stepped inside. 'Mr Bone,' Paul announced.

The man who rose from the couch was young and exuded charm. His eyes were bright with intelligence. 'I'm pleased you could come,' he said and extended his hand.

While Bone shook, his eyes flickered over Costandi's shoulder to the bird seated on the couch. She was a world-famous American film star whose films Bone usually happened to like. She had a glass in her hand and a sardonic smile on her face.

Bone swiftly took in the room. The floor, the walls and the roof were all of stone. The roof itself was arched. A metal spiral stairway curled up one wall to where a platform jutted out from an alcove. Bone glimpsed an unmade bed. His nose wrinkled from the stale smell of sex.

After introducing himself, and making a few pleasantries, Costandi said, 'Perhaps you'd be good enough to show Mr Bone into the club, Paul. I have a few more things to attend to here and then I'll join you. I hope you don't mind?'

Bone murmured that he didn't, and made his exit. Already he knew he didn't like Costandi. He couldn't have said why, it was merely his natural reaction to that type of man. As he and Paul walked back the way they'd come Bone wondered idly what it would be like screwing a film star. He came to the conclusion that they probably weren't very different from any other piece of skirt. But what the hell, it might be fun to find out someday.

The club room itself was cool to the point of being chilly. In the centre of the flagstoned floor stood a plinth, and on top of this rested a ball of worked stone. On closer inspection the ball turned out to be fashioned in the features of a fat man with blubbery lips. The expression was cruel, the laughing, sadistic kind. Bone didn't have to ask to know this was Bacchus, the God of booze and revelry.

'Drink, sir?' asked the bartender. Another big man with the inevitable Nasser moustache. Bone ordered up a Coke and leant against the bar. His nose twitched from the warm, rich scent which invaded it, and it was a full minute before it dawned on him that the odour was coming from the bar itself. He leant closer and smelled.

'Cedar wood,' said a female voice over his shoulder, 'The Lebanon's famous for it.'

Bone turned to find himself staring into the face of the film star. A white hand limped towards him. 'Hi! Shawki forgot to introduce us. My friends call me Lorri.'

Bone smiled and shook the offered hand. 'Mine call me Jack.' There was the tinkle of ice and a frosted glass slid on to the bar. The barman waited patiently while Lorri ground out her cigarette in an ashtray. She said throatily,

'Usual for me, Kamel.'

After the barman had moved off, Bone said, 'I know you

probably think it's a bore but I'd like to say it anyway. I'm a great fan.'

She studied him intently before nodding. 'Thank you. I can see you mean it.' A fluffy green concoction was placed in front of her, which she picked up in well-manicured fingers. The slashed mouth seemed to have a life of its own as it sipped. For some reason Bone thought of a spider tucking into a fly.

'How do you like our little watering hole?' she asked.

Bone's eyes flicked around as he took in the decor. Mostly it was stone, the only real ornamentations being some costly Persian rugs tacked to the wall. At one end of the room there were several glass topped cases upon which an entire battery of spots played.

'Very nice, if you like that sort of thing,' he said. He'd already decided he didn't. There was something about the atmosphere that bothered him, gave him the creeps almost. It reminded him of the last time he'd walked through a graveyard late at night.

Lorri crooked a finger. 'Come!' she said.

Bone rose and followed her towards the lit cases. When they arrived at the first one she placed her hands at its edges and leant forward. Thick auburn hair cascaded over her shoulders, while the front of her blood-red dress gaped open in a V. Bone caught a glimpse of snow-white Gossard.

'Shawki brought all these up from the sea bed himself. He's a great one for scuba diving you know,' Lorri said. Her eyes flamed with excitement. 'He's promised to teach me, so I can go with him on some of his dives.'

There were ancient coins, beads, bracelets, rings, plates, all manner of loot inside the case. Most of them were black with age.

'You haven't known Mr Costandi long, then?' queried Bone.

The slashed mouth curled upwards as Lorri went back to looking sardonic. 'Long enough,' she said sweetly.

Bone shrugged. 'They say time's relative.' He was beginning to wish he'd never met his idol, her films would never be the same for him again. He thought her a phoney, and knew if you scratched her surface a first-class bitch would be revealed, which was a pity, for Bone had never gone in for bitches.

'I see you're being well looked after,' said Costandi, materialising out of the gloom. He wore a dealer's smile on his face. He clicked his fingers twice and a few moments later the bartender Kamel came hurrying over with a glass of whisky.

'Could yours do with a little freshening up?' Costandi asked.

Bone shook his head. 'It's only Coke. I don't drink alcohol.'

An eyebrow was raised while his host's mouth pursed. 'Well, well.' He gestured Bone and Lorri towards a table. 'I think we'll sit while you tell me what I can do for you, Mr Bone,' he said. Like Duff, his American accent came and went.

Bone was suddenly aware of figures moving in the shadows behind him. Several times he heard the scrape of chairs being pulled out from tables. He said slowly, 'I'm looking for a girl called Nova Foster.' If he was expecting a reaction from Costandi then he was disappointed. So, leaving out all references to Duff, he started at the beginning and told his story. When he came to the bit about Costandi's business card being found in the evening bag, the Arab's smile stretched even wider. Bone finished and lit up, aware that every eye in the room was riveted on him.

'And you think I might know where this Nova Foster is now?' asked Costandi.'

'That's right.'

The Arab threw his head back and laughed, a deep, warm brown gurgle that erupted from the back of his throat. His chest heaved up and down as his fingers played with his moustache. 'I like it, oh I like it!' he gasped.

Bone frowned as fairy fingers danced up and down his spine. At that moment he knew for a certainty that his instincts had been right all along, that there was a lot more to this than just a missing girl.

'If you tell me what the joke is then maybe I can have a laugh as well,' he said. He felt a presence at his back and was just about to spring out of the way, when Costandi snapped, 'Kamel!'

A thin wire whipped round Bone's neck, and he froze.

There was the shuffle of feet on stone and four other men, one of them Paul the chauffeur, sidled into view. Costandi nodded and the wire was pulled a fraction tighter.

Bone gagged and desperately fought for air. Through bulging eyes he saw that Lorri was laughing quietly. The film star was thoroughly enjoying herself.

'Search him,' said Costandi.

It was Paul who did the honours. 'He's clean,' he muttered after patting Bone down. He laid the contents of Bone's pockets on the table in front of Costandi.

Lorri stared in fascination at the wire round Bone's neck. She licked her lips and rubbed her thighs together. Her breath was coming in short sharp gasps, sensation was crowding her belly and she knew she could bring herself to orgasm any time now. She trembled at the thought of hearing Bone scream. When he did that it would be time.

Costandi methodically went through the contents of Bone's wallet. He frowned as he read the card identifying Bone as a member of Alcoholics Anonymous. When he threw the card down Lorri picked it up and scrutinised it eagerly.

The pressure on Bone's throat was relaxed a little and he managed to get out, 'Do you mind telling me what this is all about?' Instantly Paul's hand flashed twice to crack against his cheeks. His heavy signet ring gouged flesh and a trickle of blood spurted through the air. It landed on the floor in a myriad of tiny drops.

Costandi grunted when he came to the pastel pink business card bearing his name. 'Fool!' he hissed through clenched teeth. When he saw the figures scrawled on the card's back he shook his head sadly from side to side. He repeated the gesture when he came to the receipt for the Hittite pot. His gaze zeroed in on Bone.

'If you're merely what you claim to be, then where did you get the money to come out to the Middle East?' he demanded.

Bone replied thickly, 'I told you, the parents gave me all the money they had. When I told them Nova's trail led here then they agreed I should come. We thought Nova might be working one of the clubs.'

Costandi grunted, 'Plausible, but I think you're lying. I can feel it.'

'Can I make him talk? Please?' whimpered Lorri. Her hands were trembling with excitement. Costandi turned to stare at her before bringing his gaze back to Bone.

'I advise you to tell me what you know now. If you don't, I'll turn you over to Lorri here, and I can assure you what they say about the female of the species is certainly true in her case.'

Bone stared at the woman in disgust. He'd always presumed the sadistic parts she played to be acting, now he knew better. 'I told you, I haven't a clue what you're on about,' he jerked out.

'Aaah!' breathed Lorri as Costandi gave her the nod. The wire slid from Bone's throat and he was firmly gripped by his arms and legs. He again had the sensation of watching a spider as Lorri scuttled out of view behind him.

'I tell you, I don't know what you're driving at,' protested Bone. 'I was hired to find a missing girl and that's what I'm trying to do.'

'Sure,' said Costandi cynically. 'And when you find her you also find Rupert. Are you sure he isn't the one you're really looking for?'

Bone shook his head. 'It's the girl I want.' There was the patter of feet and Lorri was back by his side. She held one hand behind her back.

'Now you're going to tell Shawki what he wants to know, aren't you lover boy?' she crooned. The breath that curled round Bone's face was tinged with garlic. She went on, excitement vibrating in her voice. 'I could make you scream till you would be only too happy to go down on your knees and beg to tell us what you know. But I've had a better idea. Something a little more subtle.' She jerked her hand out from behind her back and waggled a bottle of whisky in front of Bone's face. 'How about a little sundowner, Jack?'

Sweat drops broke out all over Bone's skin as he stared at the bottle of booze. Fear gnawed in his belly and his mouth was suddenly a wasteland. He watched while the woman twirled the cap from the bottle and then recoiled when she lifted it towards his face. He found himself hard against the iron wall that was Paul's chest.

'Smell!' taunted Lorri and rammed the neck of the bottle under his nose. The old, familiar fumes wafted their way up his nostrils, and the craving that was only dormant sprang fully into life.

'No,' he mumbled.

Lorri smiled viciously. 'Oh but yes, unless you tell Shawki what he wants to know.'

'I've told you the way it happened. I swear,' he lied.

Lorri pouted. 'I don't believe you.'

Bone knew it would be futile, but he made his play anyway. His foot smashed downwards and there was a howl of anguish as it made contact with the arch that was Paul's right instep. 'I told you I damn well don't know anything else!' shouted Bone as his elbow shunted backwards into Kamel's gut. He whirled, his hand raised to knife downwards into the bartender's exposed larynx. Then there was a bang on the back of his skull and the lights in the room did a crazy minuet in slow, slow time. As he fell a voice he recognised as his own said:

'I'm telling the truth!'

The pain that throbbed through his body as he surfaced from unconsciousness told him he'd taken a bad beating. He fought down the nausea before opening his eyes, and found himself staring into the dealer's smile.

'I still can't tell you what I don't know,' he mumbled.

There was a pause before Costandi said, '*Now* I believe you. Take my advice, Mr Bone, go back to Scotland and forget about Nova Foster. Otherwise . . . ' He shrugged and his meaning was clear.

'Can I go now?' asked Bone.

'Shawki?' Lorri's voice was a demanding whine. 'You will let me have my little bit of fun?'

Costandi looked apologetically down at Bone. 'Sorry about this, but the lady seems intent on getting her jollies. Goodbye, Mr Bone.' He nodded and walked away.

Bone's hair was pulled and his mouth jerked open. The neck of the bottle was jammed between his teeth and the spirit gurgled as it flowed out.

'Swallow,' growled Kamel and clamped his free hand over Bone's nose.

Bone gagged and tears filled his eyes as he was forced to suck in a breath. Instead of air it was raw spirit that burned its way down his gullet.

Lorri writhed as her body found fulfilment. This was what she enjoyed more than anything else, making other people suffer. In Bone's case the pleasure lay in reawakening his addiction. The gushing inside her became a roar which finally blossomed into a torrent. When her passion was on the ebb she whispered, 'Oh that was fine. Real fine.' Then she gazed down at Bone and laughed. She knew all about the horrors of being an alcoholic. She was one herself.

For Bone, it was as though he was being drowned in a sea of fumes and booze. Strangely, he found himself thinking of Susan Sweet, and that somehow he'd let her down. The mists had already begun to close in when the feet tried to kick their way through his rib cage. His last conscious thought was that the alcohol now seeping back into his soul was an old friend, one from whom he'd been parted for far too long.

He giggled, and then oblivion came.

Chapter 8

Home was a gutter where the soft rain trickled. A younger Bone lay in his filthy rags and stared out into the gloaming. Filth-caked hands scrabbled at the kerbstone as he tried to haul himself to his feet. He grunted, lost his balance and rolled on to his back. It didn't matter any more, nothing did, except where to find the next drink. There was a beast to be fed and the beast was a demanding master.

'Hey, would ye look at the state of that, Ally!' cried the young voice. Two teenagers edged into view.

'Whit's the matter wi' him?' asked the companion.

Ally smirked, he knew the answer. 'He's pished as a fart. Have ye never seen a drunk man before?'

Through, bleary, gummy eyes Bone noted that the youngsters were well-dressed. Was it not possible he might be able to tap them for a couple of bob? The sour pit that was his gut whined its protest as he flopped on to his side and started the long climb to his knees.

'Phew, what a stink!' muttered the companion. 'It's enough to make ye boak!'

'Aye,' Ally agreed sagely. 'It is that.'

An empty bottle clinked as it rolled from Bone's pocket. It took the path of least resistance and rolled downhill till it came to rest at Ally's feet. The boy bent down, picked up the bottle and sniffed its open neck. His face screwed up with distaste. 'Jesus Christ, it's bloody red biddy he's been on,' he said.

Nectar, thought Bone, soothing balm for the troubled soul. You adjusted what taste buds you had left to the rotgut wine and tried not to think of the meths that had been added for spice. Too much and you went blind, more than that and you were dead.

'A drink, I need a drink . . . please?' he pleaded.

'We canna help you,' said the companion. He wanted to go home, away from this apparition. His skin crawled just to look at the filthy rag-bag that was Bone.

Ally, however, had other ideas; a bud called power was born in his young mind. He sauntered closer, ready to turn and run should his judgement prove wrong. The foundation of his cockiness was that he was the fastest runner in all of Govan. At nights he dreamt of the Olympic Games, but he knew that was a dream which would never reach fruition. There were eight in the family and money was needed. In two more years he would leave school and go to work in the yards. He stuck his hands jauntily in his pockets and peered down at Bone. 'What was that you said, mister?' he asked innocently.

Bone croaked, 'A drink, I need a drink. If you could just see your way to letting us have a couple of bob, son. I would sure appreciate that.'

The companion had a tanner that he'd kept for gob stoppers. His hand dug in his pocket. 'Here, I think I've – '

He was cut short by Ally's scowl. Ally turned back to Bone and smiled sweetly. 'Wasn't there something else you said? A word I think.'

Bone tried to make saliva and failed. He panted and then ran his hand over a bristly chin. Cracked and broken nails scratched at what a lifetime ago had been a white semmit. 'What word?' he managed at last. He peered up at the boy's smirking features.

'Didn't you say "please"?'

Bone's head sank downwards. He knew the game, he'd been forced to play it many times before. But now it was two kids who were calling the tune. Kids! Shame welled through him, that and disgust. He hated himself with a passion he'd never have believed possible.

'Please,' he whispered.

'Here,' said the companion and the sixpenny piece chinked on to the ground. Bone's hand flashed and he grunted with satisfaction as the coin was scooped into his palm. It was enough for one drink, a beginning.

'Let's go now,' said the companion.

Ally made a face and dug in his own pocket. He was thoroughly enjoying himself. A half crown twinkled as it spun through the evening air. Bone heard the faint whirr it made and raised his face to watch the coin with eager anticipation.

'And again,' said Ally.

'Please,' choked Bone. 'Please, please, please . . .'

'Pretty please?'

The important thing was to get his hands on the money, then the rest of the day would take care of itself. His stomach griped and he shook with the dry heaves. He had to have a drink and hc had to havc it soon.

'Pretty, pretty please,' he mumbled.

Ally flashed a triumphant look at his appalled companion. Ally liked his first taste of power. He wanted more. He chuckled to himself and said, 'Now sit up and beg. Say bow-wow, like a dog!'

Bone's fist impotently pounded the ground. 'Not that, not that,' he pleaded.

Ally glanced round to make sure that the coast was still clear before going on. He displayed the half crown tantalisingly between finger and thumb. 'Don't you want it eh? Don't you want it?'

Bone licked cracked lips as he focused on the coin. It was an easy thing to do and no one would see apart from these two boys. Not that it mattered much if anyone did; Bone was a joke and he knew it. He struggled into a kneeling position and raised limp hands in front of him.

'Bow-wow! Bow-wow!' he said and joggled up and down.

'A drink I promised, and a drink you'll have,' said Ally tremulously. There was the screech of a descending zip and and then an amber jet was arching through the air.

'How's that then!' Ally cried exhultantly.

Bone yelled and desperately tried to protect his eyes from the stinging urine that spattered against his face. 'You promised, you promised,' he moaned.

There was a single laugh, followed by the clatter of boots as the boys fled the alleyway. Bone tried again to stagger to his feet and this time he made it. He leant against a red brick wall and clutched the sixpence so tightly in his hand it almost penetrated his flesh. He jabbed at his sodden front before closing his eyes. 'Oh God, oh my God!' he muttered. Then, 'I'm sorry Nick. I'm sorry.'

Waves were lapping gently at his feet when Bone came to. For a few moments he stared into the Lebanese sky before he was able to recollect what had happened to him at Club Bacchus. Then he started to shake and he knew it wasn't cold or water but the D.Ts.

There was a flurry of sand, and a running figure whirled to a stop beside him. When it sank to its haunches he glimpsed Zena's concerned face.

'Are you all right?' she demanded. Her hands poked and prodded his body as she searched for a wound or broken bones.

'I must have passed out,' he said. He smelt the whisky and shook some more.

'Can you stand?'

He managed a nod. 'I think so.' With the girl's assistance he managed to struggle into an upright position. His legs buckled twice as they staggered to beyond the tide line.

'How did you find me?' he asked. His head was thundering with the full 1812 Overture.

Zena said, 'The receptionist at the hotel promised to buzz me should anyone inquire about you. I got downstairs just as you were leaving with the chauffeur so I decided to follow in my own car.'

'I'm glad you did,' grunted Bone and stumbled again.

As they tottered towards the road Zena told him how she'd waited by the pier while he was inside the club and how she'd seen a body being brought out and bundled into the back of the Jag. 'They dumped you here and I had to wait till they were gone before I could come down,' she said. 'When they threw you in the shallows I thought you might drown.'

'Where's *here?*' Bone asked.

Her reply was that they were a few miles beyond Byblos on the coast road to Tripoli. When they reached the car Bone collapsed into the front seat and searched his pockets for fags. They were wet when he found them so he had to borrow one from the girl. He lit up and stared down at his hands; one thing was certain, he wasn't going back to the U.K. with his tail between his legs.

His thoughts on the subject were interrupted when he gagged from stomach gripe. As Lorri had known it would, the whisky whirling round his bloodstream was doing its work. His entire system was clamouring for another drink. He shuddered and said, 'I don't want to go back to the hotel. Is there someplace we can lay up for a few days? Somewhere quiet where Costandi and his circus are going to have trouble finding us?'

Zena thought before replying. 'Some friends of mine have a villa further down the coast. They're abroad at the moment, and the place is lying empty. I'm sure they wouldn't mind us using it.'

'Fair enough,' said Bone and clanged his door shut. He huddled in his wet suit and tried not too shake too much.

Later he fell into a restless sleep which was occasionally punctured by tiny cries of, 'Babs!' and sometimes, 'Susan!' He would have been more than surprised if he'd been aware of the latter.

The villa was white and full of space. Luckily for them it had been left well-provisioned, so while Zena made noises in the kitchen he filled the enormous marble bath. He soaked for a little while in the luxurious green warmth and then, just as he was drying off, the door banged open and an arm appeared waving a thick Turkish towelling dressing gown.

'Coffee and eats are ready in the other room,' Zena said.

Later, when the grub and coffee had been demolished, the Palestinian girl asked her question.

'Do you want to talk about it or is it something I shouldn't know about?'

Bone lay back in his chair and stared at the ceiling. It wasn't plaster he saw, but Lorri's face, wriggling with ecstasy as the whisky was forced down his gullet. Thinking of it brought the smell back to his nostrils and that made his insides heave as they pleaded with him for more booze. His teeth chattered when he spoke.

'Do you know what an alcoholic is?' he asked.

The surprise mirrored in the girl's eyes mellowed into pity. She nodded.

'Well, I'm one.' He told her about the A.A., the card he carried and what had happened in the Club Bacchus. There was a silence before the girl said slowly:

' "You cannot separate the just from the unjust and the good from the wicked;

For they stand together before the face of the sun as the black thread and the white are woven together." '

This time it was Bone who registered surprise. 'Who said that?' he queried.

'A Lebanese poet and philosopher called Kahlil Gibran. I've always thought him a very wise man. In another part of his sayings he said, "Much of your pain is self chosen.
It is the bitter poison by which the physician within you heals your sick self.
Therefore trust the physician, and drink his remedy in silence and tranquillity:
For his hand, though heavy and hard, is guided by the tender hand of the Unseen,
And the cup he brings, though it burn your lips, has been fashioned of the clay which the Potter has moistened with His own sacred tears." '

Bone sipped his coffee and tried to digest the words the girl had just spoken. 'I don't know, I'll have to think about that,' he said at length. His eyes slid to where several bottles of booze were standing on top of a cabinet. One part of him was repulsed at the thought of having a drink, while the other part cried out for one. He took a deep breath and lit another cigarette.

Zena nodded towards the bottles. 'Shall I put those away?'

'No!' he said emphatically. 'They stay there in plain view so I can see them. That's the way it's got to be!'

'Well, I suppose you know best.'

'Yes,' he said heavily. 'I have a great deal of practical experience on the subject.'

She smiled tentatively. 'Is there anything I can do?'

'To paraphrase your man, it's a case of "physician, heal thyself". Mind you, I have one thing going for me. I didn't want that drink, it was forced on me. That makes a big difference.'

She stood framed in her bedroom door. 'How long do you think?'

He shrugged. 'How long is a piece of string? I'll be ready when I'm ready. If it's a case of money . . .'

She cut in quickly, a hint of anger flicking across her face: 'It's not. I was merely asking in case you might have an idea.' The anger faded as swiftly as it had appeared: 'Good-night!' Then she was gone.

The voice inside Bone said smoothly, 'Just one little drink, there's no harm in that.'

'No!' Bone thundered in reply.

'It'll cure the shakes and get you through the night. You can always knock it on the head in the morning. You can control it now, you're strong enough.'

'Lies!' Bone screamed inside himself. The D.Ts came back to make his coffee cup rattle.

The voice oiled on, 'Just one nip to steady the nerves and get you sorted out. A good night's sleep and then you can go back on the wagon if you want. After all, you've managed it for years now, one more jar after what's happened today isn't going to make that big a difference.'

Bone jumped to his feet and strode up and down the parquet floor. 'I won't listen, I won't,' he mumbled over and over again. He conjured up a picture of the wreck he'd been in his drunken days. He made himself recall that sharp, aggressive stink all alkies give off, and suddered to think he'd once smelled like that.

He thought of the really bad times when all he'd been able

to lay his hands on was a container of cheap hair lacquer. The drill was to rip the top off the can and add water to the liquid contents. The result was a cloudy mixture like aniset which blew your mind into instant release.

And then there were the lies and the thieving. There had been a wide eyed, young social worker who pulled him out of the gutter and helped him to a flop for the night. And while she was doing this his hand was in her pocket, nicking the small change. Anything for a drink, it didn't matter how or where you came by it, all that counted was the drink.

Bone stomped across the floor, through french windows and on to the patio that lay beyond. The Med was a midnight mirror, the moon a silvery ball sunken in its depths. He scuffed along the sand, occasionally bending to pick up a pebble which he threw seawards as far as he was able. He found a minor satisfaction in the plopping noises they made when they entered the water. His guts were sausages frying in a pan. The voice inside him pleaded and cajoled, tempted and promised. Bone refused to listen; instead he thought of Mathew Pamm and the state his friend was in. He told himself over and over again that if he took even one voluntary drink then he was finished. It would be the last mad dash down boozer's alley, the street with a graveyard at the end. He didn't have to take the advice of the quacks who'd told him, he knew it instinctively.

He wondered what Susan Sweet was doing and if she thought of him. He found himself jealous at the idea that she might still be parading her tits in front of a bunch of lechers. He shivered in the moonlight and wondered if he was going to catch a cold.

'Just a little one, for medicinal purposes,' whispered the voice.

'Get lost,' growled Bone out loud. He threw a stone and tried to hit the moon. He missed by a couple of million miles.

One thing he was certain of, Costandi knew where Nova Foster was. He'd read that in the Arab's eyes. And what was all this guff about trying to find Rupert through the girl? Why was the chinless wonder suddenly so important? He toyed with the idea of phoning Duff and then finally decided against it. He didn't quite know what his reasons were, one of them might have even been pride.

'You'll catch your death out here in nothing but a dressing gown,' Zena's voice said behind him.

'I thought you'd gone to bed.' He turned with a half smile on his face.

'I got worried when I heard you prowling around outside.'

Bitterness crept into his voice. 'Are you also paid to play nursemaid? Well I can assure you I'm a big boy, and quite capable of looking after myself.' He hated himself for having spoken the words as soon as they were out, and saw the hurt look on the girl's face before she turned away.

'It's a lovely night,' she said. 'Very different from your Scotland I'd imagine.'

'I'm sorry, Zena. I didn't really mean that.'

'I know,' she said softly.

He flexed his fingers. 'I'll need at least a couple of days to sort myself out. If you want to go back to Beirut I can always give a buzz when I need you.'

Zena appeared to consider that. Then suddenly, 'What sort of cook are you?'

Bone laughed at the unexpectedness of the question. 'Rotten!'

She waggled a clenched fist under his nose. 'Then there's your answer. Mr Duff would never forgive me if I allowed one of his men to starve to death.'

Bone persisted. 'There's bound to be a café close by.'

Zena stood on tiptoe and glared into his face. 'My mind's made up, and that's an end to it.' She gabbled something unintelligible in Arabic before saying, 'If you're going to stay out here all night, will you at least put some warmer clothes on?'

'OK!' laughed Bone. 'You win.' Arm in arm they ran across the sand to the villa and their respective beds.

Bone was wrong about one thing; it took a lot longer than a couple of days for him to reconquer his booze problem. Most of the time he spent sitting on the sand staring out to sea, and when he wasn't there he sat huddled in a comfy armchair staring into space. Zena once asked him what he thought about but the only reply was a grunt.

On the seventh day Bone roused himself from his reverie and said, 'I'd like you to get hold of a few things for me.' He handed her the list which he'd already made out.

When Zena came to the end of the list she frowned. 'No gun?'

Bone shook his head. 'I told you, I had a nasty accident with one once. I swore then I'd never use a gun again, and I haven't.'

The girl tapped the list. 'I presume from the things you want here that you're going back to Costandi's?'

'Correct.'

Zena sighed, then she looked puzzled. 'You mean you'd actually go in there without a weapon?'

Bone came to her shoulder and his finger jabbed at the final article on the list. 'There's my weapon,' he said.

Zena laughed, a belly-laugh that boomed from deep inside her. She clapped her hands at what she thought was a joke. 'You're teasing me,' she gasped.

Bone said evenly, 'I was never more serious in my life.'

Her laugh died and crinkled frown lines came back to her eyes. She asked in amazement, 'But how can childrens' marbles possibly be used as a weapon?'

Bone took the girl by the hand and led her out to the patio. He pointed southwards and said, 'That way's the Negev, a desert, like most of the places where you people do your fighting. Now, out there you can spot an enemy miles away, so consequently your entire mode of warfare has been developed round that one fact. Planes, tanks, missiles, those are your weapons because they ideally suit the terrain.

'But where I learned my business it was very different. There your enemy could be two feet away and you wouldn't know he was there until it was too late.

'I was trained in stealth, quietness, where an advance of less than a hundred yards left you exhausted at the end of the day. Part of my training was to go out into the jungle totally unarmed and to not only exist, but also be able to convince my superiors at the end of the exercise that I was still an effective fighting force. And to do that I had to find myself an indigenous jungle weapon.'

Bone knelt, picked up a small pebble that lay on the patio and hefted it in his hand, gauging its weight and familiarising himself with its contours. He straightened and pointed to an old bird nest tucked neatly under the gable. 'See that?'

Zena nodded.

Bone's hand blurred as it flashed forward, and a second later there was an explosion of twigs as the nest disintegrated. Bone turned to the girl.

'And now you're going to ask why marbles in particular?'

Zena smiled. 'I was.'

'Simple. Marbles are round, which is best for accuracy, and secondly, if you buy the same size of marble from the same manufacturer then you don't have to bother about any difference in weights.'

'And you'd go up against an armed man using only those?' Zena asked incredulously.

Bone laughed. 'It's not as crazy as it sounds. Don't forget, I'm very skilled at using them, and as long as I have some advantage of surprise I'm on a very good wicket.'

'I still think you're mad!'

'We'll see,' he mused.

'Tell me,' she asked curiously. 'Can you actually kill someone using one of them?'

'Of course,' said Bone. He tapped her on the temple. 'Clock him there and he's dead on the spot, but there . . . ' He tapped the centre of her forehead. 'You can stun as well as kill.'

Zena said, 'So, presuming you get through to Costandi, what then?'

'I put the frighteners on him till he coughs.'

'I see.' Zena picked up a small stone and stared at the remains of the bird nest. She threw in that particularly awkward way women do, and missed by at least a couple of feet. The stone rattled down the far side of the roof.

Bone smiled. 'It's like anything else, only easy when you know how.'

Zena didn't reply. Instead, she lay flat on top of the patio wall and angled her face towards the sun. Her tan was already lusciously golden brown. 'I'll be coming with you, of course,' she said matter-of-factly.

Bone considered that. He wasn't adverse to company, especially the company of someone trained as a guerrilla. 'Is it part of the deal?' he asked.

Zena contemplated the reasons why she'd volunteered to stick her neck out. The more she thought about it, the more she came to the conclusion that it was simply because she liked this raw man with the grey voice. She'd discovered depths to him that intrigued and fascinated her.

'It's included in the fee,' she lied. She rolled on to her side and fixed Bone with her gaze. 'But I go with a gun – as you've just seen I'm lousy with marbles.'

It pleased Bone that she was coming. 'OK!' he said.

The next morning Zena drove into Beirut to pick up some more bits and pieces and also to find out where Costandi was. It had been agreed between them that if he was at the Club Bacchus then the play was to be for that night.

While she was gone, Bone climbed into his gear to get the feel of it. Tennis shoes, socks, trousers with pockets and roll neck sweater. All in black. He'd also asked for a balaclava in the same colour, but that had been beyond the girl. It seemed balaclavas weren't to be found in the Lebanon.

The marbles she'd bought were large and blue. He caressed one between thumb and forefinger, judging, gauging, making it an extension of himself. He checked each marble in turn, discarding one that was a fraction lighter than its brothers. Then he sat by the sea and wondered again where Nova Foster was. He'd had Zena check every club in town but, as he'd half expected, she'd drawn a blank. Neither a Heather nor a Nova Foster had ever been heard of. There had been six British birds working the clubs who fitted Nova's description and these Bone himself had surreptitiously checked out, to no avail.

He was going over the layout of the Club Bacchus in his mind when Zena's car returned, screeched to a halt and she jumped out. She excitedly waved a copy of the local Arab rag in front of her as she dashed down the path which led to the patio. The paper was thrust into Bone's hands and the girl stabbed a finger at the picture which dominated the front page. It was one of Shawki Costandi in his best non-smiling executive pose. Bone noted he was wearing an Ivy League suit.

'So what happens now?' Zena jerked out.

Bone said patiently, 'If I could read the squiggle then I might be able to tell you. It's in Arabic, remember.'

'Oh!' said the girl. 'He's dead.'

Bone experienced a horrible sinking feeling. 'Who?' he asked already knowing the answer.

'Costandi. He was killed in a car crash last night.'

Bone took a deep breath before returning the paper. He lit a fag and jetted smoke through his nostrils. 'Start at the beginning and read it through,' he said.

The gist of the story was that Costandi had been en route to Byblos when another car had come screaming in off a side road to totally write off the Jag. Costandi, Paul the chauffeur, and the three Arabs who were in the other car were all dead.

'Crazy Saudis,' said Zena. 'They always drive as though theirs is the only car on the road.'

'You think it's gen, then?' Bone queried.

Zena nodded. 'Without a doubt. It's the sort of thing that happens every day around here, and it's always desert Arabs who're to blame. They go mad once they get behind a wheel.'

Bone sat down heavily and puffed on his fag. After a long time he said, *'Shiiiiiiiitttt!'*

'I guess that blows it, eh?' queried Zena.

Bone made a face. 'Let me think. I want to be on my own for a little while, if you don't mind.' He jumped down on to the sand and strode off down the beach.

'Damn!' he muttered to himself. 'Damn! Damn! Damn!' At that moment it seemed he was back at the brick wall and this time there was no way round or over. 'Of all the rotten, lousy, bloody luck,' he mumbled. 'My one and only lead and he goes and gets himself creamed in a car crash!' He kicked a grassy tussock in the hope that it would make him feel better. It didn't.

An hour later he was back at the villa and smiling. He hummed *All the Blue Bonnets Are Over the Border* as he took the girl by the hand and plunked her into a seat. He perched himself on its wing and said, 'Costandi was knocking off the Hollywood frightmare and it's crossed my mind he might just have confided to her Nova's whereabouts. What do you think?'

Zena caught his buoyant mood and grinned, 'I think it's worth a try.'

'Good lass!' He jumped to his feet and crossed to the

window. Fingers drummed on glass. 'If you were going to set a trap for a film star, what sort of bait would you use?' he asked.

Zena shrugged. 'A man?'

'No, something even better. Every woman I've ever met has the same weak spot, and it seems to me that in the case of an actress that spot would be big enough to ride one of your camels through. Can't you guess?'

'No.' The girl was genuinely puzzled.

Bone smiled to himself. It was thinking of Jaime Swan that had given the idea. The pop star and the film lady were in the same entertainment business, and each shared a common indulgence that made them the type of people they were. 'Vanity,' he said. 'I want you to use your contacts to find out whether or not Lorri Lane has a fan club here in the Lebanon. Can you do that?'

'Sure,' said Zena, and headed for the phone. Half an hour and fourteen calls later she had the answer. There wasn't one, official or otherwise, in this part of the world.

'Good,' said Bone. 'Now, how are you as an actress?'

'I don't know. I've never tried.'

'Well, now's your chance to find out. Just remember this, acting's only another name for telling lies. And I've never heard of a member of the fair sex who wasn't good at doing that!'

'You're a cynic, Jack Bone,' Zena retorted. She pretended to be insulted, but Bone wasn't buying. He went on, 'Now, you're going to ring Lorri Lane at the Club Bacchus – '

'Providing she's still there!'

'As long as she's still in the country I don't mind. We'll root her out and you'll give her the spiel.'

'Which is?'

Bone was in full spate now. He paced up and down the parquet floor, his finger jabbing the air as he emphasised each point he made. 'You say you're the president of her fan club here in the Lebanon, and that you'd like to set up a meeting between her and the doting fans. And when you talk lay the marzipan on with a trowel, she'll lap it up.' He paused and furrowed his brow. 'And in case that isn't enough we'll give her a little bit more cheese to come sniffing at.' He picked up the paper containing the news of Costandi's death and shook it so that it rustled. 'Tell her you've got a photographer coming along who's doing some pics which'll be shown in all the local rags.'

'I like that bit,' said Zena. 'Do I use my own name?'

'No, too risky in case something goes wrong. Make up one, anything as long as it's Lebanese.'

'And where do we arrange this meeting for?'

'Somewhere that's quiet and where we can get her alone.'

Zena clicked her fingers. 'There's a ruined temple at a place called Khalde further down the coast. There shouldn't be anyone there at this time of year and it's an ideal suggestion if one was going to do a real picture session.'

'I'll buy that,' said Bone. 'Now, do you want to have a bash straightaway or do you want to think about it for a while?'

Zena went over all the facts in her mind, putting them in order and deciding how she would present them in the forthcoming conversation. When she was satisfied she had everything clear she said, 'Now, what time should I suggest for the meeting?'

'The sooner the better, this afternoon if she can make it. But if there's any trouble in that direction, play it by ear. The important thing is that we do meet up at some time.'

Zena rose and walked to the phone. She hesitated for a few moments and her hand hovered over the receiver. She said in a shaky voice, 'I know it's stupid, but I feel nervous. I've never ever done anything like this before. I'm going to feel terrible if she realises I'm a phoney, she is a famous actress after all!'

Bone crossed the room and took the girl by the shoulders. In his most reassuring voice, he said, 'Listen, kid, the more nervous you are the better. That's probably the way a real fan club president would be when speaking to her idol for the first time. Just lay the adulation on as thick as possible when you say your piece. Her vanity and ego will do the rest, I promise you.' He was feeling a lot less confident than he sounded, as he was only too aware that his plan contained a lot of 'ifs'. He knew that if this didn't work then it was back to breaking into the Club Bacchus, providing the woman was still there of course, and this he wasn't keen to do now. He suspected the place would be in a turmoil with all sorts of bods rushing around as a result of Costandi's sudden demise. The nagging thought at the back of Bone's mind was that he might already be too late and the Hollywood refugee was already winging her way back to glitterville, or whatever hole she was about to crawl into next. He hitched on his best false smile and hoped that the girl was a better actor than he was. He patted Zena's bottom, at the same time giving her an outrageous wink.

'Pull this off and I'll personally see you get nominated for an Oscar,' he joked. Then he walked swiftly to the window where he pretended to stare out to sea. He positioned his back to the phone so he wouldn't distract the girl in any way.

Zena grinned and picked up the receiver. There was a burst of Arabic as she asked for the number followed by a pause. Then she said breathlessly, 'Oh hello, I wonder if it would be possible for me to speak to Miss Lorri Lane, please? It's the president of her fan club here in the Lebanon speaking . . . thank you, yes of course I'll hang on.'

Bone heaved a sigh of relief; that answered the first question. Nasty woman hadn't done a bunk yet.

Five minutes later Zena hung up and whirled to face Bone. Her eyes shone with accomplishment. 'Half past three this afternoon. She'll make her own way there.'

Bone strode forward, grabbed the girl by the waist and lifted her clean off the ground. 'I think you're a smasher!' he said. 'And when I see Mr Duff I shall tell him how pleased I am with you.' He grunted with pain and dropped her back to the floor.

'What's the matter?' she asked.

Bone rubbed his front. 'I'm still sore from that kicking I took recently.'

Zena winced when he showed her the mottled black and blue patches which covered his torso. Then it was his turn to grimace when she gently poked and prodded.

'Well at least there's nothing broken, so I suppose it's a case of having to grin and bear it,' she said.

Bone smiled and pointed to a particularly grisly piece of blue discolouration. 'Did you know my ancestors used to paint themselves this colour? I think they thought it pretty.'

Zena made a face. 'Well I can't say it does anything for

you,' she teased. She laughed loudly as Bone chased her round the room.

They arrived at the ruins outside Khalde at two-thirty. Bone had insisted on having a fair amount of time to have a good shufti round, so he could get familiar with the place. He reckoned his luck was riding high when they discovered that, as Zena had suspected, they were the only ones around.

Despite Bone's insistence that it wasn't necessary, the girl had brought along the vicious-looking Ingram sub machine-gun. She'd also brought a canvas bag which clanked when she moved. Bone asked what was in it and was rewarded with a mysterious smile and the cryptic advice that he should mind his own business.

Bone had brought his marbles.

The ruins themselves were a mixture of Roman and Greek, part temple, part villa, contained in a basin of worked marble and stone. Even in the bright afternoon sun the various columns and pillars seemed forlorn. They seemed to Bone to be like fingers pointing accusingly at the Gods who'd forsaken them. The Med looked tired again, a sea poisoned in its old age by pollution. Somewhere a bird cried, otherwise there was silence.

Bone glanced at his watch and saw that there were five minutes to go to the pre-arranged time. He didn't think Lorri Lane was the punctual type somehow. To the girl, he said, 'Now you know what to do?'

Zena sighed, this was the hundredth time she'd been over it. 'I meet the car, introduce myself using the false name and ask Miss Lane if she'll accompany me over to the ruins. If she has a driver with her I bring him as well.'

'Plus anyone else who might be in the party. It'll be a lot tidier and safer that way.' Bone lit himself a fag and noted absently that the backs of his hands were turning a pale shade of pink. He wished he'd brought a pair of sunglasses with him, the bright sunlight bothered his eyes at times. He mused that it had been a long time since he'd left the greyness of Scotland. Then he thought of Susan Sweet, and that made him frown. He wondered what it was about the Scots lassie that made her occupy his thoughts so much. She was hardly a great looker nor could it ever be imagined she'd come top of the class, and yet Bone had felt at ease with her. He knew it was an incongruous comparison, but in a funny way she reminded him of Nick Byers.

Zena carefully checked the Ingram before secreting it under the mound that was her jacket. The jacket lay in a pile close to the spot where Bone stood. The girl cocked an ear and listened.

'Car,' she said.

Moments later Bone heard it also. There was the screech of mangled gears followed by the rattle of the car as it bounced over open ground. 'It's them,' said Bone and stepped behind an ornately carved column. As an afterthought he added, 'Good luck!'

Bone ground his cigarette out underfoot and glanced at his watch. Ten minutes past the appointed time, not bad for a film star with an image to worry about, he mused. He took a deep breath and cleared all irrelevant thoughts from his mind, then bent his knees a fraction and waited.

Zena smiled profusely as she waded through the cloud of dust the car's tyres had kicked up. She did as Bone had suggested and allowed her nervousness to show. When her hands weren't busy washing themselves her fingers fluttered. She didn't know why, but suddenly, as a woman, she felt vulnerable. In her mind she went through the greeting she'd rehearsed with Bone over and over again.

Inwardly, she sighed with relief when she saw there were only two of them, Lorri Lane and a driver. A door crashed shut and the driver emerged. He lumbered round the front of the vehicle, paused for a fraction in front of the rear door, then with a flourish opened it.

A hand waved imperiously for assistance, was given it by the driver and the glittering confection that was nasty lady slid into view.

Zena took one look at the Hollywood spectacle and hated her. The Palestinian girl felt positively dowdy beside the ultra-groomed American. She gulped and introduced herself, not forgetting to use the false name she'd given on the telephone.

'Thank you,' Lorri said to the driver. Then looking at Zena for the first time, 'It's so kind of you and your people to invite me here today. Has the photographer arrived yet?'

'Oh, yes,' Zena gushed. 'He's all set up over in the ruins there. If you'd like to come over we're all dying to meet you.'

'Yes,' said Lorri. She patted her hair and then smoothed imaginary wrinkles on her dress. 'And you say this'll be in all the local papers?'

'Oh, positively. There's no doubt about that. In fact we're hoping the story and pictures will be run in all the Arab countries. You've a big following here you know.'

The actress swelled visibly. 'I was never aware that I was even known here,' she simpered. 'After all, I'm not that famous.'

'But you are, and we all think you're absolutely marvellous!' said Zena. She did her best to look wide-eyed and awestruck. 'And I'm sure everyone will want to tell you that when they meet you.' She gestured towards the ruins. 'If you'll just follow me.'

The driver was about to climb back into the car when Zena spoke to him in Arabic. She said conspiratorially that she thought he ought to come and meet the fans as well as she was sure lots of the *girls*, she put a lot of stress on the last word, would simply love to meet the man who drove Miss Lane's car. The driver grinned lecherously and grunted his approval, and Zena led the way.

The beginnings of suspicion crowded the driver's eyes when they came into the apparently empty ruins. His body stiffened and his head swung from side to side as he clocked the area which should have been bustling with fan club.

'Where is everyone?' frowned Lorri. 'I thought you said they were already here?'

It was Bone who answered. He stepped from behind his column and smiled at the driver. 'Hello Kamel, remember me?' he asked.

Kamel stared blankly for a fraction of a second and then his meaty fist was snaking towards his left armpit. Fast as he was he never had a chance. Bone's arm snapped forward and a small blue ball whizzed through the air. There was a sharp crack as it took the Arab squarely between the eyes. The eyes swayed inwards till they were staring directly at one another across the bridge of the nose. Soundlessly, Kamel dropped to the ground.

Bone wasn't taking any chances, and besides, he had a kicking to repay. He reached the falling Kamel in time to bring his knee up smartly beneath the Arab's chin. After that Kamel had no further interest in the proceedings for a while.

Bone rolled him over on his face and swiftly tied him up with the length of rope he'd brought along for that purpose. The gun he found in a soft chamois holster was a .9mm Spanish job. Bone clicked the magazine out of the butt and then threw gun and mag in opposite directions. He turned to face the howling, squealing furies that were the ladies. Guerrilla trained or not, it was Zena who was getting the worst of the hair-pulling, nail-raking, teeth-biting encounter. One eye was puffed to the point of closing while thin trickles of blood oozed down torn and battered cheeks. Lorri Lane rolled on top of her smaller adversary and spat full in her face. Fingers curved into talons as the actress prepared to go for the eyes. Zena saw what was coming and thrust her head forward and up. Strong white teeth found their target and Lorri screamed in agony as the Palestinian girl bit savagely into her nipple. Zena had the satisfaction of tasting blood before Lorri was hauled free.

It was a full five minutes before the film star calmed down sufficiently to speak, and during this time she and Zena glared ferociously at one another. Zena had retrieved the Ingram from beneath her jacket and now she sat nursing the weapon in her lap, looking as though nothing would please her more than to use it.

'What do you want?' Lorri hissed. Her foot stamped downwards and Bone was lucky to get his own out the way just in time. He whipped her hands behind her back and, using the remains of the rope, lashed them tightly together. Then he pushed her away from him, allowing her to stumble about four feet, before jerking her to a halt.

'I'm still looking for Nova Foster,' he said.

The film star laughed and then in the middle of it stopped to spit in Bone's direction. She missed by inches. 'Get stuffed, Scotchman,' she replied.

'Scotsman,' Bone corrected. 'Now do you tell me what I want to know, or will I turn you over to my friend here?'

He gestured towards Zena. 'Who I don't think likes you very much.'

Lorri looked sly. 'What makes you think I know anything about this Foster woman?'

'Call it a hunch.'

Lorri smirked. 'Then your hunch is wrong. I don't know a thing. Shawki was notoriously tight-lipped, not exactly one for chattering in bed, if you know what I mean.'

'She's lying, I can smell it off her,' said Zena.

'I'll kill you for this,' said Kamel. The now conscious Arab had managed to roll himself into a sitting position from where he now blinked at Bone through cracked sun-glasses.

'Shut up,' said Bone and turned again to nasty lady. 'I think you're lying as well. Now give!'

Lorri gazed contemptuously down at Zena. 'We Americans don't frighten easily. Anything happens to me and you'll have Uncle Sam plus the good ole U.S. Marines breathing down your butt. Now what do you think of them apples, *honey*?'

Zena's reply was to cross to where she'd left her canvas bag. It clanked ominously when she lifted it.

Bone knew Lorri had some relevant information, he'd seen it in her face even as she'd denied it. He blinked in the harsh sunlight and wondered what Zena was up to.

The girl said, 'I thought you might prove difficult, so I brought along a little persuader, My guerrilla compatriots have found it most effective in the past, especially with women.'

Bone watched in fascination as Zena unzipped her bag and took out a grey canister. Next came a grey coloured metal attachment which the girl plugged into the can after first removing its plastic top. 'Could I borrow your lighter, please?' she asked Bone.

The lighter sparked and then there was a great whoosh as a jet of orange flame shot out of the nozzle of the handy home blowtorch.

Lorri gulped and went deathly white. Her gaze was riveted to the two foot racketing flame. Zena grinned fiendishly. 'You turn the control so . . . ' She twiddled a knob at the rear of the attachment. 'And you adjust the flame to the intensity you require.'

The flame now shooting out the nozzle was thin, blue and about six inches in length. Zena continued, 'This for example would be about right for stripping paint or . . . ' She leered maliciously at Lorri. 'My, *honey*, what a lot of make-up you're wearing!'

The film star gagged. 'You're joking, you have to be!' Then, hysterically to Bone, 'You wouldn't let her use that thing on me!'

Bone swung his gaze away from the blowtorch. He stuck his hands nonchalantly in his pockets and pretended to stare out to sea. He said slowly, 'You were saying, about Nova Foster?'

Lorri Lane's resistance crumbled. Her head sagged and her shoulders drooped. Her voice shook when she spoke, 'I don't know very much at all and that's the truth . . . ' Her eyes slid sideways to the blowtorch. She couldn't control herself, the feeling in her belly surged to fruition. She moaned as shudder after shudder rippled through her body.

'Go on,' said Bone.

Through clacking teeth the film star said, 'There was some sort of gold deal between Shawki and this guy Edwards, involving a transfer of money . . . '

'Where to?' snapped Bone.

The actress shook her head. 'I don't know, I swear. The name of the country was never mentioned in my presence.'

'And Nova?'

'She's with Edwards, I heard Shawki say that when he was on the phone to the guy. Wherever those two are, they're together.'

Bone said heavily, 'And it's not in the Lebanon?'

'The call was long distance, abroad. I know that because the line was bad enough for Shawki to say something about it.' Lorri yelped as Zena moved closer. In the background Kamel was being studiously quiet, it seemed he didn't fancy the idea of the blowtorch either.

Zena said, 'Now, I'm sure if you try there's more you can remember for us.' Her voice was a cat's purr.

'I swear to God there's nothing more! I swear!' She tugged furiously on the rope and Bone had to jerk her back into position. Lorri's eyes bulged as the flaming jet wavered inches from her face. The heat from it caused her heavy make-up to melt and run.

'Please!' Lorri whined. 'I'm telling the truth!' Then in a rush so that the words tumbled over one another, 'Wait, there was one thing. Just as he was about to hang up, Shawki said something about enjoying themselves on Clifton Beach. He'd heard it was a great place to pick up a sun tan, he said.'

Bone looked at Zena. 'Mean anything to you?'

The Palestinian girl bit her lip. 'No, I've never heard of it,' she replied.

Lorri sank to her knees. 'There's nothing more, I swear. I swear,' she mumbled.

Bone took the blowtorch and twisted the black knob to the shut off position. The flame spluttered and died. 'Let's go,' said Bone. When he passed the actress he saw that tears of relief were streaming down her cheeks.

'What about us?' Lorri blubbered.

Bone remembered the way she'd wriggled with ecstasy as the bottle had been thrust down his throat. He remembered the cruel face gazing sardonically into his as it revelled in his pain and anguish. He stared at the woman who'd found pleasure in trying to turn him into an active alcoholic again. 'If you walk around long enough you're bound to bump into someone who'll untie you. Then you can do the same for lover boy here,' he said.

They were half-way back to Beirut before he spoke again. 'Tell me something, would you really have used that blow-torch?'

The answer was a strangled whisper, 'No.'

It was the reply Bone had hoped to hear. He stared out at the world and thought that maybe it wasn't such a bad place after all. It only seemed that way at times.

'I think you'd get on well should you ever decide to come to Glasgow,' he said. 'They'd appreciate your sense of humour.'

Chapter 9

Jack Bone took a deep breath of salty, fresh air and stared down at the churning Atlantic. It was the vision that every travelogue promised and somehow never delivered. It was paradise with a capital P.

Dark shapes sliced through the water and for a moment he thought they were sharks. He grinned with delight and relief as a shape burst from the surf to flip over in a somersault. It was the first time he'd ever seen dolphins at play.

There were two signs on his right-hand side, the first said 'SLEGS BLANKES', the other 'CLIFTON BEACH'. It had taken Zena four days and a lot of graft to come up with the answer that had brought him to the toe of Africa. As far as the Arab girl had been able to ascertain, there was only one beach called Clifton, and he was staring down at it now.

Bone put his hand in his pocket and touched the scrap of paper that was a cable from Susan Sweet. At his request she'd checked out old man Foster's health; he was still the same. The dust hadn't claimed its victim yet. The last line of the wire said simply: I MISS YOU.

Bone made his way down the flight of rocky steps that led to the beach. When he arrived he lit a fag and blew smoke at the hundreds of bronzed bodies which stretched before him. It was Sunday and the good people of Cape Town were out in force. He noted that the majority of the sunbathers were young and female. The sand they lay on was a shimmering gold.

Nasty lady had said gold was involved in the deal between Edgerton-Thomas and Costandi, and this was the land where a lot of it came from. Again he heard Duff's laughter and wondered what else he hadn't been told. One thing he was certain of, gold was the motivator, the key to the puzzle.

'Hey man! You swelter in that suit!'

The voice was nasal Afrikaans, high-pitched and whining. The bird it belonged to was a sun-bleached blonde with budding breasts. She smiled brazenly up at Bone, her indication clear.

Bone nodded. 'Come back when you're full grown,' he said and turned away.

The girl scowled and poked holes in the sand. Then she rose and waggled her bum towards the sea. The scent she left behind was Brylcreem.

Clifton was certainly the place for spare, he decided as he patrolled the ranks of prostrate bodies. All sorts, shapes, sizes, a horny man's delight. He thought of Susan Sweet's white skin and how she could use a couple of weeks in a gaff like this. His own pinkness was gradually turning a light shade of brown.

There were a lot of blondies on the beach, most of them with arrogant sneers plastered all over their mugs. He passed one young Adonis and heard the word 'kugle' mentioned. He wondered what it meant.

An hour later he'd covered every face on the beach. Nova Foster wasn't one of them. With a sigh he wiped streaming sweat from his brow and trudged towards the steps which led to the small hotel perched on top of the cliffs. When he reached the bar he flopped on to a stool and ordered a large ice cold orange juice.

'Ever see her in here?' he asked, and pushed the photo across the formica bar surface.

The smiling Bantu barman became suddenly ill at ease. He looked apprehensively at Bone. 'You police, baas?' he asked in a tremulous voice.

Bone shook his head. 'Nope.'

The barman picked up the photo and studied it. A pink tongue flickered over black lips as he did so. 'Sorry, baas, I never see this madam before.'

'You sure?'

'Yes, baas. A's positive.'

Bone stuffed the photo back in his pocket and wondered where he went from there. He decided on the phone company, dialled the operator and explained that friends of his had recently moved to Cape Town and he was trying to locate their number. The name he gave the operator to look for was Rupert Edgerton-Forbes. When that drew a blank he thanked her and hung up. Then he dialled again, spoke to a new voice and this time gave the name Rupert Edwards. After that he tried Heather and Nova Foster. As he'd expected, he got no joy from any of them. If the chinless wonder and Nova were in town, then either they didn't have a telephone or else they'd gone back to their old habit of changing names. Bone was convinced it was the latter. He climbed into his rented Volks and started back towards Cape Town and his hotel. He came to the conclusion that that evening a lot of leg work was in order, and groaned at the prospect. Bone reckoned he had two things to go on, the first being that Rupert liked to gamble and secondly that they both enjoyed their gargle.

Back at his hotel, the Mt Nelson, Bone sounded out the white receptionist about gambling casinos and where the best ones were to be found, his reasoning being that if Rupert had a lot of poppy burning a hole in his sky then he would naturally gravitate towards the better establishments. The receptionist's reply was a dampener. There were no casinos in the Republic at all, the nearest being in Swaziland and Lourenco Marques.

Bone reckoned there had to be some local action somewhere and was determined to find it. He compiled a list of the more expensive bars and clubs and, after a kip, shower and meal, sallied forth. He went armed with a wallet full of Rand.

Midnight found him sitting in the bar on the 32nd floor of the Heerengracht Hotel. The walls were glass and afforded him a panoramic view of the city, the mountain and the docks. He asked his question for the thousandth time:

'Ever see this woman?'

The bartender shook his head. 'Sorry, can't say I have.' Then eagerly, 'Say is that a Glasgow accent you've got?'

Bone said it was.

'That's where I come from. Sure is good to hear a voice from home, man.'

'Ever think of going back?'

The bartender polished a glass. 'Naw, it's the good life here. The only thing that would budge me is if those kaffirs up north get really uppity. When that happens then I'm on my way. Not home, mind you, I reckon the old country's dead.'

Bone smiled. 'If it is, then someone should tell it to lie down . . . ' He paused as fear sprang into the bartender's eyes. A voice behind him said, 'Do you mind if I sit and talk with you for a few minutes.' It was said as a statement not a question. The newcomer sat down without waiting for a reply.

'I hear you been asking a lot of questions, man. That right?'

Bone sized the newcomer up. The body was burly and exuded the suggestion of power. Baby blue eyes gazed out of a bland face; the voice was guttural Afrikaans.

'Who wants to know?'

The blond man gave a chilling smile and reached into his inside pocket. The card he produced proclaimed him to be a member of the Bureau of State Security.

'Yes I was,' Bone admitted. Behind the bar the man from Glasgow furiously polished a glass that already shone like crystal. His eyes were lowered and even in the subdued lighting it could be seen how pale he'd suddenly become.

The man from B.O.S.S. said, 'I wonder if you would care to accompany me? There are some questions we would like to ask you.'

Bone smiled thinly. 'Do I have a choice?'

'Of course.'

'What is it?'

'You either come with us of your own free will, or we take you forcibly.'

Two more men materialised out of the shadows. They were big and beefy like the one who was doing the talking. Bone noted that the atmosphere in the bar had changed since the conversation had started. People were looking anywhere but at him, and those that were talking were doing so more loudly than was normal. 'Let's go then,' said Bone and slid from his stool.

Once out in the street he was hustled towards a black saloon and told to climb in the back. When they drove off he was sandwiched on either side.

'Mind if I ask your name?' he said to the one who'd approached him and who was obviously the leader.

The reply was: 'Pieter Wankie.'

Bone fought to keep a straight face. 'I'll bet you had a rotten childhood,' he said at length.

Wankie frowned and glared into the night, his breathing slow and regular. Bone knew he'd made a mistake.

The building they parked in front of was grey and forbidding. The air was scented with flowers. 'Shouldn't I call a lawyer or something?' Bone asked.

'Why, do you need one?' Wankie replied. His eyes glittered malevolently. One of his companions laughed. 'Quiet, Johann,' he rapped.

'I don't know. What do you think?' Bone said.

'I think you'd just better follow me, man,' said Wankie and strode purposefully towards the doorway. Bone stumbled when he was pushed from behind. He fought down the impulse to turn and smash the one called Johann in the face. Bone had never been a man who liked being pushed.

He was ushered into a near empty room and told to sit on a hard-backed chair. He grunted more with surprise than pain when Wankie slapped him across both cheeks.

Wankie paced up and down. 'Why are you in South Africa?' he snapped.

Bone had hardly started on his story when he was smacked again across the cheeks. 'Lies!' Johann shouted. This time it did hurt. The third member of the trio said, 'Tell us the truth, Meneer Bone, that's what we want to hear.'

Bone waited till the stinging had subsided. 'I don't know what I'm supposed to have done, but I think it's time I got in touch with the British Consul here,' he said.

Wankie chuckled. 'Next you'll be telling us it's your right to do so.'

'Isn't it?'

The three roared with laughter. Johann said, 'In the Republic we decide what rights you have, Meneer. *Us*, you understand?'

Bone nodded. He understood only too well. He was in the hands of secret police in a country where their word was law. He said, 'In what way can I help you gentlemen?'

Wankie said patiently, 'You've been going around town asking a great many questions. Why?'

'Only one question, if anyone knows where I can find a

girl called Nova Foster.' Then, hopefully, 'Do you mind if I have a cigarette?'

'Go ahead,' said the third member.

Bone lit up, savouring the first tasty drag. Three pairs of eyes bored through him while he smoked. Finally, Johann said, 'Can we see your passport?'

'It's at the hotel.'

'And which one is that?'

'The Mt. Nelson.'

Wankie crossed to a desk, opened a drawer and took out a passport. He leafed through it slowly. 'You list your occupation as being a "sorter". What exactly is that, please?'

Bone explained.

'I see.'

'There was no need to break into my hotel room. If you'd wanted to see anything all you had to do was ask. I've nothing to hide.'

Wankie's top lip curled. 'We did not break into your room, Meneer, we opened the door with a key.'

'What were you doing in Beirut?' Johann rapped out.

'The same as I'm doing here, looking for a girl called Nova Foster.'

The third member of the trio beamed and then walked slowly towards Bone. 'You've been advised to tell us the truth,' he said in an accent so thick Bone had trouble understanding the words. Then the man took the cigarette from Bone's mouth and stabbed it into the back of Bone's hand.

Bone yelped and hurriedly flicked smouldering ash from his singed skin. The man beamed even more and ground the butt out underfoot. 'The truth,' he repeated and walked away.

Bone licked his wound. 'I'm telling it,' he growled. That earned him another smack across the face from Johann.

Wankie went back to pacing up and down. 'Who are you working for?' he asked.

Bone had no intention of mentioning Duff's name. 'The girl's parents, like I told you.'

Wankie shook his head from side to side. Piggy eyes darted towards Bone. 'I'll ask again, who are you working for?'

'The Fosters,' replied Bone. He yelled in agony as a lighted cigarette was thrust into the back of his neck. Third man smiled innocently. 'You're not listening, Meneer. We said we wanted the truth.'

Wankie said patiently, 'We know your type, Bone, or whatever your name is. We've seen a lot of them here in South Africa.' His eyes narrowed. 'And I can assure you we don't like them.'

'What type is that?' asked Bone.

'Like you,' replied Johann. 'Men who think they're tough. They come to this part of the world and meddle in affairs which do not concern them. Some are motivated by political reasons, others are simply out for as much money as they can get. They sell themselves to the highest bidder.'

'Which black country employed you?' snapped Wankie. 'Eh?'

'Eh?' echoed Johann and third man simultaneously.

The light dawned for Bone. 'You think I'm some kind of mercenary?' he asked incredulously.

Wankie snorted. 'What is your job here in the Republic? Who are you supposed to contact, and are they white or Bantu?'

'There's no use lying. You were overheard, you know,' said Johann.

'Overheard saying what?'

Third man leered. 'Shoot him, shoot the bastard, Nick,' he mimicked in an appalling Glasgow accent.

'Where was that, Meneer Bone?' asked Johann.

Wankie added viciously, 'Was it Rhodesia? Were you working with the Frelimo, perhaps?'

Bone shook his head. 'Nick who? I don't know any Nick.'

'You lie,' said third man. 'We heard you, we heard you say his name.'

'Where?' shouted Bone. He had begun to suspect the answer.

Wankie leered. 'It's dangerous to have a conscience like you have, Meneer. It can get you into trouble without you knowing about it.'

'Especially when we're listening,' crooned Johann.

Third man stuck his face close to Bone's. 'I forgot to introduce myself. I'm called Van Krug.'

'Is Nick your contact?' thundered Wankie.

'Bantu, perhaps?' added Johann.

Van Krug smacked Bone viciously across the cheeks. 'The truth now,' he smiled.

Bone fought down the bile that was mounting in his gullet. He said slowly, 'I take it you have my hotel room bugged in some way?'

There was a pause while Wankie lit a cigarette. 'You were noticed at Jan Smuts airport, you know. One of our men was with you when you flew down to the Cape.'

'The Arabs have a lot of money to spread around nowadays. And they don't always use it wisely,' snarled Johann.

'True, true,' muttered Van Krug. Then, 'Are you working for them, Meneer? Are they your masters?'

Bone shook his head from side to side. 'No, you've got it all wrong, you –'

'Shut up!' screamed Johann. 'Speak only when you're told!'

'I thought you –'

Van Krug's hand flashed and Bone cried out in pain. Then Bone was out of his chair and heading for the Dutchman. His hands wrapped themselves round Van Krug's throat and his fingers were feeling for the pressure points when the world exploded. Blackness rushed towards him and there was a sensation of falling. Then there was nothing.

When he came to, he was strapped to the chair. Wankie smiled. 'You're very quick. You almost caught us there.'

Bone groaned, his head a solid core of pain. 'Could I have a glass of water?' he croaked.

'Certainly,' said Johann. He disappeared from the room to return a few moments later holding a chipped cup. 'Here you are,' he smarmed and held the cup to Bone's lips.

Bone sighed with satisfaction. 'Thank you,' he said.

'You see, we're not the monsters some people try to make out that we are,' said Wankie.

'We can be very nice sometimes,' added Johann.

'Very,' beamed Van Krug.

Bone said, 'Nick Byers was the name of my Corporal in Malaya. I killed him accidentally. What you heard through your bug was me having a nightmare about it. I've been having them for years.' Wankie laughed. 'Oh that's very good. I like that!'

'Why don't you tell us about it? Start at the beginning and don't worry about how long it takes. Time doesn't bother us,' said Van Krug.

'True,' echoed Johann. The three men leant against the wall and stared expectantly at Bone. They were all gently smiling.

Bone took a deep breath to try and settle himself. His eyes were burning in their sockets and he felt as though his eyeballs were covered in grit. This was crazy, he told himself. But then the whole thing had had that element to it ever since he'd gone to London and been picked up by Jonno. He started at the beginning of his army days and told the story of his friendship with Nick Byers. Van Krug laughed at the part about Beverley Robertson and Nookie Rider.

'Very interesting,' said Johann after Bone had finished. 'Pieter?'

'Clever. Well thought out,' agreed Wankie.

'You tell a good tale, I'll give you that, Meneer,' said Van Krug. 'You certainly held my interest. I applaud your imagination. I never had much of that myself.'

Bone said, 'Why did your man tail me at Jo'burg? What was so special about me?'

Wankie answered, 'We develop an instinct in our business . . . ' He tapped his nose. 'We get so we can smell trouble and those who cause it.'

'Our man smelled you out, Meneer,' interjected Johann. 'He took one look at you and his nose told him that you were trouble.'

'And we don't like troublemakers here in the Republic,' smiled Van Krug. 'We give them very short shift.'

'I told you why I'm here. It's to find a missing girl.'

Van Krug came close and breathed on Bone's face. 'You won't be told again. Speak only when you're asked.' He grabbed hold of Bone's nose and viciously twisted it. 'And tell the truth, man!'

Bone's vision swam as tears poured out of his eyes. 'I am, I am,' he mumbled.

Wankie clapped his hands. 'So, let's start at the beginning, and this time we'll do without the funny stories.'

'Who is your contact in Kaapstad?' queried Johann.

'Is it Nick, and if so who is he and where can we find him?' asked Van Krug.

'Nick's dead,' muttered Bone. He wondered to himself where the bug had been located. He'd never thought to look for it, for the simple reason that it had never crossed his mind that the security forces would be interested in him. When he'd woken that morning to find his body lathered with sweat he knew he'd been in Malaya the night before. The craving for booze had been strong, so he'd stood under an ice cold shower and followed that up with endless cups of strong coffee from the bedside coffeemaker. Thinking of Nick conjured up a vision of Susan Sweet. He remembered the crumpled cable in his pocket. I MISS YOU the last line said. He derived a great deal of comfort from that. The tears flowed even more copiously as his head was savagely tugged backwards by the hair.

'What is your job here in the Republic?' snarled Wankie. His piggy eyes glittered with fanaticism.

'Which of the Arab groups hired you?' thundered Johann.

Van Krug added, 'Where and when are you supposed to meet up with the Frelimo?'

'I've never even heard of them,' said Bone. He grunted as a fist sank into his belly.

'Don't play games with us,' snarled Wankie.

Johann said: 'We don't like that one little bit.'

'Cigarette?' asked Van Krug sweetly.

The pressure was released from Bone's hair and his head slumped forward. He hoped none of his hair had been pulled out, he was already short in that department as it was. He grinned inwardly; what a stupid thought to have at a time like this! He clamped his lips round the fag and sucked the smoke into his lungs, then coughed at the unexpected different taste of South African tobacco. He said, 'What are the Frelimo?'

Wankie frowned. 'You're very good, Meneer Bone. You almost convince me.'

'I honestly don't know.'

Wankie cleared his throat and went back to pacing. He clasped his hands behind his back as he walked. 'The Frelimo are a guerrilla organisation dedicated to the overthrow of white Africa. They have sworn to sweep our folk into the sea.'

'I see,' said Bone. 'And you think I'm a mercenary working for them?'

'Correct,' said Johann.

Van Krug said sweetly, 'If you confess now and give us all the information you can, then we'll promise to see that no harm befalls you.'

'It could be very nasty if you don't co-operate,' said Johann.

Van Krug added, 'There's a place not far from here called Robben Island. You'll be taken there and forgotten. Understand?'

Bone nodded.

Wankie said with a smile, 'But help us out and we'll even give you a plane ticket. Say, eh . . . , a U.T.A. flight to Brazzaville. How does that appeal to you?'

'Sounds great,' muttered Bone.

'Marvellous. Then you'll co-operate?'

'Sure. Only there's one snag.'

'And what's that, Meneer?'

'The truth is I only came here to look for a missing girl. I don't know where you got this idea that I'm a mercenary, but it's just not true.'

Wankie shook his head from side to side. 'And I thought we were beginning to understand one another.'

'Such a pity,' said Van Krug. He cracked his knuckles one by one.

'Listen,' said Bone. 'We all know that given time you can make me confess to being the man in the moon if you want to. But if it's really the truth you're after, then I've been telling it.' He screamed as a flaring match was laid against his neck.

'You're being checked out now,' grinned Van Krug. 'You'll save yourself a lot of pain if you just come clean. Because if there's a chink in your story, Meneer, then we'll find it. I warn you, the Bureau of State Security doesn't like having its time wasted. We tend to be severe with people who try.'

'Tell me about this Nova Fraser,' said Wankie.

'Foster,' corrected Bone. 'Her real christian name is Heather, but she changed it to Nova.'

'Why was that?'

'I was told she didn't think Heather exciting enough. She wanted a name to go with the image she had of herself.'

'And who told you this, Meneer?'

'A girl in London who knew her.'

Johann nodded. 'You do get around don't you?'

'Only on this job,' said Bone. 'It's never happened before.'

Wankie mused, 'What puzzles me is how this father of hers, you did say he was a miner?'

'Yes.'

'What puzzles me is how he got the money to send you careering round the world. The flight to Beirut and your stay there, you were in a hotel I presume?'

Bone nodded.

'And then your flight down here, plus your room at the Mt. Nelson. That's all going to add up to quite a bit, isn't it? Now where would an ordinary British working man get money to pay you for the likes of that?'

Bone decided it was still best to stick to his original version of the story, which did not include any references to Duff's involvement. 'I've no idea,' he said. 'Maybe some of his mates chipped in to help him out. Our miners aren't exactly paupers any more, you know.'

'And how long does this Meneer Foster have left to live?'

'Any time now. Today, next week. He could go at any moment. At least that's what his quack says.'

Van Krug frowned. 'What's a quack, please?'

The Afrikaners spoke English so fluently that Bone had forgotten it wasn't their basic language. It seemed they weren't quite up on their colloquialisms. 'A doctor,' Bone explained. He went on, 'It's like I told you, the old man and his daughter are very close and it's his wish to see her once more before he snuffs it. You can check that out if you like.'

'We already are,' said Wankie. 'Our people in London are attending to it.'

'The Fosters live in Glasgow, like me.'

'You have aeroplanes in Glasgow, hey, man?' smirked Johann. The trio laughed.

The door opened to admit a newcomer carrying a sheet

of paper. Wankie carefully read the paper through before passing it to Van Krug in turn.

'You will stay the night with us, Meneer Bone,' said Wankie. 'We will talk again tomorrow.' He wheeled and left the room.

Van Krug unstrapped Bone and roughly hauled him to his feet. Bone sensed the Afrikaner was dying for him to make another play, so just to be perverse he didn't. Van Krug shrugged when he read from Bone's expression that he'd been rumbled. He poked Bone in the ribs with a stubby finger. 'Think of Robben Island tonight, Englishman. It's a place you're going to get to know very well.'

'Scotsman,' said Bone. 'There's a difference.'

Johann made a mock frown. 'Scotsman,' he muttered. 'Aren't they a sort of English Bantu?'

Bone smiled back. 'That's the first compliment I've had since coming to your country,' he said. Pain lanced through his foot when Van Krug stamped on his toes.

'This way,' said Van Krug and pushed Bone ahead of him.

The cell was dark and smelled of damp. There was a solitary light built into the brick wall that illuminated the conveniences which lived in a corner. The wc brimmed to the point of overflowing with water and human waste. The stench was almost unbearable.

'It'll be cleaned out in the morning,' said Johann. 'We'll get a coloured down here first thing.' Then surprisingly he reached into his pocket and pulled out a packet of cigarettes. These plus a book of matches he gave to Bone.

'Good-night,' he said. The metal door clanged shut behind him and Van Krug.

Bone lay down on the raised stone platform that was his bed, and wrapped himself in the one threadbare blanket provided. He spat in the palm of his hand and rubbed the saliva into the burns on his neck, then he lay back and stared at the ceiling.

'Poor wee soul, you're looking awful thin, a puckle of hair covered over with skin . . . ' He sang softly. He wondered what he'd ever done to deserve the unholy mess he was in now. He had no illusions about the sort of men who'd captured him. Fanatics, with total belief in their own cause, like most secret police. They were a breed that could be found in any country. Bone held them in contempt, at the same time not underestimating their power.

He remembered the fear in the Scots bartender's eyes when Wankie put in his appearance. The bartender had known, he'd seen the sort of things these men were capable of. And now they held Bone, and not a soul knew. Panic fluttered inside him, so he comforted it with a cigarette. He still didn't like the new tobacco taste, but it was better than nothing. The shreds he picked from his tongue were sweet tasting, which made him wonder where she was at that moment. Would he ever see her again? He knew he'd be denied access to anyone who could help or furnish evidence to his innocence. As Wankie had said, they had their own men and it would be their findings which would be all-important.

'Bally bally, bally bally bee, sitting on your Mammy's knee greetin' for a wee baubee, tae buy some coulter's candy,' he sang.

He must have dozed off, for he was startled awake by the sound of a key grating in the metal lock. The door swung open to reveal a leering Van Krug.

'Time for another little chat, Rooi Nek,' the Dutchman said. A coloured man, armed with a bag of tools and plunger, bustled past him and made for the overflowing loo.

'Phew, what a stink, man,' said the coloured. He made a face and rolled his eyeballs round and round.

Johann stood in the corridor, his jacket unbuttoned and pulled slightly to one side. Bone glimpsed the butt of a gun protruding from a shoulder holster as he was hustled past.

'It's a lovely morning outside,' said Johann. Then, playfully punching Bone on the arm, 'I tell you what, you confess right away and I'll see you get a swim before breakfast. What about that, hey?'

'Thanks a bunch,' Bone replied. He gently touched the back of his neck where the burns were. The flesh was inflamed and tacky, he thought it was probably suppurating.

Van Krug giggled, a surprisingly effeminate sound to come from such a big man. He gabbled something in Afrikaans and then pointed to Bone. 'Rooi Nek!' he guffawed. Johann applauded the joke.

Bone was escorted to the same room as the one he'd been

taken to the day before. Pieter Wankie sat behind a desk studying a sheet of paper. Johann gestured Bone to sit on a chair facing the desk. The minutes ticked by while Wankie carefully read through to the end of the paper. Then he lifted his piggy eyes and fastened them on to Bone. 'Coffee?' he asked. Without waiting for a reply he pushed a steaming plastic container across the desk.

Bone nodded his thanks and sipped. The coffee was black without sugar. Normally he would have hated it that way, but this morning he didn't complain.

'So!' said Wankie. He smiled and made a pyramid with his hands. 'What would you say if I told you there is no record of an Edgerton-Forbes, Edwards or a Foster entering the Republic in the past few months?'

Bone shrugged. 'There are such things as phoney passports.'

'I grant you that, man, but how would ordinary people like them know where to get such things?'

Bone sat in silence and watched the steam rise gently from the coffee. 'I don't know, but I suppose it's possible,' he mumbled.

'He's lying,' snapped Van Krug.

'I think so too,' added Johann.

Wankie tapped the side of his nose. 'I agree. I can smell it.'

Johann sighed and looked pained. 'And after us being so considerate towards you, Meneer. What a pity.'

Bone said, 'The girl's in South Africa, I'm sure of it. All I want is to find her and tell her about her Dad. I promise you that's the truth. I have no other motives for coming to your country.'

Wankie pulled out a packet of cigarettes and lit one. His chair scraped back as he rose. 'Our reports confirm your story about the corporal, Byers,' he said. He went back to his old game of pacing up and down. As he walked he left ribbons of smoke behind him. 'So why do all three of us think you're lying and holding something back?'

Van Krug said gleefully, 'I'm told you sang in your cell last night.' He chuckled evilly. 'A few hours with me and I'd have you singing another song.'

'I don't doubt it,' said Bone. 'You can break anyone, provided you've got enough patience and know-how.'

'You forgot flair; that can be a great asset when it comes to that line of work. I enjoy making them squeal, Meneer Bone. I derive a great deal of satisfaction from it.'

'I'll bet,' mumbled Bone. He was surprised when he wasn't thumped. He made up his mind that it had all got too heavy and that he'd spill the beans about Duff during the next round of questions. After all, he wasn't going to be much good to anyone if he had to rot out the rest of his life in some stinking concentration camp, for that was the conclusion he'd come to about what Robben Island had to be.

Wankie stopped pacing and swung to face Bone. 'Our men have also confirmed that you are what you claim to be. You have no known political associations that would interest us. As far as we can ascertain, you are clean. A Mr Foster does exist and has corroborated the fact that he hired you to find his missing daughter.'

Bone heaved a sigh of relief. His fingers were trembling slightly as he lit up his last cigarette. He blew smoke at the floor and licked dry lips. He could feel his heart thudding against his rib cage.

Johan said, 'If we ever find out that you've been trying to make fools of us, then we'll jump on you from a great height. Is that perfectly clear?'

Bone nodded as wave after wave of relief surged through him. He tried not to let it show on his face.

'I have taken a special interest in you, Meneer Bone,' said Wankie. Then, 'Good-bye . . . for now.'

'Does that mean I can go?'

'Of course.'

Van Krug grinned sadistically. His heavy shoes clattered on the floor as he crossed to Bone. 'I hope we see you in here again, Rooi Nek. I really do.' Then he laughed.

Wankie pulled open a drawer in the desk and picked out Bone's wallet. It had been the only thing removed from Bone's person prior to the interrogation. Wankie said, 'You carry a lot of Rand (he pronounced it 'Ront') around with you. If you'll take my advice you'll put some of them in the bank.'

'I'll think about that,' said Bone. He scooped up the wallet and riffled through the notes. The total was as it should have been. He said to the scowling Van Krug, 'Well you know what they say about Scotsmen and their money. They just can't bear to be parted.'

'Good-bye, Meneer,' said Johann.

Bone paused at the door. He knew he shouldn't push his luck, but the B.O.S.S. men's arrogance really got on his tits. 'If you ever get to Glasgow, look me up.' Then to Van Krug, 'You in particular. I'd love to show you the sights.'

Outside, the sun was blazing down. Bone blinked and ran a hand over his stubble. More than anything he wanted a bath to clean away the stink that was clinging to him. His nose wrinkled in disgust as he thought of the smell in his cell. He felt sorry for the coloured who'd had to get to work on the bowl with his plunger. Bone stopped at the sign which said APTEEK/CHEMIST and bought himself some salve for the burns on his neck. Then he hailed a passing cab and told the driver to take him to the Mt. Nelson, he'd collect his car from Clifton later. That was when he remembered that he hadn't been given his passport back.

'You look like you had a good night, man. Been on the razzle, hey?' said the cabbie. He winked knowingly. 'Somebody's husband away on a trip, eh?' He brayed with laughter.

Bone shot him a sour look. 'I'm a tourist who's been out having a ball with a welcoming committee,' he said dourly.

The driver bobbed his head. 'They can say what they like about us overseas, but one thing they can never accuse us of is not being hospitable. We're sure lavish with that, man.'

At the hotel, Bone paid off the driver, bought a carton of cigarettes and picked up his key. The moment he let himself into his room he knew he wasn't alone.

'Hello,' said Jonno. He rose from where he was sitting to shake hands.

Bone laid a finger across his lips and then tugged his ear. Jonno got it straight away. He gestured Bone to take one side of the room while he took the other. Bone found the bug behind a radiator. They then moved into the bedroom and this time it was Jonno who found one. The bug, a tiny metal and plastic device, was screwed in behind the bed's headboard. When they'd ascertained that the bathroom was clean, Bone turned the hot water tap on to full and closed the door.

'What gives?' whispered Jonno.

Bone told him how he'd been picked up by the Bureau of State Security the night before and of the grilling he'd gone through.

'*I* wasn't tailed from Johannesburg, I'm certain of that,' Jonno said after Bone had finished.

Bone could well believe it. Jonno was immaculately dressed, well groomed and had a clean cut appearancce. He looked like a successful young executive rather than what he actually was.

'I'd be very careful about carrying,' said Bone. 'They rumble you, and that might be enough to haul you out to this Robben Island of theirs.'

'Thanks,' said Jonno.

'Did Zena give you the guff?'

'You must have realised she would make a full report to Mr Duff about your progress. I'm to tell you that Mr Duff's very impressed with you so far.'

'Good,' said Bone.

Jonno sat on the edge of the bath. 'Have you found the girl yet?'

'Nope, but she's around here somewhere. I'm sure of it.'

Jonno pursed his mouth and nodded. Breath whistled out from between his lips. 'Fine, he murmured. 'Fine.'

'You booked in here too?'

'I've got a room just along the hall.' Jonno rose. 'You have your bath and I'll contact you later. I think I'd better give Mr Duff a buzz and inform him of these latest developments.'

'I'd use an outside phone if I was you. These guys seem to have a liking for gadgetry.'

Jonno said, 'One thing; you're sure you didn't mention Mr Duff's name?'

'Nope, although at the end I thought I might have to. That Wankie character's no dope. Either he or one of his boys are going to be watching me from here on in. I hope you get my point.'

Jonno nodded. 'Mr Duff likes you. He never considered you expendable.'

'Good, I was worried about that. What happens to the girl then, when I find her?'

Jonno's face was inscrutable. 'I'll be back in about an hour,' he said. 'You can tell me what your next move is then.' The bathroom door clicked shut behind him.

Bone stripped and eased himself into the piping water. He groaned with pleasure as the aches and stiffness melted from his body. He fell asleep wondering what sort of honey would draw this particular fly.

Chapter 10

'I belong to Glasgow
dear old Glasgow town,
there's nothing the matter with Glasgow
for it's going round and round.
I'm only a common old working chap
as anyone here can see,
but when I get a couple of drinks on a Saturday
Glasgow belongs to me.'

Bone sang softly through blue smoke. Clifton beach was the key; his job was to find the lock it fitted. He watched Jonno move amongst the sun-bronzed bodies and thought that the man reminded him of a cat. There was definitely something feline about Jonno, the way he had of staring at you. Giving nothing away as he watched and waited.

Ten minutes later, Jonno eased himself down beside Bone. He shook his head in reply to Bone's unasked question, and Bone pushed a cold bottle of Lion Lager in his direction.

'I bought you a wet. Thought you might like it,' he said.

Jonno nodded his thanks and ripped the can open. He sipped delicately and said, 'There's a geezer giving us the fish eye over there.' His glance wavered fractionally to the right.

'I know,' murmured Bone. 'He arrived a few moments ago. One of the B.O.S.S. men, I reckon.'

Jonno chuckled. 'Well, whatever else you call them, you can't exactly use the word subtle, can you?'

'True.' He licked the still sore spot on the back of his hand where Van Krug had used it as an ashtray.

'What now, do we just wait?'

'Getting bored?' Bone asked.

Jonno shrugged. 'Makes a change, but doesn't exactly get the job done. Too much hanging around and Mr Duff's going to start wondering what we're up to. He likes results, does Mr Duff.'

'Yeah,' said Bone. A familiar bum waggled past and he recognised the chick who'd chatted him up on his first day at the beach. She still left a scent of Brylcreem trailing behind her.

Bone adjusted his sun specs and stared out at paradise. He wondered why the old Will Fyffe number kept running through his mind.

'I belong to Glasgow . . .' His thoughts drifted back to the days when he'd been a kid. One year, he remembered it well because it had been such a treat, he'd been taken for a fortnight's holiday at Rothesay on the Firth of Clyde. There'd been a present the day he arrived, a strong brown fishing line wound round a wooden frame. The sinker had been a dull lead circle. As soon as they'd unpacked he'd excused himself and, scrounging the end of a loaf from the landlady, run as fast as his legs could carry him on to the pier. Although it was mid-August the rain had been bucketing down. The paddle steamers had come and gone, and still he'd caught nothing. He remembered the tears welling from his eyes to join forces with the rain water already streaming down red cheeks. He knew he'd be due for it when he got back, he'd have his backside tanned for standing out in the rain. And yet he had to catch a fish; it didn't matter what its size was, as long as *he* caught it. It was the most important thing in the world to him that day.

'What sort of bait are ye using, son?' asked the old fisherman. Pale blue eyes twinkled out of a crusty face.

'Bread,' the kid stammered.

'Oh aye,' said the fisherman scratching his cheek. 'Ye haven't done much fishing before, I take it?'

'No, this is my first time. We only arrived today.'

'Wait here,' said the old man and walked away. Five minutes later he was back with a handful of black mussels. 'Now, watch what I do,' he said.

Bone watched in fascination as the old man inserted the tip of a gully knife into the crack of the shell and forced it open. A gnarled finger pointed to a small black spot which lay cradled in an orange mess. 'The eye,' said the man. 'Always mind the fish like that part best.' He scooped out the the black spot and edged it on to the silver hook. 'Like that, see?'

Bone nodded.

The old man pulled the bait from the hook and chucked it into the sea. He beckoned Bone to squat beside him and when Bone had done so he laid the gully and a fresh mussel in front of the boy. 'Now you do it,' he said.

The eye was so slippery Bone had trouble hooking it, but at length he succeeded.

'Fine,' said the old fisherman. 'Now, lower it into the water and let's see what happens.'

While Bone waited expectantly, the old man opened the rest of the mussels. As he worked, he told Bone how to hold the line, gently between thumb and forefinger. The fisherman also explained to the boy that he shouldn't get overexcited and jerk the hook out of the fish's mouth when the first nibble came. 'Wait until it feels like a good bite, and then pull sharply to one side,' said the old man. 'That should do the trick.'

Moments later Bone was shouting with pleasure as he felt the brown line buck madly between his fingers. 'I've got one! I've got one! I've got one!' he cried and pulled in as fast as he could.

The old man clucked his approval. 'As fine a wee herring as I've seen in a long time. Why don't you take it away home for yer tea?'

'You mean I can eat it?'

'Of course. I'm sure your Ma'll know how to dress it for you.' The old man laughed. 'Now, away with you before you catch your death, but before you go, sonny, remember this. Always use the right bait. That's the important thing: The right bait!'

'I'll no forget,' said Bone. He scampered down the pier clutching the herring tightly to his chest. 'I'll no forget!'

Bone drifted back to Clifton Beach. He took off his glasses and wiped the corners of his eyes. He noted that the tail from B.O.S.S. was still watching them intently.

'I've got an idea. Want to come with me or do you want to stay here?' he asked.

Jonno rose. 'I'll stick with you.'

Once they were both in the rented Volks, Bone wheeled the car round and headed for town. As he drove, he said, 'You know, the funny thing about Scots people, and Glaswegians in particular, is how sentimental they get about the old country when they're abroad. Do you know the first thing two Scotsmen would do if you marooned them on a desert island?'

Jonno shook his head.

Bone laughed, 'Form a Caledonian Society.'

'Is there one in Cape Town?'

'Bound to be, and that's where we're headed.'

'Do you think Nova might have joined?'

'No,' said Bone. 'Or at least, if she has, not under her own name. What I have in mind is something slightly different.'

They found the Society headquarters in Keerom Street. Bone made a lot of Celtic noises at the door and that gained them admittance. He found the man he was looking for wrapped round a large glass of malt whisky, and said in his best Kelvinside:

'Pipe Major Struan McDonnell?'

'I am.'

Bone smiled at the caricature of the Erse race, a pudgy white face dotted with freckles and topped by a carroty thatch. He spoke the magic words, 'Can I buy you a drink?'

'Och, now, that would be very kind of you indeed,' said the Pipe Major. Then, 'I don't recall having seen you around here before?'

'We've just arrived,' said Bone. He introduced himself and his 'English' friend. Pipe Major McDonnell sipped his Glenmorangie. 'Now what can I be doing for you?' he asked.

'I'm told you run the band here.'

'That is so.'

Bone said, 'I'd like to buy a second-hand set of pipes. Do you know of any going?'

'For yourself?'

'Aye.'

The Pipe Major frowned. 'There's no that many kicking

around, you understand. But if you were to join the band I'm sure we could help you out.'

'I'll only be staying here a short time,' said Bone. 'But if I couldn't buy a set then I wouldn't mind renting. A couple of weeks would probably be enough.'

The Pipe Major swallowed his whisky and ordered another round. There was a slight argument over Bone insisting on a soft drink, but when Bone confided that he suffered diabolically from ulcers the Pipe Major was instantly contrite.

'And who've you played with?' the Pipe Major asked.

'The Boy's Brigade for six years.'

'Is that so? Which company was that?'

'158th Glasgow.'

Carroty eyebrows waggled up and down, 'Not Charlie McCracken's lot?'

'The very same,' said Bone.

McDonnell beamed. 'Och, Charlie's an old friend,' he said. 'We've known each other from way back.' To Jonno he added, 'A rare piper Charlie. Could have been born a McCrimmond.'

Jonno stared blankly at Bone. He wondered what all this chat about bagpipes had to do with finding Nova Foster. Bone laughed gently when he caught the look. 'The Scots are like the Mafia, Jonno,' he said. 'We stick together.'

Bone's explanation left Jonno none the wiser.

'Aye we do that,' agreed McDonnell. 'But tell me, what do you want pipes for?'

Bone slid a Rand on to the bar and ordered a large malt. 'I'd like to get a couple of weeks practice in. Just for my own pleasure, ye ken.'

'Och, aye,' replied the Pipe Major. He knew there was more to it than that. He stared again at Bone and made up his mind. 'Now, as it so happens I do have a spare set I could lend you, which I'm of a mind to do, seeing as how you know Charlie McCracken. You'll take care of them, of course?'

'You have my word,' said Bone.

The Pipe Major said cannily, 'Now, about payment; what do you think?'

'I'll leave that up to you.'

McDonnell indicated a small wooden box that stood at one end of the bar. 'We're kind of fond of the Black Sash ladies round here,' he said. 'If you'd care to make a donation for their good works.'

'Do you mind if I ask what they do?'

'Let's just say they're a group of white women who're no too pleased with apartheid and the like.' He smiled as Bone pushed fifty Rand through the slit in the box.

'Och, that's real generous of you. Now, if you give me your address I'll drop the pipes off tonight. I'll treacle the bag and put in some new drones if you like.'

'I'd be obliged,' said Bone. 'And if you could stick in a practice chanter, I'd really be in your debt.'

Once they were back outside Jonno said, 'What's all this about the bagpipes? Can you actually play them?'

'Well, I used to be able to. Let's just hope I still can.'

Jonno shook his head. 'I can't see what you're driving at.'

'It's all a matter of bait,' said Bone mysteriously. 'And the name of ours in sentimentality.'

It was the old Harry Lauder syndrome. He'd never yet known a Scot abroad who wouldn't come running when they heard the sound of pipes. Which was funny when you thought about it; at home most of them wouldn't even have crossed the road to hear the same thing. And Nova/Heather Foster was a Scot all right. And, better still, a Glaswegian. They were the most sentimental of the lot.

'That joker's still with us,' said Jonno. His eyes flicked to one side, indicating behind him.

The man from the beach had been joined by a companion whom Bone recognised immediately as his old friend Van Krug. He resisted the temptation to wave. At this stage there was no advantage to be gained from making the Dutchman angry. Except from a certain amount of personal pleasure, that was.

The local paper was called the *Argus*, and lived in an old grey building in Adderley Street. Bone spoke nicely to the bag on reception and as a result was ushered straight into the presence of the features editor. He and Jonno sat in harsh sunlight while the woman talked on the phone. She flashed them a smile when she finally hung up.

'My name's Kat Swanepool. What can I do for you, gentlemen?'

Bone replied, 'I have a story that might interest you, a real schmaltzy tear-jerker.'

Pencilled eyebrows were raised. 'Go on.'

Bone noted that, although she was listening to him, it was Jonno she looked at. Her gaze was frank, the sex light bright in her eyes. Like the girl on the beach, her meaning was clear.

'What do you think?' asked Bone after he'd said his piece.

Carmine lips pursed. 'It's a possible. I'll send a photographer along to cover it, and after that we'll see what happens.'

'Great,' said Bone.

Kat Swanepool leaned across her desk and addressed Jonno, 'I'm having a lunch party at my place this Sunday. Perhaps you and your friend would like to come along? Nothing fancy, mind you, just a few drinks and a *braai*.'

Jonno hedged, 'Sounds interesting, but I'm afraid I might be working.'

Incredulous: 'On a Sunday?'

The faintest of smiles drifted across Jonno's mouth, 'It's a full-time job I've got. Seven days a week.'

The lady editor thought she was getting the brush off. 'I see,' she snapped and sat back. The end of a pencil rattled between her teeth.

Bone said hurriedly, 'Please, don't misunderstand, we're both here on very important business and our employer wouldn't like it if we didn't put it first. However, if we can get free then we'd be delighted to attend.' He flashed Jonno a look and the bodyguard caught the message. 'Sure, we'd love to,' Jonno said. His expression was inscrutable.

Carmine lips formed themselves into a bow. 'Good, and if you do manage you can tell me all about this fascinating job of yours. You have me intrigued.'

Jonno said softly, 'I may even do better than that, I may even give you a personal demonstration.'

The woman's lips quivered, and Bone wondered what it was about Cape Town that produced such randy women; en mass they reminded him of a school of hungry sharks. He said, 'Every hour on the hour, starting at ten tomorrow.'

'You'll both be there?'

'Yes.'

The sex light became a gleam. 'Then I may cover the story

myself. I do that in special cases sometimes.'

'We'll look forward to it,' said Jonno.

The phone rang and they excused themselves. Kat Swanepool's eyes followed Jonno all the way to the doorway.

'What happens now?' asked Jonno once they were outside.

Bone replied, 'I suggest I tout Nova's photo round a few more bars and see if I come up with anything. Apart from that, all I can do is wait for tonight and have a practice on the bagpipes.'

'Good day, Meneer,' said Wankie, stepping out of a doorway. He stared up at the brilliant blue sky. 'And a great one for a swim, eh?'

'I'll maybe get around to that later,' replied Bone.

Wankie stared directly at Jonno. 'Welcome to our fair country. I believe your friends call you Jonno.'

'S'right.'

'And you're a friend of Meneer Bone's here?'

'Correct.'

'How long are you planning to be with us?'

Jonno shrugged. 'Not long, a couple of weeks, maybe.'

Wankie chuckled. He stuck a cheroot in his mouth and then lit it in cupped hands. When the ritual was over he said, 'All this fuss over a missing girl. She must be very important, man.'

'Her Daddy loves her,' Bone replied. He staggered as an elbow thudded into his ribs.

'Don't be cheeky,' snarled Van Krug. Then to Jonno, 'I don't like the look of you, either.'

'I'm sorry,' said Jonno. 'I don't like making unnecessary enemies. It's such a waste of time, don't you think?'

'I take it you two knew each other in the U.K.?' snapped Wankie.

'We've met casually several times,' answered Jonno. 'We have mutual friends.'

'I'll bet you have.'

Van Krug said, 'And I suppose you've never heard of the Frelimo either?'

'I've heard of them, all right. I do read the papers, you know.'

Van Krug grunted, 'What are you doing in Kaapstad?'

'I'm having a holiday and, before you ask, I'm quite apolitical. I don't even bother to vote.' Jonno had come out into the open on instructions from Duff. He knew that, no matter how hard the men from B.O.S.S. checked up on his background, they wouldn't come up with anything incriminating. As far as British records were concerned, he had no form and was up to date on both his taxes and insurance stamps. Besides, he had no intention of committing a crime whilst in South Africa. Duff had been quite clear on that point. The action was scheduled for the U.K.

Bone slicked down the hair flapping round his neck and made a mental note to get a haircut. He was beginning to look scruffy and that wasn't good for inspiring confidence in the punters. He winced when he accidentally brushed against a burn spot.

Wankie said, 'I've been doing a little more homework since I saw you last, man. There are four females in the Province by the name of Foster. None of them could be the party you're looking for. So that brings us back again to the idea of a false passport. You do realise that anyone entering the Republic on one is automatically deported?'

'If he comes across the girl then I'll see he reports her,' said Jonno softly, 'I promise you.'

Wankie sucked on his cheroot while his piggy eyes tried to bore through the bodyguard's bland expression. He nodded, 'You do that small thing.'

Van Krug was impatient. He turned to Bone. 'What were you doing in the *Argus* building?'

'Why don't you buy tomorrow's paper? Chances are you can read for yourself.' Then to Wankie, 'Can we go now or are we going back to your place for another round of Perry Mason?'

'You can go, Meneer.'

Bone said sarcastically. 'I'm sure you'll keep in touch.'

He and Jonno turned and strode off down Adderley Street. They'd only gone a few paces when Jonno said gently, 'You shouldn't let them get to you. Although they make a lot of noise, they're only amateurs underneath.'

'I know that, but we're still in their territory, where they hold most of the cards. I don't fancy the idea of ending up on this Robben Island of theirs.'

Jonno replied, 'When Mr Duff hires a man, that man gets his full protection. In other words, Mr Duff gives his men the loyalty he expects in return. You do take a trip to Robben Island, you won't be there for long. That is a fact.'

'It's something about their attitude that gets under my skin,' said Bone. 'It's not just the arrogance, it goes deeper than that.'

'It's a weakness, and that's good; a weakness can always be exploited. Let them think they're more clever and sophisticated than they actually are, because that gives us the advantage.'

Bone glanced sideways at his companion. 'Mr Duff thinks very highly of you. He told me he thought you were the best.'

Jonno smiled secretly. 'I think I can honestly say Mr Duff and I understand one another. It's a pleasure working for him.'

'That bird at the Argus really took a shine to you. Will you take her up on it?'

'Only if it's necessary. She's not my type.'

'Mind if I ask you what your type is?'

Jonno's smile broadened. 'Yes I do,' he replied.

Bone left it at that.

They toured more plush bars and pushed the photograph about. One barman vaguely recalled seeing the girl but he couldn't be certain when. Then the barman renegued and said maybe it wasn't Nova after all but someone who'd looked like her. He couldn't remember an accent.

When Bone returned to the Mt. Nelson he found a black pipe box waiting for him. There was a note from Pipe Major McDonnell saying he'd put in well-played drones and reed. The bag had been treacled. Bone sat on his bed and stuck the practice chanter between his lips. He smiled at Jonno.

'This may be a bit painful to begin with. Want to go downstairs?'

'I'll be in my own room. Give me a shout if you need me.' As always his exit was silent.

Bone glanced towards the bug and wondered what the men from the Bureau Of State Security were going to make of this little lot. He started with the THE PIBROCH OF DONALD DHUI. It was amazing how the fingers remembered. At first they were stiff and slow, but the more he played the more his skill and dexterity came back. After half an hour he was playing grace notes and doublings. He ran through the old repertoire. The tunes of glory: SCOTLAND THE BRAVE; HIELAND LADDIE; BROWN HAIRED MAIDEN; ALL THE BLUE BONNETS ARE OVER THE BORDER. The sound of Scotland had the same effect on him as it always had. Excitement bubbled in his stomach, the hair on the back of his neck rustled and threatened to stand on end. His blood danced and sang in his veins.

At length he laid the practice chanter on the bed and picked up the pipes themselves. They were a beautiful, blackwood set, mounted in ivory, the bag tartan Black Watch, the mouthpiece silver. Bone blew, ending with the little suck that brought the leather flap back into position, thereby effectively cutting off any air from escaping back up the blow tube. The bag expanded and the drones groaned. He grinned to himself; that would have earned him a reprimand from the good Pipe Major. Two more blows and he elbowed the pipes into life. He played his favourite: THE MIST COVERED MOUNTAIN.

He stopped half an hour later when the manager appeared at the door to say that complaints had been made. Bone said he fully understood, and that he was finished anyway. He whistled as he packed the pipes away. It was later as he tried to go to sleep that the homesickness came to him. He tossed and turned before finally dozing off. He dreamt that he was going to kill Van Krug, but as he pulled the trigger of the Sterling the Dutchman's face shimmered and became Nick Byers.

'*Noooo!*' Bone screamed into the night.

The next morning he picked up Jonno and headed for Clifton Beach. Kat Swanepool was already waiting for them. 'My photographer,' she said and indicated a weedy-looking specimen. The weed gabbled his pleasure at meeting them.

The sun was high in the sky as Bone unpacked the pipes. He hoped he wasn't going to get nervous and muck up his playing. He glanced at the hundreds of bronzed bodies on display and, just this once, wished he'd been a natural born extrovert. He started tuning up. Kat said, 'You must find us very forward here. I've heard a lot of your countrymen say that.'

'A little bit,' Jonno replied.

'You'll get used to it, you know.'

Jonno smiled blandly, giving nothing away. 'We'll see.'

Kat held a cigarette to her lips and waited for Jonno to light it. When he'd done so she said, 'When we South Africans want something, we go after it. Psst! Straight to the mark like an arrow. You understand?'

'Perfectly.'

'You don't sound as though you approve.'

Jonno's eyes were flickering through the crowd that had already gathered as he searched for Nova. 'It doesn't bother me one way or the other,' he said. He eased himself round a fraction so he could survey another section of the gaping onlookers. He glanced down when a card was slipped into his breast pocket.

'Why wait till Sunday,' said Kat. 'If you find yourself free anytime before then, give me a buzz.'

'I'll say this for you; you're persistent.'

'That's a qualification you need for my job. Which reminds me, don't forget you promised me a demonstration of yours.'

A faint smile creased Jonno's lips. 'I'll just give you a hint. I don't think you'd like the full works,' he muttered.

Kat Swanepool grinned. She was determined to have this man, and she was a woman renowned for always getting what she went after. She wondered what it was about him that attracted her so much, and came to the conclusion it was the feeling of menace he sometimes exuded. She'd felt it like a slap across the face the moment he'd walked into her office. Just looking at him made her quiver with anticipation to a degree of intensity she'd never previously experienced.

'I like you,' she said. 'You're different.'

Bone blinked behind his sun specs and swung into AUSTRALIAN LADIES. He hoped Jonno wasn't being too distracted by the Swanepool woman, as he was finding it difficult to play and search the crowd at the same time. He hoped it would be easier after he got the hang of things.

Ten minutes later his puff gave out, so he packed it in. He

was momentarily startled by the round of applause the crowd gave him. As he crossed to where Jonno stood he saw the girl who'd been on the beach the first day he'd arrived. She gave him the come-on, but he ignored her. She went into her bum-waggling retreat routine again.

'Got your story then?' he asked.

Under her tan Kat Swanepool looked a trifle flushed. 'Sure,' she said. 'But don't ask me yet if it'll be printed. That depends on what other copy comes in.'

'Fair enough,' Bone replied. He glanced at Jonno, who shook his head. One up, one down. There was still a long day ahead.

Kat said to the weed, 'Get some good pics?'

'Oh yes,' he oiled. 'They should come out really great.'

Kat nodded before rounding on Bone. 'One thing puzzles me,' she said. She jerked her thumb in a gesture that took in him and Jonno. 'Neither of you two strikes me as the type who goes looking for publicity, at least not the corny sort, anyway. So what gives?'

'The story's gen,' lied Bone suavely. 'Cross my heart and hope to die if it isn't.'

'Balls!' retorted Kat. 'I'm sure there's more to it than that.'

Jonno cut in smoothly, 'I think I'll go up to the hotel and have a beer. Anyone fancy coming along?'

'Not me,' said Bone. 'I'll hang around here for a while. Why don't you go, Kat? I'm sure you could use a wet after broiling in his sun.' The day was rapidly turning out to be another scorcher.

'I'd be delighted,' the Swanepool woman said, and looked it. To the weed she added, 'You get back to the office and get these pics printed. I'll expect them on my desk before noon.'

After they'd left, Bone packed his pipes back in their box and asked a prostrate Adonis to keep an eye on them for him. Then he did the tour. It took him well over half an hour to peer at every face on the beach. As usual, he drew a blank.

He found Jonno waiting for him when he got back.

'OK?' he queried.

'Sure. No sweat.'

Bone pretended to shiver, 'I've never been taken with the man-eaters myself.'

'I know what you mean,' said Jonno laconically.

Bone sat on the sand and lit up. 'One thing, is it the girl or the man Mr Duff's really after?' he asked.

'He wants Edgerton-Forbes, or Edwards as we knew him.'

Breath whistled through Bone's teeth. He'd hoped that was the way it was. He kept thinking of the old couple, the husband who was dying from the dust. He'd taken a liking to the pair of them; he wanted the old man to see his daughter again before he pegged out. Casually, he said, 'Do I take it then you're here to persuade him to go back?'

'That's right.'

'Where does the gold come into it, Jonno?'

The bodyguard scooped up a handful of sand and allowed it to trickle between his fingers. 'No offence, Mr Bone, but Mr Duff'll tell you that if he wants you to know. I have my instructions.'

'I understand.' Then: 'You've known Mr Duff a long time, haven't you?'

'Yeah. We go way back to the days when he first came over from the States. I was a friend of his first wife.'

'Oh? What happened to her?'

'She died.'

'You make it sound like she was a close friend.'

Jonno leant back and closed his eyes. Drops of sweat formed at his hairline and rolled down to his nose. 'She was,' he said so softly that Bone almost missed it.

At eleven o'clock, Bone tuned his pipes and treated the crowd to a medley. He could hear quite a few Scots voices dotted amongst the Afrikaans and English speakers, but none of them belonged to Nova Foster. When he sat down again Jonno said, 'You really think this will work?'

'Can you think of anything better?'

Jonno shook his head wonderingly. 'You know, this is ridiculous.'

'Yeah,' Bone replied, 'I'm very good at being that.'

Later that afternoon Jonno came back with the latest copy of the *Argus*. 'You made page twelve,' he grinned.

Bone glanced at his picture and grimaced. He reckoned he looked like a well-worn gargoyle. The skin on his face came up so clearly it could have been used as a close up of the moon. He read aloud, 'Jack Bone, a Scotsman from Glasgow, keeps a promise. Five years ago Mr Bone's old mother lay dying, and her last wish was to hear the bagpipes played once more by her son. The old woman, a highland lady from Tomintoul, sat up in bed for five consecutive mornings while Jack serenaded her with all the tunes she remembered from her youth. On the sixth day it was discovered that Mrs Bone had miraculously recovered, and so great was his happiness Jack Bone swore there and then that, no matter where he found himself during the anniversary of that week, he would play his pipes in honour of the occasion.' There followed a blurb about Bone being on Clifton beach and that he would play every hour on the hour during the day for the next five days.

'You had it taped when you described it as a real tear-jerker,' said Jonno. 'You'd have me blubbering if I thought it was true.'

Bone neatly folded the paper and laid it by his side. He noted that several bronzed faces were being raised occasionally to stare in his direction. The news was travelling fast.

'Hey, Jimmy, you this Bone chap?' It was a poison dwarf with a mouth full of Glasgow.

'Aye, that's right,' acknowledged Bone.

'When ur ye going tae play again, then?'

'On the hour.'

The dwarf said, 'Good on ye, Jim. I'll wait around to hear that!'

When the man was out of earshot Bone flashed Jonno a grin. 'Sentimentality,' he said. 'It's a national characteristic.'

The trap was baited, the jam on display. All Bone could do now was keep on playing and hope his fly would put in an appearance. Session after session he marched up and down the sand while Jonno mingled with the crowd and peered at faces. Nova Foster was never one of them.

At the end of three days he began to think he was backing a loser. Then she came.

He was in the middle of THE EARL OF MANSFIELD when the face from the photograph stared at him from out of the crowd. Such was his excitement that his fingers slipped and the pipes squealed. He swiftly looked away and brought the pipes back under control, and his eyes flicked from group to group as he tried to find Jonno. Oh shite, he thought when he looked back and saw the girl pushing her way through the press. Where are you Jonno? The bodyguard was nowhere to be seen.

Two burly pairs of shoulders snapped together and somewhere a baby cried. Nova was gone, hidden from view. Bone whipped through the last remaining notes and elbowed the bag into silence. He bobbed his head up and down in response to the round of applause.

'Have you seen Jonno?' asked a voice at his side. He whirled to find Kat Swanepool staring up at him. He thrust the pipes into her hands.

'Hold these for me till I get back. When Jonno shows, tell him she came and I'm going after her. She went that way!' He gestured in the general direction of Cape Town.

Kat was bewildered. 'Who came?'

Bone grabbed her by the arms. 'He'll know. And please, tell him right away. It's very important!'

Then he was running, his feet scuffing in the sand as he bulldozed his way through the crowd.

'Hey, that was great!' said an Edinburgh voice. Bone brushed on past, oblivious to the angry shout behind him.

'Cheeky bugger!' said irate Edinburgh.

Bone snatched off his sunglasses and dashed sweat from his eyes. He blinked as a combination of wet and harsh sunlight dazzled him. 'Oh no!' he groaned. Then there was a flash of Liberty print and he had her again.

His feet thundered on the rock steps as he raced upwards towards the small hotel that squatted on top of the cliffs. His chest heaved with exertion and the breath was tight in his throat. 'Too many fags,' he gasped, but forced himself on.

He reached the top just as the Lincoln Continental eased itself out of the gravel driveway and wheeled towards the city. He clocked the girl's profile before turning and racing towards the rented Volks, then he slewed to a halt and almost yelled with frustration. The car was neatly hemmed in by a couple of old bangers.

Bone gulped down several deep breaths and made himself think. There wasn't time to go into the hotel and roust out the cowboys whom the bangers belonged to. He needed instant transport.

The bike was a Raleigh ladies' model and had seen better days. Bone didn't care about that as he wrenched it from the rack. Pebbles flew as the wheels spun and then he was on the road and barrelling after the Yankee car.

He pumped his legs and kept his head down as he flipped through the Sturmey Archer gears. He laughed as he suddenly had an objective view of himself. 'Come on, Reg Harris,' he muttered, pretending he was wearing the yellow jersey.

The road dipped and then inclined into a hill. Bone lifted his backside off the saddle and strained. A river of sweat flowed down his back as his legs whirled round and round. At the top of the hill he knew he couldn't take much more. He was too old, too tired and his body was a wasteland caused by too much booze and even more nicotine. His stomach heaved and for a moment he thought he was going to have to stop and throw his guts up. He clamped his teeth together and forced the sensation back down his throat.

He had just passed a sign saying BANTRY BAY when the Lincoln's tail light flashed and the girl did a left. She pulled into the driveway of a smart-looking house overlooking the sea.

Bone gulped and sat back. He freewheeled past the house before applying his brakes, then dropped the bike to the ground and leaned against a lampost while he waited for the world to stop spinning. That was the way Jonno found him.

The rented Volks screeched to a halt and the bodyguard leapt out. He grasped Bone by the shoulders, 'You OK?'

'Yeah, just give me a few minutes.'

'Kat said Nova showed.'

Bone jerked his head towards the house. 'That one. She's inside.'

'You sure it's her?'

'I'm positive. I got a good look.' Bone stuck a fag in his mouth and lit up. That made him want to be sick again. Jonno said:

'You hang about here a few minutes while I look the place over.'

'OK,' gagged Bone.

Jonno picked up the fallen bicycle and laid it against a brick wall. Then he casually sauntered past the house Bone had indicated. The building was expensive-looking, the architecture Cape Dutch. It was surrounded on three sides by lawn while the back was a sheer drop into the Atlantic. There was a large swimming pool on the right hand side.

Jonno checked the location of all doors and windows before returning to Bone. 'How are you feeling now?' he asked.

Bone nodded, 'I'll live.' He wondered why the burns on the back of his neck had suddenly started to sting so ferociously. He put it down to the sweat. 'What now?' he asked.

'You do what you were paid to do. You go in and give the girl the message about her old man.'

'And you?'

'I'll say my piece after you've said yours.'

Bone wiped his sunglasses with a handkerchief and then slipped them back on his face. He was hot, sticky, and desperately needed a bath. He was sure he smelled. 'Let's go,' he said.

They crunched their way up the drive to stand before a massive, wooden door. There was a huge brass knocker in the shape of a fairy. Bone thought it might be Joan The Wad. He banged it once.

'Yes? Can I help you?' The servant was an enormous African who towered above Bone. The man was built like the proverbial brick shit-house. Bone smiled and said, 'We'd like to speak to the madam.'

'Is she expecting you, baas?'

Bone put on his friendliest grin, 'I think you'll find she'll see us.'

The Zulu stepped back. 'If you'll step this way, baas, I'll tell her you're here. What name shall I give?'

'Bone.'

'Thank you, baas.'

The room they were ushered into screamed money. On one wall there was a huge painting signed Klee. It looked like an original to Bone. From another room came the sound of voices, the male of which spoke with an Eton-type drawl. Bone couldn't hear what they were talking about.

Jonno positioned himself in front of the Klee in such a manner that his back was presented to the rest of the room. He stood relaxed, hands dangling by his side.

A door opened and a man who looked vaguely like the older Edgerton-Forbes entered. The face was weak, with a suggestion of decadence about it. His colouring was high Anglo-Saxon. Rupert said, 'My wife will be down in a few moments. Can I help you?'

'No,' said Bone. 'It's her I want to speak to.'

'Would you care for a drink while you wait?' asked Rupert pleasantly. His expression was puzzled as he glanced from Bone to Jonno's back. He asked the inevitable: 'Are you the police?'

'Neither my friend nor I drink,' said Bone. He smiled and didn't answer the latter.

'M'senga,' said Rupert. The Zulu servant padded to the drinks table and poured a large whisky into a cut crystal glass. He added soda before handing it to Rupert.

'Cheers!' said Edgerton-Forbes. His eyes were suddenly furtive.

There was the patter of bare feet on wood and Nova breezed in. She wore a kaftan and her hair had been caught back in a bun. She smiled in recognition.

'Why, the man from the beach! You know, the one I told you about, Rupert. He plays the pipes.' To Bone, 'I came along to hear you, you know.'

'Yes,' said Bone. 'I saw you.'

'Oh, really?' Her voice held only the trace of a Glasgow accent. She crossed to the drinks and poured herself a large Cane, topping the glass up with lime.

Bone studied her while she did this. He was slightly disappointed; he'd expected a better looker. In the flesh the face was hard, calculating, the figure somehow mean. He'd have bet she was the selfish type in bed.

Nova said, 'M'senga said you wanted to speak with me.'

Bone lit himself a fag. It amused him to see that, although Jonno was still standing in front of the picture, it was as though his physical presence somehow wasn't there. It was the true art of camouflage. Bone reckoned Jonno would have done well in Malaya. He said, 'Your father hired me to find you. He wants you to know that he's dying.'

Nova looked stunned. 'What?'

Bone repeated the message. Edgerton-Forbes gulped and

swallowed his drink. 'You mean you traced Nova here from London? But that's impossible!'

'I'm here,' said Bone.

The girl licked her lips while her fingers beat a tattoo on the brocade of her sleeve. 'How did you find me?' she asked.

Bone ignored the question. 'Your father's time's running out, he could go any day now. I know he's hoping you'll come home so he can see you before the end. He told me you're very close.'

'We are,' muttered the girl.

Jonno turned and faced the room. 'I bring a message as well. Mr Duff would like a word with you, Rupert.'

Edgerton-Forbes went first white, then green. His eyes bulged like poached eggs. 'Jonno!' he gargled.

The bodyguard said, 'We've a few business details to see to, you and I, and then I'm taking you back. If you want to go on living you'll come with me.'

Green turned to puce. Edgerton-Forbes pointed a finger dramatically at Jonno. 'Kill him, M'senga!' he screamed. A glass whizzed through the air as Edgerton-Forbes dived for a knobkerrie lying in a corner.

'Yes, Nkosi,' said the Zulu and sprang into action. Jonno and the African went down to the sound of thudding fists.

Bone had only taken a step forward when the female threw herself at him. A leg locked round his as razor sharp nails raked his face. He grunted, and grabbed at the talons which threatened his eyes.

'Run, Rupert! Run!' shouted Nova.

Edgerton-Forbes was a matchstick man galvanised into action. He hurriedly skirted the tangle of arms and legs that was Jonno and the Zulu and ran for a door. There were white flecks on his lips and he was sobbing.

M'senga screamed in agony and doubled up as Jonno kneed him in the crutch. A flattened hand knifed sideways to take the Zulu full in the throat, and Jonno finished his man with a piledriver that squashed the already spread nose even further.

Bone threw the girl to one side and turned into the flying knobkerrie. The heavy wooden stick took him full on the left shoulder. The breath whooshed out of him and his left side and went completely numb. His right hand groped in his pocket as he crumpled towards the floor, the hand flashed forward and a blue ball hissed through the air.

The marble took Edgerton-Forbes squarely on the forehead. Rupert staggered backwards to smash against a picture window which lined the back wall. There was an explosion of glass as he vanished from view.

Jonno thrust his head through the window frame and stared down at the Atlantic. Bone gasped, 'He'll be unconscious. He'll drown.'

Nova screamed, the noise of hysteria mounting and mounting as she shredded her throat.

With a calmness that belied the speed of his actions Jonno removed his jacket, shoes and socks. Then he dived into the sea.

Postscript

Duff handed Bone a St Clements and then pulled himself a pint of London Pride. He nodded in appreciation as he sipped the beer. It was every bit as good as he'd been led to believe. He gestured towards the notes stacked in front of Bone.

'OK?'

'Three thousand, plus expenses in full. I've no complaints.'

'Good.' Duff sat facing Bone and they both lit up. 'Jonno rang this morning, Edwards' broken leg is well on the mend and he'll be able to travel soon.'

'You're bringing him back here, then?'

'Of course. That was always the intention.'

'Do you mind if I ask what happens to him now?'

Duff gave a thin, chilling smile. 'You know what they say about justice; it shouldn't only be done, it should be seen to be done. Edwards, or Edgerton-Forbes as his name is, was a very foolish man.'

'And the girl?'

Duff smiled mysteriously. 'Now that she's home, she's

been advised to stay there. I'm sure she had a lot to do with egging Edwards on, but I feel she and her family have paid enough.'

Bone wasn't quite sure what to make of that statement. He said, 'I asked Jonno how the gold fitted into it, and he said that you'd tell me if you thought I should know.'

Duff grunted and finished his pint. He pulled himself another before answering. 'I guess I owe you that.' He took a swallow and leaned on the bar. 'Edgerton-Forbes was a bad gambler who was into one of my casinos for a hefty sum. When time came to pay, he couldn't. So I came up with an idea. The man was born and brought up in India, and still had a lot of childhood friends there, one of whom was a customs official. I had Edgerton-Forbes make contact and sound the official out about a little deal I had in mind. The official was buyable, and we were in business. What do you know about gold?'

'It costs a lot,' Bone said.

'Quite, but in some places it costs more than in others. Gold in India sells for up to three times its value in this country. Are you with me?'

'You were smuggling gold?'

'Precisely. You would be amazed at the amount of gold that comes into my possession in lieu of debts of one sort or another. The Indian run was my way of selling it and making an inflated profit.'

Bone said, 'Only Edgerton-Forbes got ideas of his own, I take it?'

'Right. Twice he did the run, and everything was OK. The third time he got the gold through customs, and then he and it disappeared. I was out about quarter of a million nicker.

Bone whistled. It was a lot of mazoola.

'Edgerton-Forbes knew he couldn't sell the gold himself in India without me getting a line on him, so that was where this Costandi came in. He made a deal with Edgerton-Forbes, whereby the money he paid for the gold was paid into an account in South Africa. The gold itself would be disposed of through various Arab traders, but that bit's guesswork on my part.'

'Will you get any of your money back?' Bone asked.

'Most of Edgerton-Forbes's share was still in his bank account. That, plus the capital realised from the sale of the house in Bantry Bay, will be transferred to an account in my name. Should I decide to, I can have the money brought back to this country at a later date. Costandi's share, of course, is gone.'

'And Edgerton-Forbes has agreed to co-operate?'

The chilling smile was back. 'Jonno gave him a very plausible argument. He believes if he returns the money he'll get off with his life.' Duff chuckled.

They smoked in silence for a while before Duff said, 'Now that oil has been found north of the border, Scotland has become a very exciting proposition. All sorts of new avenues have now been opened up. I hope to be in touch with you soon, that's if you're interested?'

'I am.' Bone knew the interview was at an end. The men shook hands and said their good-byes, and Bone was at the front door when the thought struck him. He turned to Duff.

'The old man, Foster, *is* dying, isn't he?'

Duff's eyes twinkled. 'I knew if I could find the girl then I'd have her man. I also knew how close Foster and Nova were. What I wasn't sure about was that the Fosters weren't lying when they told my man they had no idea of their daughter's present whereabouts. So I engineered a fake medical report, and then sat back to wait for something to happen. That something was you, Jack.'

'Don't you think it was a bit much, conning the old geezer like that?' asked Bone.

'Oh, I don't know. He'll doubly appreciate what he thinks is an added lease of life, and as a bonus he's got his daughter back alive. That wouldn't have happened if I hadn't had to use him the way I did. You may be interested to know that the doctor who arranged the fake report has now told the old man a mistake was made.'

'I'm glad of that,' said Bone. He clamped his floppy felt hat on to his head and pulled up the collar of his Crombie. He wondered if it was merely the weather that had suddenly made him feel chill.

He slid behind the wheel of the brand new Mini, an added token of appreciation from Duff. The car was black with tinted windows; Duff said it fitted his personality.

London was behind and he was on the A1 proper before he spoke. 'A penny for them?' he asked.

The pixie face was soft and loving. 'It's good to be going home,' said Susan Sweet.

END

Also by Iain Blair in Sphere Books:

TRUE

It was crazy . . . unbelievable . . . I was just an ordinary sort of guy, an actor getting the odd part in TV plays and commercials, spending my spare time boozing, chatting up the birds and all the everyday things people do. The next minute I found myself staked out as victim in a bizarre game of cat and mouse.

A megalomaniac nutcase was sending an assassin after me. He thought I'd killed his daughter! So he gave me £1,000 to make the contest a bit more even, then set his paid sadist on to me – armed with a recorder to tape my death throes.

The whole thing was like a very bad dream. But it was actually happening. To me . . . !

0 7221 1707 8 65p

and

DUFF

You *can* actually taste freedom, Duff decided as he walked out of the Scrubs. And what he meant to do with his freedom was to avenge Julie . . .

Julie, his pretty blonde wife – only twenty-four years old when she was wiped out in a road accident – now rotting in an untended grave in a London cemetery. Duff knew it was no accident that had left him with the agonizing, gut-wrenching sense of loss. For eight years in prison his rage festered into cold determination to kill Julie's murderers.

But when he had watched Julie's kid brother burned alive and had almost been finished by thugs himself, Duff realised that his plan to take a life for a life was not to be lightly achieved. For a start, there were now two lives to avenge.

0 7221 1708 6 75p